# THE LEDBURY LAMPLIGHTERS

# THE LEDBURY LAMPLIGHTERS

A Victorian Crime Story

*Kerry Tombs*

ROBERT HALE · LONDON

© Kerry Tombs 2009
First published in Great Britain 2009


ISBN 978-0-7090-8908-7


Robert Hale Limited
Clerkenwell House
Clerkenwell Green
London EC1R 0HT

www.halebooks.com

2 4 6 8 10 9 7 5 3 1


Typeset in 11/13pt Plantin
by Derek Doyle & Associates, Shaw Heath
Printed in Great Britain by the MPG Books Group,
Bodmin and King's Lynn

# CONTENTS

*Prologue*    Dinard, Northern France, November 1888    7

Chapter 1    Ledbury, Christmas Eve, 1888    13
Chapter 2    Ledbury, New Year's Eve, 1888/89    21
Chapter 3    Ledbury, New Year's Day, 1889    32
Chapter 4    Ledbury, New Year's Day, 1889    48
Chapter 5    Ledbury, 2 January 1889    64
Interlude    London, 2 January 1889    79
Chapter 6    Ledbury and London, 3 January 1889    85
Chapter 7    Ledbury, 5 January 1889    99
Chapter 8    Ledbury, 6 January 1889    111
Chapter 9    Malvern Wells and Ledbury, 7 January 1889    128
Interlude    London, 7 January 1889    145
Chapter 10    Ledbury, 8 January 1889    148
Chapter 11    Ledbury, 9 January 1889. Morning    170
Chapter 12    Ledbury, 9 January 1889. Evening    188
Chapter 13    Ledbury, 10 January 1889    210

*Epilogue*    Ledbury, 17 January 1889    221
*Postscript*    224

*For Samuel and Joan*
*Fond memories of Ledbury*

# PROLOGUE

## DINARD, NORTHERN FRANCE, NOVEMBER 1888

He had always known – of course – that eventually he would have to kill her.

That much was certain.

The outcome of their liaison had never been in dispute. The only question that now remained was when, and how, the deed would be performed.

Four weeks previously he had sought her out in the drinking taverns of Whitechapel. There he had watched her, as she had flaunted her crude charms in front of her prospective customers. Later he had followed her down the dark alleyways of the neighbourhood, where he had observed with almost clinical aloofness the coarse nature of her trade, while he had waited for his opportunity to speak with her alone. Finally one night, he had felt sure of himself and had confronted her in the alleyway near her lodgings. At first she had laughed at the elderly shambling man with his grey hair, flowing beard and polite speech, but as he had shown her the gold coins in his gloved hands, he had witnessed the look of greed flutter across her eyes, and knew that she would eventually undertake all that would be demanded of her. After that initial conversation, he had always been careful that they had only met in places where they could remain unobserved. Slowly, as he had gained her confidence, he had discovered her fancies and desires, and it had been easy to make her believe that if she went with him, and him alone, then he would grant her everything that she wished for. At the same time he had been sure to swear her to secrecy, declaring that their association would end if she told anyone of his existence.

When he had informed her of his impending visit to France, he had known that she would be only too anxious to accompany him, and it had been easy for him to send her on ahead to Portsmouth, while he had used her room to complete the work he had begun so earnestly earlier that autumn. Before the body had been discovered, he had left the capital well behind him, and by the time the news of his latest atrocity had been printed in the newspapers, they had arrived safely in Brittany.

At first she had wanted to travel on to Paris, but he had insisted that they remain in Saint-Malo for a few days, and when he had taken her to the costumiers to purchase some new clothes for her, she had been more than pleased to comply with his request.

As they had made their way down the narrow winding streets of the historic town, or sat in pavement cafes, he had become used to people turning their heads to observe the unusual couple – the old man with his walking stick and large hat, progressing slowly on his way, and the young, laughing woman full of charm and good looks, her arm looped through his, seemingly dependent on her new benefactor for everything.

Then he had deemed it prudent to move on – that had always been his way – and they had travelled the few miles along the coast until they had arrived at Dinard and the Hotel Gandolphi. As they had alighted from their carriage, however, he had been momentarily taken aback when he had seen that nuisance Ravenscroft and his new wife departing from the hotel. For a brief moment he had been afraid that the interfering policeman had recognized him, but as he had shuffled his way up the steps of the front entrance and the other carriage had driven away, he had recovered his confidence, knowing that his disguise had served him well.

For several days after their arrival, they had enjoyed the late autumn sunshine, sitting out on the balcony of the Gandolphi overlooking the sand and the sea, visiting the town of Dinan to admire its steep cobbled streets and gentle river, stopping off for refreshment at cafes in small Breton villages. And all the time he had been careful that they had kept to themselves, shunning the polite after-dinner conversations of their fellow guests, always travelling alone and above all making sure that she had no opportunity to read the London papers, where she might have learnt of the outrage that had taken place at her former lodgings.

Now, however, he had become restless and unsettled. The quiet, unhurried pattern of their existence, which had at first been so welcoming and enlightening, had begun to bore him. Worse still, he had grown tired and embarrassed by the attentions of his young companion, whose pretentious French mannerisms and silly conversation had started to irritate him. And when she had cast glances at one or two of the more eligible male single diners in the hotel dining-room, he had known that it would be only a matter of time before she abandoned him for another perhaps more appealing prospect – or worse still, would reveal her true identity to some passing stranger.

When he had announced that they were about to return to London, she had become annoyed, still believing that he had intended taking her on to Paris, but he had bought off her displeasure with the promise that once they returned to England he would visit his lawyer to instruct him to draw up his will, leaving his entire estate to her and her alone.

'We are sorry to see you leaving us, Monsieur Cranston, Mademoiselle Kelly, and trust that you have enjoyed your stay at the Gandolphi,' said the manager of the hotel on the morning of their departure.

'Yes, thank you,' he had replied, and she had laughed and squeezed his arm.

'We wish you a safe journey, and hope to see you both again some day.'

'Thank you, I'm sure that we will.'

They had made their way out the hotel and down the steps to their waiting carriage.

Later that afternoon, as they had boarded the ferry, the sun had already begun setting over the fortress walls of Saint-Malo, bathing the town in a gentle autumnal glow. He had been sure to book a cabin in a quiet part of the boat, and once there he had complained that he was unwell, lying on the bed and requesting that his companion read to him so that they would not have recourse to mix with the other passengers.

Presently, they had dressed for dinner and had begun to make their slow way towards the dining-room.

Suddenly he paused as they were about to climb the steps on to the deck.

'What is the matter?' she asked anxiously, looking into his face.

'I am still feeling unwell, my dear.'

'Shall we return to the cabin?'

'No. I shall be well in a moment. I think if we could go up above for a brief moment or two, I would be much better after some air. I find the close confines of the boat somewhat oppressive, my dear.'

Taking his arm, they made their way up the steps and out through the door that brought them up on to one of the promenade decks.

'It is far too windy!' she recoiled, drawing her shawl close around her, and wishing to return indoors.

'I am sorry, my dear, to bring you up here. I promise we will not be very long. I feel a little better already. Perhaps we could walk for just a minute or two, before we go into dinner,' he suggested.

She gave him a look of momentary displeasure, then remembering the reason for their journey, smiled and complied with his request.

The couple made their way along the empty, dimly lit deck. He looked out across the wide expanse of sea, to where a solitary lamp somewhere in the far distance broke the intense darkness of the night – and knew that the time had come.

'Please can we go into dinner? It is so cold and dark out here!' she pleaded, shouting above the noise of the crashing waves.

'I think you are right, my dear. I am so sorry to have brought you up here,' he replied.

Suddenly he let out a groan and staggered forward. She moved quickly and reached out to prevent his fall.

'Shall I call someone?' she said anxiously, holding his arm tightly.

'Over there,' he muttered, moving towards the rail.

'Do let me call someone. You are not well.'

'No. It will pass,' he replied, reaching out for the rail. 'Just hold on to me. All will be well in a moment.'

'Of course, but—'

'Just hold me tight.'

She complied with his instructions. 'Let me fetch someone.'

'I am so sorry it has come to this, but believe me, there is no other way.'

She said nothing, but as she looked into his eyes she saw the sudden flash of hatred there, and as the hands closed quickly around her neck she knew that she was powerless to prevent the draining away of her short life. A few seconds later her head fell silently on to his shoulder. He held her close, feeling the fragile, limp body against his own.

'Madame is not well?'

The unexpected voice startled him. He had been so sure that they had been alone.

'Madame does not like the sea air?' enquired the new arrival.

'Madame will be well in a moment. It is just the motion of the vessel. Thank you.'

'I understand, Monsieur,' replied the fellow passenger, smiling and taking his leave.

He watched as the stranger made his way back along the deck, continuing to support his victim as he waited for the sound of the door opening and then closing.

He waited for a few seconds, his face close to hers, listening and looking for anything or anyone that could possibly disturb his next action. Then, sure that he was alone and unobserved once more, he quickly thrust her forwards over the rail, and stepped backwards into the darkness as the body fell into the water.

He stood silently on the deck for a few moments, hoping that no one would have heard the sound, before quickly retracing his steps through the door and down the steps to his cabin.

Locking the door behind him, he stared into the mirror without emotion and began to slowly remove his beard and grey hair. Opening his case he took out another set of clothes, which he placed neatly upon the bed.

The Old Man had served him well but it was now time to move on and leave Cranston as nothing more than a brief passing memory.

He would again become Monk, the man of the shadows. He had covered his tracks with his usual expertise. There had been nothing to suggest that it had been anyone other than Marie Jeanette who had perished in that room that night, and now that he had ended her short life as well, there would be nothing to link him with the crimes of the previous few months. The police would continue to make enquiries, but he would never be found.

His secret would continue down through the generations.

Now he could begin again – a new life!

Tomorrow he would assume his new identity, slip away unnoticed from the boat and return to the capital, where he would again seek out others who would have need of his services.

# CHAPTER ONE

## LEDBURY, CHRISTMAS EVE, 1888

'A very Happy Christmas to you sir!'

Anthony Midwinter looked across at the old lamplighter in Church Lane. 'Yes, thank you, Mr Sanderson, and to you,' he replied quickly, anxious to continue his journey.

'Looks to be a cold one. Snow falling already, sir,' continued the other, reluctant to let his new listener depart, and attempting to rectify the spluttering flame.

'Yes, I think you are correct,' said Anthony, turning up his collar against the cold air and the falling flakes as he made his way across the cobbles.

'My best wishes to your good lady, sir,' called out the lamplighter.

The old church clock of Ledbury struck four. Another hour and Anthony knew that he would be free to attend to his own celebrations, not that they would amount to a great deal. There would be no excited children to open presents before an open fire, no unexpected guests to disturb their Christmas dinner, no long-lost relative returning to arouse their curiosity. He would merely exchange gifts with his wife later that evening. They would attend church on the morrow, where they would pass a few words of greeting with their fellow townsfolk, many of whom he had served in a professional capacity for the past forty years. On the day following they would make the tiresome journey across to the nearby village of Eastnor, where they would be welcomed by his wife's irritating brother and his dull wife. No, he was long past the time of life when Christmas had come to hold any appeal to him. But then he remembered that there would at least be the hunt to watch, where he would again pay his respects to the local gentry, and an opportunity perhaps to read one or two books in the evenings, seated before a roaring fire. In fact, the more he considered the prospect of Christmas, the more he found himself growing to like the idea.

Suddenly he felt himself sliding as his foot slipped on the wet surface of the cobbles, and he flung out one of his hands in a vain attempt to soften his fall.

'My dear sir, let me be of assistance,' said a concerned voice somewhere above him.

Anthony accepted the outstretched hand and regained his footing. 'Thank you, sir, you are most kind.'

'A treacherous afternoon. Are you hurt in any way? I live in the cottage over there. You would be most welcome to enter and rest with my wife and myself until you feel reassured to continue with your journey,' said the speaker, smiling.

'No. I am quite well, sir. That will not be necessary, I thank you,' he replied, brushing the wet flakes away from his coat.

'If you are quite sure? My name is Samuel Ravenscroft,' said his saviour, offering his hand.

'Anthony Midwinter of Midwinter, Oliphant and Burrows, at your service, sir,' replied the solicitor, shaking hands with the middle-aged man with thinning hair and pleasant manner.

'I am pleased to make your acquaintance, Mr Midwinter.'

'You are a new arrival in the town, sir?' inquired Anthony, always anxious to acquire new prospective clients.

'Yes, although my wife has lived here for over three years. You may have known her as Miss Armitage?'

'I know of the name but cannot recollect having ever met the young lady in any professional capacity. If you will excuse me now.'

'Yes, of course. It is a busy time and I must not detain you.'

'I thank you once again for your kind assistance, Mr Ravenscroft. Should you ever feel in need of my legal services, you will find my offices across from the marketplace.'

'I wish you the compliments of the season, sir,' said Ravenscroft, giving a slight bow before walking across to his cottage.

Anthony continued on his way, down the narrow lane where the old black and white buildings looked across at one another from opposite sides of the walkway. He exchanged greetings with one or two of his clients at the bottom of the lane. The flakes of snow began to increase as he entered the busy marketplace. He drew his coat closer to him as he paused to listen to a group of carol singers.

'A penny for the poor of Ledbury,' said one of their number, shaking a box in his direction. Anthony dug deep into his inner pocket and produced a coin, which he placed in the slot. He doubted whether the poor of Ledbury would ever have need of his services, but he knew the gesture would be expected of him as one of the prominent businessmen resident in the town.

'God bless you, Mr Midwinter – and a Happy Christmas to you!'

Anthony nodded and quickly made his way through the crowd towards one of the open shops.

'Good day to you, Mr Midwinter. Can we interest you in one of our lovely birds?' said the cheery, red-faced shopkeeper, raising his arm and sweeping it majestically across his display.

'I'll take that goose, if you please,' replied Anthony, pointing to the bird at the end of the open table that had first presented itself to his casual gaze.

'A good choice, sir, if I might say so; a very good choice. This bird would do justice to the finest table in Ledbury. I'll have my boy deliver it to your house within the hour.'

'Thank you.'

'The compliments of the season, sir, to you and your good wife,' shouted out the butcher, as his latest customer hurried away.

'And to you and your family.'

Anthony turned away from the marketplace, crossed over the road, and walked a few yards before entering an old building which bore a brass plaque with the words 'Midwinter, Oliphant and Burrows. Solicitors'. Seeing the highly polished plate with its neat lettering never ceased to remind him of the day when he had first joined the practice as an articled pupil some forty years before. Then the business had been merely Burrows and Son. When old Burrows' son had died unexpectedly, however, Anthony had used his meagre inheritance to buy his way into the partnership, and when Burrows himself had passed away some fifteen years previous, he had assumed the sole ownership of the firm. That was when he added the Oliphant. There had never been any Oliphant, of course, but Anthony had added it nevertheless, believing that it created the impression that the firm was larger than it first appeared.

'Any news, Perkins?' he enquired of the young clerk who rose from his desk as he entered.

'No, Mr Midwinter. I think everyone is far too busy at the moment preparing for Christmas to require our services, sir.'

'No matter, Perkins. At least we are here should anyone have urgent need of our services. The pen and our expertise are always available. Have you completed the copying yet?'

'Another page to go, sir,' replied the young man smiling.

'Good. Let me know when you have finished,' said Anthony, opening the door of the inner office as the clerk resumed his labours.

After hanging his coat on the single peg, he warmed his hands in front of the dying embers in the grate before seating himself behind his large desk. Opening a folder before him, he read intently for some minutes before uttering a deep sigh and leaning back in his chair. As he gazed up at the stained ceiling, thoughts of expansion again crept into his mind, as they had done from time to time during many an idle moment in the past five years. He really could do with taking on a new partner, someone younger, who would attend to the more mundane work of the practice and to whom he could eventually sell his share when he needed to seek retirement – but then there was the continual worry that such a move might not support two partners. Since that new practice had opened up further along the Homend six years ago, with its two young partners, he had seen a steady decline in the fortunes of his own business as his clients had slowly drifted away.

His thoughts were disturbed by a knocking at his door.

'Begging your pardon, sir, but there is a gentleman who would like a word with you. He is most insistent, sir,' said his clerk, entering the room.

'Is this gentleman known to us, Perkins?'

'No, sir.'

'Did he give a name?'

'No, sir. I've never seen him before. He says his business is most important and that he must see you before Christmas.'

'Then you had best show him in.'

His clerk closed the door, only to reopen it a few seconds later.

A tall, thin gentleman, wearing a long overcoat with a turned-up collar, grey hat, and sporting a turned-down carroty-type moustache, entered the room.

'Good day to you, sir. Good of you to see me at such a late hour. Mr Oliphant, I presume?' said the stranger, extending an arm.

'Midwinter,' corrected Anthony, rising from his seat and shaking the new arrival's hand as his clerk left the room. 'Mr Oliphant is away on business at present.'

'My apologies, sir. Mr Midwinter.'

'Would you care to take a seat, sir. And whom do I have the honour of addressing?' he enquired.

'My name is of little consequence,' said the other.

'And how can I be of assistance to you, sir?'

'My business is of a highly serious and delicate nature, Mr Midwinter,' said the stranger, accepting the seat and removing his hat.

'Most of my clients would say the same,' replied Anthony.

'I would need to be assured, sir, that what I tell you in this room tonight would not go any further than these four walls.'

Anthony observed that the new arrival spoke in a London accent, and that his delivery was of a hurried, almost nervous, nature.

'You would have my word on that, my dear sir,' said Anthony, trying to sound reassuring.

'I would also need to know that you would not seek to question me further about my affairs, or my motives in the matter that I intend placing before you. I can assure you that you would be paid well for undertaking a task that would require little effort on your part.'

'I see. I cannot see a problem in that respect,' replied Anthony, leaning back in his chair and becoming intrigued as to what was about to be revealed to him.

'Good. I can see that I have made the correct choice,' said the new arrival, unbuttoning the top two buttons of his coat, reaching into its inner pocket and producing a large brown package, which he placed on the table before the solicitor.

Anthony stared down at the package, not knowing whether he should leave it where it was or examine it.

17

'This envelope, Mr Midwinter, contains papers of a delicate and sensitive nature. The package must never be opened, by anyone, least of all by yourself or anyone in your employ. There are others out there who would seek to do so. Should these documents ever find their way into the public arena, the very foundation and stability of our country would be put at risk,' said the stranger, leaning forward and tapping the envelope with one of his fingers.

'I see,' said Anthony, somewhat taken aback by what was being imparted to him.

'I have two requests of you, Mr Midwinter. One is that I leave the package with you, for safe custody. No doubt you have a secure safe?'

'Over there.' Anthony indicated to the corner of the room, where the tall metal device was located.

'Excellent. And the keys?'

'There is only one set of keys to the safe, and I have it upon my person at all times. Not even my clerk has access. Be assured sir, that your package will be safe with us.'

'Good,' said the stranger, again reaching into his coat pocket and taking out a wallet from which he extracted a five pound note. He placed it upon the desk in front of Anthony.

'I will return on 1 May, when I may have further instructions for you, and when you will be paid a further five pounds for your services. I trust that will be satisfactory?'

'Yes, that will be more than satisfactory. We are often asked to look after important papers for our clients. I will have my clerk issue you with a receipt.'

'That will not be necessary, Mr Midwinter.'

'As you wish. But you mentioned two requests?'

The stranger paused for a moment, shifted uneasily in his chair and frowned deeply before speaking. 'My second request may not need to be carried out, Mr Midwinter. Should I not return to your offices on 1 May, however, you are to take the package and present it to the manager of the bank here in Ledbury.'

'We have two banks here in Ledbury. There is Martins Bank and there is Cocks and Biddulph. To which bank am I to take the package?' asked Anthony, looking puzzled.

'Cocks and Biddulph. You must insist on seeing the senior partner, and him alone, and present him with the package. He will see that it is returned to its rightful illustrious owner.'

'Forgive me, sir, for enquiring, but why have you chosen me to look after your package? Would it not be more convenient for you to leave it with Cocks and Biddulph in the first place?' asked Anthony, becoming somewhat perplexed by the whole matter that was unfolding in front of him.

'Mr Midwinter, sir, I have requested that you do not enquire into my affairs. It is you whom I have chosen to look after the envelope. You are only to carry out my second instruction should I not return to your offices on the appointed date. I think I make myself clear on that point,' said the stranger, hastily rising from his seat.

'Of course, my dear sir. There is no address where I can contact you?'

'None. I shall be leaving Ledbury on the evening train for London. You will not see me again until May. I wish you the compliments of the season, sir.'

'And to you, my dear sir.' Anthony rang the bell on his desk, rose to his feet and shook the other's hand.

The door opened and his clerk entered.

'Ah, Perkins, will you show this gentleman out?'

'Of course, sir. If you would care to follow me, sir.'

The stranger hurried from the room, and Anthony listened to his clerk opening and closing the door of the outer office.

Anthony stared down at the package for some moments before picking it up. He estimated that it perhaps contained a dozen papers or so. Crossing over to the safe, he placed his key in the lock and opened the large, heavy door. Before depositing the package on the second shelf from the top, he observed that the envelope had two initials written in pencil in the top left-hand corner – 'A.V.' Anthony scratched his head. The initials obviously meant something to the man who had ensured the package to his safe custody, and had probably been written on the outside of the envelope so as to distinguish it from any others of a similar nature.

As he locked the door to the safe, he went over in his mind once more the words that the stranger had used – 'should any of these documents ever find their way into the public arena, then the very foundation and stability of our country would be placed at risk'. It all sounded very mysterious and important. But what had the stranger meant by those words? If the envelope and its contents

19

were all that important, why had he been chosen, above all others, to be the guardian of such property? Why had he been instructed to take the package to Cocks and Biddulph if the stranger failed to return in May? Why had the stranger not chosen to take it there in the first place? The more he thought about it, the more puzzled he became.

Finally he came to the conclusion that no amount of deliberation on his part would throw any light on the intriguing matter. Extinguishing the light in his room, and after dampening down the remainder of the small fire and buttoning up his overcoat, he closed the door to his office and turned the key in the lock.

'I think you can safely leave off that now, Perkins. What is not done now can safely wait until the festive season is over.'

'Right you are, Mr Midwinter,' replied the clerk, closing his ledger with an eager flourish.

'Put out the candles and let us return to our families for the festive season.'

'As you wish, sir.'

Closing the outer door behind him, Anthony shook hands with his clerk. 'A very Happy Christmas, Tom, to you and your family.'

'Thank you most kindly, sir. May I wish the best of the season to you and your wife, Mr Midwinter. Strange sort of gent, sir, to seek us out at such an hour,' replied his clerk, stamping his feet on the snowy ground.

'Strange indeed, Tom. Strange indeed.'

# CHAPTER TWO

## LEDBURY, NEW YEAR'S EVE, 1888/89

'Damn this collar stud!' exclaimed Ravenscroft, pulling a face as he looked into the mirror.

'Samuel! I do believe that is the first time since our marriage that I have heard you use such language,' reprimanded his wife, shaking her head.

'I am so sorry, my dear. It's just that collar studs and I never seem to get on well together. I don't seem to have too much of a problem during the morning, but these formal occasions can be irksome. No, it's no good. It just won't fasten.'

'Let me, Samuel,' said his wife, crossing over to where he was standing and reaching up to the offending collar. 'Just breathe in a little.'

'I am breathing in. If I breathe in any more I will be dead!' complained Ravenscroft.

'There we are. All done.'

'Thank you. The joys of having a wife who can be employed to do up one's collar studs.'

'I hope you did not marry me just on that account?' teased his wife.

'Indeed not. There was your cooking to be taken into consideration as well.'

'Samuel Ravenscroft, may I remind you that it was I, rather than yourself, who was instrumental in securing our union.'

'And it was the best day's work that you ever managed. I cannot believe that such a miserable fellow as me could have been so

21

fortunate to have married such a beautiful woman as yourself. Hardly a day passes by when I do not give thanks for the salvation of my soul!'

'Now it is you who is being foolish, Samuel.'

'You are right as always, my dear. What is this ball we are attending, anyway?' asked Ravenscroft, picking up a brush from the dressing table and vigorously employing it upon his trousers.

'The Lamplighters' Ball.'

'Strange name to give to such a social occasion.'

'It is an old Ledbury tradition. The lamplighters see in the New Year.'

'And how do they do that exactly?'

'Well, between the hours of eleven and twelve the lamplighters go round the town extinguishing all the lamps that they can see. Then at twelve o'clock they light them all again. Something to do with dampening down the flames of the old year and letting in the light of the New Year. I believe that they also attend the ball, which is named in their honour, and do something with all the lights there.'

'All seems rather quaint and old-fashioned,' remarked Ravenscroft, replacing the brush on the table.

'In the old days I believe the lamps were lit with oil, but now the town has gas. But each lamp still has to be turned on and off by hand.'

'You seem remarkably well informed about all this, but I still don't know why we have been invited.'

'You are now a man of importance in the community, Samuel, and as such you must take your rightful place within Ledbury society.'

'I think you are over-estimating my position, my dear. I am sure that the majority of the citizens of Ledbury have not the slightest awareness of my presence in the town. They are all far too busy going about their everyday business to notice me. Anyway, most of my time since my arrival here has been spent either in Malvern or Worcester,' grumbled Ravenscroft, looking out of the window where he could make out the lamp flickering down the street.

'All the more reason that you – we – should attend the ball tonight. You will have a wonderful opportunity to meet at first hand all the potential lawbreakers within the community,' laughed his wife.

'Lucy, I have been here six weeks and during that time all I have managed to accomplish is the apprehension of two railway navvies who were fighting in the marketplace one night, and the recovery of one lost bicycle and a basket of washing! Hardly major crimes, by any count.'

'Dear Samuel, I suppose life in Ledbury must be rather dull for you after all the excitement of Whitechapel. Perhaps it will be only a matter of time before someone is murdered in the town, and then the good citizens of Ledbury will be more than anxious to call upon your services so that they can again sleep peacefully in their beds at night.'

'Now I know that you are teasing me. I must admit, though, that I was more than pleased to put London behind me. Everyone chasing around, looking for that awful Ripper character and having no success; police being blamed for everything, uniformed officers being jeered at in the street. No, I thank God for my appointment here – even if life is somewhat unexciting at present. But then if I was still in Whitechapel I would not now be here with you, my love, and that is what I most desire in all the world.'

Lucy came forward and kissed him on the cheek.

'And now, my dear, it is time that we put in an appearance at your Lamplighters' Ball before they extinguish all the lights in the town and we have to find our way there in the dark.'

After giving final instructions to the maid in regard to the welfare of her son, Lucy and her husband made their way slowly down Church Lane. As they walked past the old timber-framed buildings, the flickering lamps threw beams of light across the snow-covered cobbles.

Crossing the main thoroughfare at the marketplace, they entered a large black and white building on the other side of the road.

'Good evening, sir. Good evening, madam. Welcome to the Feathers. If you would care to leave your outer garments here, you will find your host and hostess in the large room upstairs,' said a smiling footman as they entered the building.

After depositing their coats with the attendant, they climbed the old wooden staircase and made their way along the landing of the hotel, being drawn forward by the sound of music further down the corridor.

'Good evening to you, sir, madam. And whom do I have the honour of addressing?' asked an elderly grey-haired gentleman at the entrance to a large room.

'Samuel Ravenscroft – and Mrs Ravenscroft.'

'Ravenscroft? Who's Ravenscroft, my dear?' said the man, shaking the new arrival's hand as he turned towards his wife.

'I believe Mr Ravenscroft is the local police sergeant, recently arrived in the town,' replied their hostess, shouting in her husband's ear.

'Inspector,' corrected Ravenscroft uneasily.

'Don't think I've seen you around,' muttered his host.

'I have only been here for six weeks, sir, although my wife has lived in the town for three years. I spend quite a great deal of my time in Malvern and Worcester. That is perhaps why I am not much in evidence.'

'Hmm. More crime in Worcester, I suppose?'

Ravenscroft smiled.

'Delighted to make your acquaintance, Mrs Ravenscroft,' said the gentleman, taking Lucy's hand and bringing it to his lips.

'I hope you will enjoy the ball,' said their hostess, somewhat nervously.

'I'm sure we will,' replied Ravenscroft, giving a short bow and guiding his wife into the room.

'I don't think I have seen so many people in Ledbury in one place before,' said Lucy, as they made their way through the throng towards a waiter who was holding a silver tray.

'Who on earth was that who welcomed us?' asked Ravenscroft, helping himself to two glasses of wine.

'I believe his name is Montacute. He is the manager and owner of Cocks and Biddulph, the local bank. I think he and his wife live at The Gables, that large, imposing house on the way out of the town,' replied Lucy.

'They must have plenty of money to live in such a house. I should think they would need to employ at least a dozen servants or more to keep them in any degree of comfort. The wife must be about half his age.'

'She is very attractive,' offered Lucy.

'I am sure I did not notice – but then you are certainly the most attractive person in the room tonight.'

'Samuel, stop flattering me.'

'You're Ravenscroft, ain't you?'

Ravenscroft turned.

'Onslow at yer service. Major Onslow. Late Bengal Lancers, and now master of the Ledbury hunt.'

'I am pleased to make your acquaintance, sir,' replied Ravenscroft, shaking the hand of a late-middle-aged man of somewhat squat appearance and freckled brown complexion, who sported a large, turned-up, white moustache.

'And who is this fine lady?'

'Allow me to introduce my wife, Mrs Ravenscroft.'

'Delighted, ma'am. Delighted. Mrs Ravenscroft, you say? What a pity. All the best women are spoken for,' said the major, giving a sigh before taking Lucy's hand and kissing it.

'There is a Mrs Onslow?' coughed Ravenscroft.

'Wish there was, my man. Wish there was. Far too busy out in India to have had time to study the field. Now I'm far too old for any decent filly to cast her gaze in my direction.'

'I'm sure that is far from the truth, sir,' said Lucy, smiling.

'You think so, ma'am? Perhaps there is hope for me yet? Should have met you before yer husband snapped you up! There would have been no faltering in the starting blocks then, I can assure yer. Me timing has always left a lot to be desired. Like a word with you about the hunt whilst yer here, Ravenscroft.'

'I'm afraid I don't ride.'

'Pity. Don't know what yer missin'. There's nothing quite like the thrill of the chase to improve one's constitution. Let me know if you fancy trying yer hand sometime or other. Sure I can fix you up with a good filly.'

'Thank you, Major. I'll let you know if I change my mind,' said Ravenscroft, smiling.

'While yer here, there's something else I need to have a word with you about.'

'How can I be of assistance?'

'It's that damn fellow Catherwood!' snorted the major.

'Catherwood?' enquired Ravenscroft.

'Sorry. Forgot you're new to the area. Owns a big farm out towards Colwall way. The man's a bounder. No respect for society. Won't let my hunt go over his lands. Says he'll shoot the first dog that he sees. Damned unsporting of him! Sorry for me language, my dear lady. Very unsporting. Want you to have a word with him Ravenscroft. Tell him to follow the laws of the countryside and all that. Jiggle him up a bit, if you know what I mean.'

'I don't think I can do that, sir.'

'Why ever not, man?' asked the major, frowning.

'Well, unless Mr Catherwood has committed an offence, I have no cause to question him. He would be perfectly within his rights to say who, and who cannot, come on to his land.'

'Rubbish, man!'

'I'm sorry, Major, but I don't see what I can do,' said Ravenscroft quietly, trying to placate the master of the hunt.

'Damn it, Ravenscroft! That sort of attitude won't go down well here. Damned unsporting of yer! Didn't have you down as a lily-faced townie!' growled the major, turning abruptly away and moving to another part of the room.

'Oh dear. I think you might have upset the major just a little, my dear,' said Lucy, squeezing her husband's arm.

'I can't help that. It is just not my job to go around telling people who they can and who they cannot allow on their land,' answered Ravenscroft.

'Never mind. I'm sure the major might eventually come round to your way of thinking.'

'I doubt it.'

'Aren't you going to ask me to dance?' enquired his wife, looking into his eyes.

'I'm not sure I would be very good at it. It has been quite a time since I took to the dance floor. I also suffer from policeman's foot.'

'Policeman's foot? Whatever is that?' asked Lucy.

'Two left feet,' said Ravenscroft, smiling.

Lucy ignored his last remark and, taking hold of his arm, led her husband out on to the crowded dance floor.

'Strange to see the lamps going out all over the town,' said Lucy, as she and her husband looked out from the upstairs window of the Feathers Hotel. Beneath them they could see the lamplighters extinguishing the lamps in the marketplace.

'Within a few minutes the whole town will be plunged into darkness,' added Ravenscroft. 'A good opportunity for housebreaking, I would say, with everyone of note attending this ball instead of safely guarding their own homes.'

'It's Mr Ravenscroft, is it not?' asked a voice at his elbow.

'Yes.'

'Anthony Midwinter. You were kind enough to assist me when I fell the other day.'

'Yes, of course, Mr Midwinter. I trust you are fully recovered, sir?'

'Indeed.'

'Let me introduce you to my wife. Lucy, dear, this is Mr Midwinter.'

'Of Midwinter, Oliphant and Burrows, Solicitors of Ledbury at your service.'

'I am pleased to make your acquaintance, Mr Midwinter,' said Lucy, smiling at the elderly gentleman.

'Strange to see the town plunged into darkness at night. An ancient but not unpleasant custom, I think you would agree, Mrs Ravenscroft?'

'Yes, indeed,' replied Lucy. 'I presume that the lamplighters must have held an important role in the life of the town?'

'Why, yes indeed, Mrs Ravenscroft. The town has always depended on light for its very survival, and the position of lamplighter has always been considered an important one. In medieval times there were just two. Over the past hundred years the town has grown in size and so we now have three lamplighters. A much sought-after position – almost an honour, you could say, to be nominated. Only men of honesty and longstanding in the town are considered to fill the role of lamplighter when such a vacancy arises,' said Anthony.

'Fascinating. Perhaps you should have been a lamplighter, Samuel, rather than a policeman,' said Lucy, smiling at her husband.

'Of course, you are the new inspector!' exclaimed Midwinter.

'I'm afraid so.'

'My husband was only saying to me, earlier this evening, that he did not have enough to occupy his time, due to the law-abiding nature of the town.'

'It has not always been so, I can assure you. Ledbury, alas, does have its crimes, like everywhere else. Why, a few years ago, there was even a robbery at Martins Bank. I remember it came as quite an affront to the town. I'm not sure that they ever caught the perpetrators. Oh, if you would excuse me, I think I can see my wife calling me from near the mantelpiece. I trust you will both enjoy our little ball, Inspector, Mrs Ravenscroft.'

'I hope we may speak again, Mr Midwinter,' said Ravenscroft.

They watched as the solicitor made his way across the crowded room.

'A pleasant gentleman,' remarked Lucy. 'Oh Samuel, do look! They have put out the last lamp by the marketplace. That means it must be nearly twelve o'clock and the lamplighters will be shortly making their way up here. It will soon be the New Year.'

'Load of old ancient rubbish, if you ask me!' exclaimed a young man, bumping into Ravenscroft and spilling some of the contents of his glass over the detective's sleeve. 'Dreadfully sorry, old man, didn't mean to cover you in the best malt.'

'It is of no matter, I can assure you. It will soon dry,' said Ravenscroft, somewhat annoyed and dabbing his suit with his handkerchief.

'Nevertheless, bad form. Not to be excused, on any account. You've met my father then?' asked the young man, taking another drink from a nearby tray.

'Your father?' enquired Ravenscroft, observing that the new arrival was rather the worse for drink.

'Montacute. Nathaniel Montacute of Cocks and Biddulph, money scrapers of this parish,' replied the young man, bringing the glass to his lips.

'We were introduced when we arrived,' offered Ravenscroft, turning away and looking for an opportunity to move to another part of the room.

'Everyone knows my father. If they don't, they won't get any money. My father owns half of Ledbury and has designs on the other half. See that he does not buy you up as well! Sorry, don't think we've been introduced. I'm Rupert Montacute.'

'And do you work in the bank?' asked Lucy.

'Lord above! Don't want to set foot in that awful place if I can help it. No, I'm what you call the black sheep of the family; sometimes referred to as the "idle layabout" by my parents. The one who is always trying to drink away the family fortune, but do you know something? I can't keep up. The more I drink, the more

28

money the old man seems to make! He's always trying not to give me any. That's money, of course, not drink. Keeps nagging me to go out and get a job. Join the army or something. God, can you see me in the army? Can you really?'

'No, I suppose not,' laughed Lucy.

'Better than the church, I suppose. God, that's a laugh. Me in the church! I suppose I'm really a great embarrassment to the old man. When all is said and done, he would rather be rid of me so he can keep up the respectability of the family. Send me off to London or somewhere else miles away from Ledbury. And do you know, I'd go like a shot, tomorrow, except that the tight-fisted old skinflint won't give me any money to go. Miserable old miser. Mean as they come. He just doesn't seem to be interested in giving me any money. What do you think of that, then?'

'I don't know what to think. Now if you'll excuse us,' said Ravenscroft, attempting to steer his wife away from the speaker.

'Oh, don't go. Have a drink with me. See out the old year and all that nonsense I know I go on rather a lot, but I can't help it, really. I'm quite a nice fellow when you get to know me. Have another drink.'

'Now then, Rupert, what have you been up to?' said a new arrival, laying a hand on the young man's arm.

'Just enjoying myself! No harm in that, is there? Go away and leave me alone. These are my new friends.'

'I must apologize for my brother. I'm Maurice Montacute.'

'Samuel Ravenscroft – and this is my wife Lucy.'

'Pleased to meet you both. I'm sorry my brother has had too much to drink. I trust he has not been annoying you?'

'No, not at all,' replied a somewhat relieved Ravenscroft.

'Come on now, Rupert. There's a young lady over there who has been asking about you all night,' said Maurice, attempting to steer his younger brother away from Ravenscroft and his wife.

'I want another drink. You've met my brother? He's always trying to keep me on the straight and narrow. Good old Maurice. What would I do without him?'

'If you will excuse us,' said Maurice, giving a slight bow in Ravenscroft's direction before taking his brother's arm.

'See you again. Can't keep the young lady waiting. Who did you say you were?' enquired Rupert, as he was led away.

Ravenscroft and his wife watched as the two men disappeared into the centre of the crowd.

'It seems as though our Mr Rupert Montacute has had rather too much to drink,' said Lucy.

'He seemed harmless enough; was probably just enjoying the occasion. Interesting – one would not have thought that the two men were brothers. Rupert, young, dark haired, outgoing and frivolous; Maurice, perhaps fifteen years older, seems more confident and reserved. Probably a banker like his father, I would say. Perhaps they are really stepbrothers?'

'Samuel, stop it! You are not on duty now. Stop trying to be the detective.'

'Sorry, my dear.'

'Ladies and gentlemen, will you please welcome the grand order of lamplighters!' a loud voice cried out suddenly from near the entrance of the room.

A loud cheer went up from the crowd as everyone turned to face the direction of the door.

'The lamplighters!'

More cheers and applause from the assembly.

Three men carrying long poles entered the room. Ravenscroft observed that people were beginning to open the windows of the room, letting in the cold night air.

'I didn't know they had uniforms,' shouted Lucy to her husband over the noise.

'Bit like Morris Men. They must just wear them for this one evening,' shouted back Ravenscroft.

The three new arrivals made their way round the room, to great applause, shaking the hands with each of the guests in turn as they progressed.

'Ladies and gentlemen! If I could have your attention for just one minute.' Ravenscroft observed that the speaker was the old banker, Nathaniel Montacute.

'Ladies and gentlemen, I give you a toast – the lamplighters!'

'The lamplighters!' chorused the crowd as they raised their glasses.

Lucy took her husband's arm and smiled as she heard the church clock begin to strike somewhere in the distance.

'Put out the lights before the last stroke!' shouted out a voice from somewhere in the centre of the floor.

'The lights! Put out the lights! Put out the lights! Bad luck not to put out the lights!'

The room quickly plunged into darkness as the cry was taken up.

'Quiet, everyone! Listen to the clock!'

A silence fell over the darkened room, as everyone strained to hear the remainder of the slow chimes of the church clock.

'A Happy New Year!'

The cry went up, as the lamplighters set about the business of relighting the room. Ravenscroft turned to face his wife.

'A Happy New Year, Samuel.'

'A Happy New Year, my love,' said Ravenscroft, kissing his wife and feeling himself the luckiest man alive.

'Ladies and gentlemen, if I could just have your attention once more?' The speaker was their host, Nathaniel Montacute, who was banging his fist on the table. Everyone turned in his direction.

'Ladies and gentlemen, please raise your glasses – to the New Year!'

'The New Year!' went up the cry.

'The New Year!'

'And a prosperous one as well, Nathaniel!' shouted out a voice from the floor.

'It will be, if the bank lets us have our money!' shouted out another, from amidst all the laughter.

'You'll all be welcome at Cocks and—'

But Nathaniel Montacute was unable to complete the sentence.

Someone in the room screamed as first the glass and then the old banker fell suddenly to the floor.

# CHAPTER THREE

## LEDBURY, NEW YEAR'S DAY, 1889

'So it looks as though we have another murder on our hands,' said Crabb.

'Indeed,' replied Ravenscroft.

'Thought things had been rather too quiet since your arrival, sir.'

'They may not be for much longer. This is Doctor Andrews. Doctor, let me introduce you to Constable Crabb, who will be assisting me in this case.'

'Constable Crabb,' replied the doctor, nodding in the arrival's direction.

'Doctor Andrews, sir,' said Crabb, returning the greeting and glancing at the dark-haired, middle-aged man who was seated in one of the armchairs.

Several hours had passed since the dramatic events at midnight, and the three men were sitting in the ballroom of the Feathers Hotel.

'Doctor Andrews was at the ball with my wife and I, and half the population of Ledbury,' explained Ravenscroft, before going on to recount the events of the evening to his younger colleague.

'So Mr Montacute was poisoned?' asked Crabb when his superior officer had finished.

'It would certainly seem that way. I was the first to examine poor Montacute. There was nothing I could do for him; he died within a minute or so,' interjected the doctor.

'We recovered the glass, Crabb. No doubt about it. Poison. Someone must have either poured it into his glass when the lights

32

went out, or made sure that the poison was already in the glass and that he drank it when the lights came back on. I saw Montacute toasting the lamplighters from his glass when they arrived in the room, and he was perfectly all right then,' said Ravenscroft, removing his spectacles so that he might clean them.

'I suppose if you were going to poison someone, you would wait for the lights to go out and then drop the poison into the glass. A perfect opportunity, sir,' suggested Crabb.

'I think our murderer must have slipped the poison into the glass before the lights went out. Everyone was far too occupied in watching the lights go out to see what he or she was up to. If the murderer had waited for the room to descend into absolute darkness he might not have been able to see what he was doing.'

'What happened afterwards, sir?'

'At first everyone was stunned by the event they had just witnessed. One or two people, including Doctor Andrews and myself, rushed forward to see if we could assist the poor man, but once it became apparent that nothing could be done for Montacute, one or two of the ladies screamed and fainted, and I could see that unless I took control of the situation straightaway a wholesale panic might have ensued. I therefore informed everyone who I was, and suggested that it would be better if they all returned to their homes as quickly as possible, with the exception of the Montacute family who were to remain. At first some of the people seemed reluctant to go and I'm afraid I had to apply a fairly strong tone of language to make sure they left. Then once Doctor Andrews had pronounced Montacute dead, I got the old man's sons to take Mrs Montacute home and the undertakers to remove the body.'

'A busy night, sir,' sympathized Crabb.

'Not the way I would have liked to have seen in the New Year,' added Ravenscroft, replacing his spectacles on his nose.

'There will have to be an inquest,' said Andrews, removing his thick-lensed spectacles and polishing them on a handkerchief.

'Almost certainly. Our task now, Crabb, is to discover who killed Montacute, and that's where you might be able to help us, Doctor.'

'Anything. Just ask.'

'How long have you known the deceased and his family?' asked Ravenscroft.

'I came to Ledbury when I completed my medical studies, some four years ago, but I did not attend to the Montacute family until two or three years ago.'

'Oh, why was that, Doctor?'

'Old Doctor Fuller was the family doctor. It was only when he passed away that I was asked to take over the care of the family.'

'I see, Doctor. Please go on. What can you tell me about them?' urged Ravenscroft.

'Well, there is – sorry, was – Nathaniel Montacute, the old man. He was the senior partner in Cocks and Biddulph, the principal bankers in the town. I believe they also have a branch in London as well. The business was apparently well established and the family was obviously very wealthy.'

'What kind of man was Montacute?' asked Ravenscroft, leaning forward in his seat.

The doctor thought deeply for a moment before answering. 'He was a very much respected gentleman in the town, but I would say that while a great deal of that respect came from his position as the town's banker, some of it also came out of fear.'

'Could you elaborate further, sir?'

'Montacute had been mayor of Ledbury on no less than two occasions. He was a local magistrate and served on a number of committees. I believe he had shares in a number of local companies and concerns, and owned a great deal of property in the town. It was generally said that he drove a hard bargain. It was known that those who had crossed him over the years had usually come off the worse for their encounter.'

'I see, Doctor,' said Ravenscroft, looking across at Crabb. 'Can you remember anyone in particular?'

'I suppose Catherwood is the name that immediately springs to mind. He lives alone in a rambling old house just outside Ledbury. Keeps very much to himself, somewhat of a recluse – but at one time he and Montacute were business partners together in a number of local concerns, until the two men fell out. All this happened, of course, before I came to the town, but they say that Montacute would not be happy until Catherwood was ruined.'

'Looks as though there was someone who had a motive for killing Montacute,' suggested Crabb.

'Maybe. Please go on, Doctor,' urged Ravenscroft.

'Well, that's all, really. There is nothing else I can add. As I said, it happened before I came to the town.'

'You mentioned that there were others who had come off the worse for encountering the old man?'

'I suppose over the years, in his role as magistrate, he had sent down quite a number of the local villains. It would have been unusual if one or two of them had not sworn their revenge on the old man,' replied Andrews.

'Anyone in particular, sir?' asked Crabb, taking out his notebook.

'None that I can recall by name.'

'Montacute's wife. She seems much younger than her husband,' said Ravenscroft.

'Edith Montacute. She is Nathaniel's third wife, I believe.'

'His third wife? Tell me about her.'

'I can't tell you much. They married just under two years ago. After the death of his second wife, Nathaniel went on a long holiday round Europe. He was away for nearly six months. When he returned, everyone in the town was surprised to discover that he had remarried during his absence and that a new Mrs Montacute was moving into The Gables. They say he had met her in Rome. I believe her family originated from somewhere in Cheshire. Other than that, I don't know anything else about her.'

'She's quite an attractive woman.'

'Yes, she is certainly a striking figure – although I must admit that I have only met her on one or two occasions, and never in a professional way.'

'Am I correct in assuming that Montacute has two children from his former marriages?' asked Ravenscroft.

'Yes. Maurice is the eldest son from Nathaniel's first marriage. He followed his father into the family bank. Straight as they come. A banker if ever I saw one. Rather dull and dry for me. Then there is Rupert, Nathaniel's son from his second marriage. He is rather fond of the drink and is generally regarded as a waster. Rupert and his father didn't get on well together by all accounts. The two boys are as different as chalk and cheese.'

'I met them both last night,' interjected Ravenscroft.

'Of course. There was also a daughter, Elizabeth, but she died long before I came to the town.'

'Tell me, Doctor Andrews, you stated that Montacute's second wife died just over two years ago.'

'Yes, I attended her during her last illness. That was when I was first called to The Gables.'

'What was the cause of her death? I appreciate you have a confidentiality to uphold, and I respect that, but the more information you can give us regarding the family, the easier it may become for us to solve this crime,' said Ravenscroft, sitting back in his chair.

'Enid Montacute was something of a local beauty, despite her years, and was a very popular figure in the town. She died of a fever. There was little I could do for her. I was not called in until it was too late. She died quite suddenly. It was a great loss to the town when she passed away.'

'And what does the town think of the present Mrs Montacute?' asked Ravenscroft.

'There has been a difference of opinion,' replied Andrews, taking out his pocket watch and looking down at the hands.

'In what way?'

'As I said, everyone was rather taken aback when old Nathaniel returned from his European excursion with his young bride, who must be a good forty years younger than her husband. Some of the townspeople were shocked. You see, Enid had been very popular in the community. It must have seemed to some as though the old man had been almost ensnared by this younger woman.'

'And what is your opinion, Doctor?' enquired Ravenscroft.

'I have none. If Edith is – was – able to make the old man happy, then that is all that matters.'

'And did she? Did she make him happy?'

'I believe so – as far as I can tell. I really must go now, Inspector. If you will excuse me, there are a number of patients I have to visit today,' said Andrews, rising from his seat.

'Of course, Doctor. Please accept my apologies for detaining you for so long. You have been most helpful.'

'Glad to have been of assistance. You know where I am if you need to call on me.'

'Oh, one final question, Doctor. You mentioned Catherwood. Is he a patient of yours?' asked Ravenscroft, standing up and shaking the doctor's hand.

'No. I have never had cause to attend to the gentleman in a professional way.'

'Thank you, Doctor.'

As Andrews left the room, Crabb closed his notebook. 'Well, sir, it seems as though we have quite a lot to go on – a former business partner who was on bad terms with the deceased, a son who disliked his father, a young bride married to a man much older than herself, and a number of criminals who had cause to see him dead. Doctor Andrews was quite informative.'

'Indeed, Crabb, but I sense that this crime will not be an easy one to solve. This room was crowded last night when Montacute was poisoned. There must have been well over two hundred people, any one of whom had the opportunity to slip poison into the glass when the lights went out. I have no doubt that there were a number of people who would have liked to have seen the old man dead – but only one of them who was prepared to go as far as murder.'

'Where do we start, sir?' asked Crabb, eager to begin the investigation.

'I asked the manager of the Feathers to provide us with a list of all those who attended the ball here last night,' said Ravenscroft, reaching into his pocket and drawing out some sheets of paper, which he passed over to his constable.

'Rather a lot of them, sir,' replied Crabb, looking down at the list of names.

'One of those names could well be our murderer, but we must also remember that when the lights went out, practically anyone could have either left or indeed entered the room completely unobserved. Our murderer may not even be on that list.'

'You and Mrs Ravenscroft are on the list. No sign of anyone called Catherwood.'

'That is not surprising. If Mr Catherwood was an old enemy of Montacute, and is a recluse, as the doctor stated, then he would not have been invited,' replied Ravenscroft.

'Perhaps we should start with him first?' suggested Crabb.

'No, I think we can leave Mr Catherwood until later. I suggest that we begin our investigations by paying our respects to the family at The Gables.'

A few minutes' walk brought the two men to the lodge gates of The Gables. As Crabb opened the wrought-iron gate and was about to enter, a voice suddenly called out from behind the hedge, 'Can I be assistance to you, gentlemen?'

'I certainly hope so,' replied Ravenscroft.

The speaker, who emerged into view, was a tall, thick-set, middle-aged man dressed in tweeds and a cloth cap, carrying a rifle under his arm. 'Who the devil are you, then? This is private property.'

'My name is Inspector Ravenscroft and this is Constable Crabb. We are here to investigate the murder of Mr Montacute.'

'Oh, I'm sorry, I did not notice your constable's uniform. Bad business,' muttered the man.

'Indeed – and you are?' asked Ravenscroft.

'Rivers. Gamekeeper.'

'Mr Rivers. Pleased to make your acquaintance. Perhaps you would not mind if I asked you a few questions as we walk up to the house?'

'If you wish.'

'Were you at the Lamplighters' Ball last night?'

'No,' replied the gamekeeper, leading the way up the path towards the house.

'Where were you, then?' asked Ravenscroft.

'Out and about.'

'Where exactly "out and about"?' Ravenscroft could see that the man was not going to be entirely forthcoming with his answers.

'I'm a gamekeeper. I go out at night, keeping an eye out for poachers and suchlike.'

'Did you catch any last night?' asked Crabb.

'No.'

'Were you out all night?' asked Ravenscroft.

'I went out about ten, and came home to find the family coming back from the ball. That's when I learnt that Mr Montacute had been killed.'

'So you were out from ten until sometime after twelve?'

'Yes, although I may have called into the kitchens for a drink,' said Rivers, stopping suddenly.

'What time was that?' asked Ravenscroft.

'Probably about half eleven.'

'Was anyone else there who can vouch for your presence?'

'Mrs Chambers, the cook. She was there. Ask her if you like. Look, what's this all about? Why am I being questioned like this?'

asked the gamekeeper, becoming annoyed.

'We need to know where everyone was at twelve yesterday evening.'

'House is over there. Just ring the bell,' grunted Rivers, turning away.

'Oh, just one final question, Mr Rivers. How long have you worked here for Mr Montacute?'

The gamekeeper turned round and gave Ravenscroft a steely look. 'I've been here for over forty years, man and boy. My father was gamekeeper to Mr Nathaniel before me, and he was gamekeeper to his father, Mr Giles, as well. Now if you've finished, I've work to be doing.'

'Thank you, Mr Rivers. I appreciate your assistance. We may need to speak with you again,' said Ravenscroft.

The gamekeeper said nothing as he walked back towards the lodge gate.

'Bit surly,' muttered Crabb.

'We will need to check his alibi. We will have words later with this cook, Mrs Chambers.'

'How old do you think this building is, sir?'

'Probably two or three hundred years old. Built no doubt by one of the earlier, wealthy Montacutes,' replied Ravenscroft, pulling the bell at the side of the front door.

'At least there are two of them to carry on the line now that the old man's dead.'

The door was opened by a housemaid.

'Inspector Ravenscroft and Constable Crabb. We would like to see either Mr Maurice Montacute or Mrs Montacute if they are available.'

'I will see if Mr Montacute will see you, sir. A terrible business, sir. If you would like to wait in the hall,' said the maid, opening the door wider so that the two men could enter.

Ravenscroft and Crabb found themselves standing in a large hallway, where fine paintings hung on the walls and where an ornate Regency table was situated along one side of the entrance way. A semi-circular staircase swept upwards to the upper levels of the house.

'So this is how the wealthy live!' exclaimed Crabb.

'I would think that those portraits are Montacute's ancestors,' said Ravenscroft, looking up at the works of art adorning the walls of the staircase.

'They certainly are. Gentlemen, if you would care to come in?' said a voice emerging from one of the rooms.

'Good of you to see us, Mr Montacute. I realize that this is a difficult time for you and your family,' said Ravenscroft, shaking the hand of Maurice Montacute. 'Allow us to express our condolences.'

'Thank you, Inspector,' replied Maurice, leading the way into what Ravenscroft considered to be the library. 'Please take a seat, gentlemen. Now, how can I be of assistance to you?'

'All this must have come as rather a blow to you, sir. I hope you will excuse our intrusion. How is Mrs Montacute?' asked Ravenscroft.

'My stepmother is as well as can be expected. She is quite distressed, as indeed we all are. I don't think she will be well enough to answer any of your questions today,' replied the banker, seating himself behind a large desk.

Ravenscroft observed that his host spoke in a slow and precise manner. Maurice Montacute was evidently a man who was used to choosing his words with care. 'Of course, sir, we quite understand. If you don't mind answering a few questions for us, it would be much appreciated. You don't mind if my constable takes notes?' he asked, accepting one of the chairs and gazing round at the book-lined walls.

'No, not at all. Anything I can do to help.'

'Can you think of any reason, Mr Montacute, as to why your father was poisoned?'

'None at all, Inspector.'

'Did your father have any enemies?'

'None that I can think of.'

'Mr Catherwood, for instance?' suggested Ravenscroft.

'Catherwood? Oh, you mean that dispute – all that was over with years ago.'

'I believe Mr Catherwood and your father were business partners at one time?' enquired Ravenscroft.

'That is so, and yes they had their disagreements, but as I said, that was really all quite a long time ago.'

'Did your father ever mention the cause of their falling out?'

40

'No. I cannot recall my father ever mentioning it.'

'You cannot think of anyone else who might have held a grudge against your father? I believe your father was a local magistrate?'

'Yes, indeed. You think that some local criminal might be responsible for his death?'

'We must consider all possibilities, sir.'

'Well, I suppose my father had sentenced a few people over the years, but I cannot recall anyone in particular who might have threatened revenge on my father in any way,' replied Maurice, rubbing the side of his nose.

'If you do think of anyone, I would be grateful if you would let us know.'

'Come to think of it, there was a certain lowlife criminal three or four years ago who was sent down for a time for stealing something or other. My father said there had been quite a disturbance at the court and that he had cause to send him down for a further term because of the unsavoury protest he had made.'

'That is interesting, sir. Do you happen to remember the prisoner's name at all?' enquired Crabb, looking up from his notebook.

'No. I'm afraid not. I expect my father probably mentioned his name at the time, but I don't recall it.'

'No matter, sir, we can check the court records,' said Ravenscroft.

'You think that this man may have been responsible for my father's death?'

'We won't know that until we look. Tell me, Mr Montacute, I believe you worked with your father at the bank?' asked Ravenscroft, changing the subject.

'Yes, I was a junior partner. I followed my father into the bank when I left university.'

'That was something you wanted to do?' enquired Ravenscroft.

'Of course. Why do you ask?' replied Maurice, a look of puzzlement on his face.

'It's just that sometimes children feel compelled by their parents to do something they don't really want to do.'

'I can assure you, Inspector, that I was only too pleased to join the bank. My family has been involved with Cocks and Biddulph for over three generations. It was natural that I should follow my father into the family business.'

41

'Quite and now you will become the senior partner?'

'I would expect so. My father had always led me to believe that one day that would be the case although, of course, there is the new will to be considered.'

'Your father made a will recently?' asked Ravenscroft.

'Yes, my father drew up a new will only a few months ago.'

'I see,' replied Ravenscroft with interest. 'Would you happen to know anything regarding the contents of this will, sir?'

'Of course not. My father did not confide in me when he drew up the document.'

'Wasn't that unusual, sir?' enquired Crabb, looking up from his notebook.

'Not really. It was entirely within my father's character. He kept his business and private affairs very close to his heart. He was not a man to consult other members of his family,' replied Maurice.

'Can you see any reason why your father drew up the will? Surely there would have been an earlier will already in existence?' asked Ravenscroft.

'Yes, of course. I suppose my father wanted to provide for my new stepmother.'

'Where is the will now, sir?' asked Crabb.

'With Mr Midwinter at Midwinter, Oliphant and Burrows, Solicitors.'

'I presume the contents of the document will be read after the funeral?' said Ravenscroft.

'That is normally the case.'

'Your brother, Rupert. There was no wish on your father's part that Rupert should join the bank?' asked Ravenscroft.

'The idea had been muted a year or so ago, but after my brother was sent down from Oxford it was evident that he was not suited to a life of banking. You met my brother yesterday evening, Inspector, so I think you can see what I mean. Unfortunately my brother is rather too fond of alcohol. He clearly has no intention at all of entering any kind of profession or occupation.'

'Was there much conflict between your stepbrother and your father?' said Ravenscroft, detecting a slight trace of sadness in the dry, measured tones of his host.

'I'm afraid so, Inspector. There were a number of heated discussions between the two of them but if you are suggesting that

Rupert would have wanted my father dead, I can assure that nothing could be further from the truth.'

'Why do you say that, sir?' asked Ravenscroft.

'My brother, would have nothing to gain from my father's demise.'

'Unless of course your father had changed his will in Rupert's favour,' suggested Crabb.

'Highly unlikely, Constable. My father would never have changed his will to favour Rupert. He knew that if he did so, it would have meant the end of the bank. You saw the state my brother was in last night. Do you think he would have been capable of carrying out such a dreadful deed in that state, even if he had wanted to?'

Ravenscroft gave a brief smile. 'Can you tell me anything about your stepmother?'

'Edith?'

'I believe your father met her in Rome?'

'That is correct. It was after the death of his second wife, Enid, Rupert's mother, that he decided to travel round Europe for a few months,' replied the banker.

'It must have come as a surprise to everyone when he returned with his young bride?' questioned Ravenscroft, discerning a slight unease breaking through Maurice's dry composure.

'Yes, certainly.'

'There is quite a large difference between their two ages?'

'Yes, but I don't see where all this is getting us, Inspector.'

'Do you get on well with your stepmother, Mr Montacute?' asked Ravenscroft, ignoring the last remark.

'I am not here a great deal, what with my work at the bank, and my club. I also spend quite a great deal of my time in London, visiting our offices there.'

'Thank you, sir,' said Ravenscroft, suddenly rising from his chair. 'We won't detain you any longer. Perhaps we could return tomorrow to see if Mrs Montacute has recovered sufficiently to answer some questions. We might need to interview your brother as well.'

'As you wish, Inspector. Look, Ravenscroft, I want whoever did this terrible thing caught. The family are quite prepared to offer a reward for any information gathered,' said Maurice, crossing over to the bell pull.

'I don't think that will be necessary, sir, at present. Rewards, I find, encourage all kinds of undesirables to come forward with all sorts of fanciful, manufactured stories.'

'As you wish, Inspector. I see what you mean,' said their host, shaking Ravenscroft's hand. 'Do everything you can, Inspector, to catch this murderer.'

'We will endeavour to do our best, sir. Rest assured on that score.'

'Will you show these gentlemen out?' said the banker, addressing the maid who had entered the room.

'Good day to you, sir. I thank you for your time. Oh, one final question sir your gamekeeper, Rivers. I understand he has been with you for a very long time?' asked Ravenscroft.

'Over forty years. He was gamekeeper here, along with his father, when I was a boy. You surely don't suspect him?'

'We have to consider all possibilities, sir.'

'That idea is quite ridiculous. Rivers was totally devoted to my father. He would have had nothing to gain from his death.'

'Thank you, sir.'

Ravenscroft and Crabb followed the maid out of the room and across the hall towards the front door.

'I wonder if we might have a word with your cook, Chambers, before we leave?' said Ravenscroft, addressing the servant woman.

'Yes, sir. She is working in the kitchens. If you would care to follow me, sir.'

The maid opened a door, and the two detectives followed her down a flight of steps which led into a large room.

'Mrs Chambers!' called out the maid. 'There are two gentlemen who would like a word with you.'

An elderly woman of stout build and a red face rose from a seat by the kitchen table.

'Good morning to you, Mrs Chambers,' said Ravenscroft, observing that the cook had recently been crying.

'Good morning to you, sir.'

'My name is Inspector Ravenscroft and this is Constable Crabb. We are investigating the murder of Mr Montacute. May we have a few words with you? Please resume your seat.'

'A terrible business, sir. Who would have wanted to have killed the master?' said the cook, dabbing her eyes.

'That's what we aim to discover,' replied Ravenscroft, seating himself at the table.

'He were a lovely man. Why would anyone want to do the master any harm?'

'You have been here a long time, Mrs Chambers?'

'Forty years, sir.'

'That is a long time. You have witnessed a few changes over the years, I'll be bound?' Ravenscroft smiled, hoping that the woman would be forthcoming with her recollections.

'I have indeed, sir.'

'People have come and gone?'

'Yes, sir. I can remember the first Mrs Montacute. She died as the result of a riding accident, when Master Maurice was young.'

'That must have been quite hard on the boy?'

'Oh yes, sir, it was difficult for him losing his mother like that, what with him being so young. Then there was his sister, Miss Elizabeth, died of a chill when she was eight years old,' replied the cook, only too happy to answer the questions.

'Could not have been easy,' sympathized Ravenscroft.

'No, sir. Then there were the second Mrs Montacute. Miss Enid. She were a real lady, no doubt about it. She knew how to run a house. She was a pleasure to work for. Everyone liked her. It was very sad when she died so suddenly.'

'And what do you think of the present Mrs Montacute?'

'Not for me to say, sir. Don't believe in tittle-tattle and all that nonsense,' replied the cook, adopting a defensive tone.

'Indeed not, but nevertheless it could not have been easy for you to have had a new mistress,' suggested Ravenscroft, knowing that she would only need the slightest encouragement to become talkative once more.

'Not like the old mistress.'

'You mean Mrs Enid Montacute?'

'Exactly, sir.'

'Difficult?'

'Very but I say no more,' said Mrs Chambers, leaning back in her chair.

'Of course.'

'She was not like Miss Enid. She were a real lady, if you take my drift, sir,' replied the cook.

'I understand.'

'Knew how to behave in polite society, and how to treat her servants right, but then the present Mrs Montacute, she's young. She may grow into it.'

'I'm sure she will. Can you think of anyone who would want to see Mr Nathaniel Montacute dead?' asked Ravenscroft, deciding to change his line of questioning.

'No one, sir. Can't see why anyone would want to kill the master,' replied the cook, beginning to wipe her eyes once more.

'Do not distress yourself, my dear lady. What did you do yesterday evening, Mrs Chambers, after the family left to go to the Lamplighters' Ball?'

'Well, sir, as it was New Year's Eve, I sat here for a while, in that chair over there before the fire.'

'Were you alone?' asked Ravenscroft.

'Yes, most of the other servants had been given the evening off. They went to one of the inns in town to celebrate.'

'But you remained here, Mrs Chambers?' asked Crabb, staring down at the large cake which lay on the sideboard.

'I just said that. I sat in that chair,' said the old woman, becoming annoyed.

'Quite, Mrs Chambers. Do you remember if anyone else entered the kitchen?' said Ravenscroft quickly.

'No, I don't think so. Oh yes, Mr Rivers came in for a while, to take a dram and warm his feet.'

'What time was that exactly?'

'Just after eleven, I think.'

'Can you be more precise?' said Ravenscroft, smiling.

'Well, I suppose it was more like half past eleven.'

'How long did Mr Rivers stay for?'

'Why, I suppose about ten or fifteen minutes,' replied the cook with a puzzled expression on her face.

'You could not tempt Mr Rivers to stay and see in the New Year with you?' said Ravenscroft, rising to his feet.

'No. I thought he might have done so, what with it being the end of the old year and suchlike, but he said he had to go outside. He said there would be poachers about, what with all the lights being out in Ledbury.'

'Thank you, Mrs Chambers. You have been most helpful to us. Please don't get up. We will see ourselves out.'

'I hope you catch the villain that did this terrible thing, sir,' sobbed the cook.

Ravenscroft nodded as he and Crabb walked out of the kitchen.

# CHAPTER FOUR

## LEDBURY, NEW YEAR'S DAY, 1889

'Well, sir, looks as though our friendly gamekeeper does not have a good enough alibi,' remarked Crabb as the two men made their way back down the path at The Gables.

'I find it strange that Rivers only came into the kitchen for ten or fifteen minutes, and did not remain there to see in the New Year with Mrs Chambers. Any other person would have taken full advantage of a good fire and a warm drink and remained indoors for longer than fifteen minutes. Either he was being over-zealous in his duties and really was on the lookout for some poacher or other, or—'

'Or he slipped into town in the dark, and put the poison in Montacute's glass, then quietly slipped away again, without anyone noticing him,' interrupted Crabb, finishing Ravenscroft's sentence.

'You could be right, Crabb. How long would it have taken him to have walked from The Gables to the Feathers? Five minutes if he hurried, ten at the outside but we are forgetting one thing, Crabb.'

'Oh, what's that, sir?'

'Rivers does not appear to have had any reason to kill his master. He had worked at The Gables for practically all his working life, as his father had done before him. What advantage could he have gained by killing off the old gentleman?'

'Perhaps Mr Montacute had found out something about his gamekeeper and had threatened to sack him?' suggested Crabb.

'And because Rivers did not want to lose his job, he killed his master? A possibility but I don't really see it at the moment. Tell me what you thought of Mr Maurice Montacute.'

'Not my kind of person, sir. Rather a dull old fish, but then I suppose most bankers are like that, when you come to think of it. Must be all that money – makes them old before their time.'

'Did you notice, Crabb, how uneasy he became when I asked him about how well he got on with his new stepmother? He was quick to divert my line of questioning,' said Ravenscroft, closing the outer gate to The Gables behind him.

'Probably did not entirely approve of his father marrying again?'

'You could be right. To have lost one's mother, and a stepmother, only to acquire a further stepmother cannot have been easy. Maurice is unmarried, I believe, so when he is not up in London he normally resides at the family home, with his father, stepmother and stepbrother.'

'At least the house is large enough to accommodate them all.'

'You would have thought that Maurice would have married by now. With his wealth and position in society, he would have been what, I believe, the ladies call "a desirable catch".'

'Time enough yet, sir. Why look at yourself,' joked Crabb.

'Enough of that,' said Ravenscroft, frowning. 'This new will interests me. I wonder why the old gentleman had decided to revise his will only a month ago?'

'Wanted to provide for his new wife?'

'Maybe. We will need to attend the reading, to see who gains and who loses from Montacute's will. We may well find our reason for the murder there.'

'Don't forget, sir, that the old banker was also a local beak,' said Crabb as the two men began to walk back into the town.

'Yes, we need to have a look at the records to see who it was that caused all the disturbance in Montacute's court, and to find out what exactly transpired there, and where that person may be now.'

'It could be a long job, sir.'

'Then we best start before the morning is over.'

The two men made their way along the main street of the town until they reached a rather drab looking building, the front of which bore a large plaque with the words Magistrates Court engraved on it.

'Perhaps there may be someone in here who can aid us in our research,' said Ravenscroft, closing the front door behind them and ringing a large brass bell which he found lying on a table in the entrance hall.

'Very fusty old smell in here, sir,' said Crabb, turning up his nose.

Presently their call was answered by a thin, elderly, bald-headed gentleman, who was wearing a suit that had seen better days. 'Ah, good morning to you. I presume you are the clerk of the court?'

'And you are Inspector Ravenscroft,' pronounced the clerk, peering over his spectacles.

'I am indeed, and this is Constable Crabb – but how did you know?'

'I was at the Lamplighters' Ball last night.'

'Yes, of course, forgive me. There were quite a number of us there.'

'Terrible business, sir,' said the clerk, shaking his head.

'Indeed. Can you think of anyone who would have wanted to kill Mr Montacute? Sorry, you are?' asked Ravenscroft.

'Simpson.'

'Mr Simpson.'

'Mr Montacute had been one of town's magistrates for nigh on twenty years. During that time he must have sentenced many of the local thieves and villains. Many of them will have accepted their sentences; one or two over the years may have felt particularly aggrieved,' replied Simpson.

'Anyone who comes to mind?'

'There was a particular nasty case some three or four years ago. One of the local villains by the name of Leewood. Came from a bad family. I think he was up on a charge of theft. There was never any doubt about his criminality. Mr Montacute found him guilty and sentenced him – but Leewood protested his innocence in quite forceful terms.'

'How do you mean?' asked Ravenscroft.

'Leewood tried to climb over the rails and attack Mr Montacute, saying he had not committed the crime and that he would get even with him one day.'

'What happened next?' enquired Crabb.

'Mr Montacute, he was having none of it, and quite right as well. He sent him down for a longer term. Perhaps you would like to see the records?'

'That would be most helpful, Mr Simpson.'

'This way, gentlemen. If you would care to follow me.'

Ravenscroft and Crabb followed the clerk down a long corridor and into a large room at the back of the building. Simpson walked over to a set of shelves on one of the walls and looked through a row of ledgers until he lifted one down which bore the year 1885 on its spine.

'I think the event you are looking for occurred in this year, although it might be a year later,' said Simpson, turning over the pages of the large volume. Ravenscroft leaned over his shoulder, looking down at the pages of neat copperplate handwriting, while Crabb busied himself by casting an eye over the contents of the room.

'Ah, here we are,' said the clerk presently, pointing to an entry on one of the pages.

Ravenscroft leaned forward and began to read. '12 June 1885. Joshua Leewood stands accused of stealing three shillings from the premises of John Freeman. Accused pleads not guilty. Evidence called from John Freeman and his servant Maggie Trubshaw who say they both saw accused take the money. Accused says he was elsewhere at the time of the theft. Accused found guilty and sentenced to three years' imprisonment with hard labour at Hereford gaol, by Mr Justice Nathaniel Montacute. Accused then attempted to assault bench but was restrained by officers and was then sentenced for a further three years on a charge of threatening behaviour.' Very interesting. So Leewood had his sentence doubled; he received six years in prison.'

'That would seem to rule him out then in regard to this murder. I reckon he has another two years left to run on his sentence,' said Crabb.

'Hmm, that would appear to be the case. I suppose there is always the possibility that Leewood was released early,' said Ravenscroft, looking up from the ledger.

'Might have escaped?' suggested Crabb.

'We need to find out what happened to Leewood. Crabb, send a telegram to the gaol in Hereford, asking what they can tell us about him. Mr Simpson, you have been most accommodating and informative. I don't suppose you can tell us anything more about this Leewood? You mentioned that he came from a bad family.

What exactly did you mean by that?'

'The Leewoods have always been a bad lot in Ledbury for as long as I can remember. The father, Rufus, went inside several times, usually on counts of stealing and poaching and suchlike. He died about ten years ago. That's when Joshua took over.'

'So this Joshua Leewood had been up before the magistrates before?' asked Ravenscroft, as the three men began to make their way to the front of the building.

'I can think of at least three former occasions. Usually petty things – bit of stealing, the odd pheasant poached, that sort of thing,' replied Simpson.

'So he had been sent to prison before?' asked Crabb.

'He was usually fined but yes, he had been inside for a few months, a year or so before this incident,' replied Simpson.

'You say the Leewoods were a problem family. Joshua Leewood was married?' asked Ravenscroft.

'Yes, sir. There is a wife and several children, I believe. One or two, I regret to say, seem set to be going the same way as their father.'

'Do you know where I can find these Leewoods?'

'You might find them living up one of the alleys leading off the Homend. Probably Smoke Alley – used to be called Smock Alley – near the Horseshoes Inn.'

'Thank you again, Mr Simpson,' said Ravenscroft, shaking the clerk's hand before closing the door and stepping outside. 'Right, Crabb. Send your telegram to Hereford. I'll go and see if I can locate these Leewoods. We'll meet up in half an hour at the Feathers for lunch.'

'As you wish, sir.'

The two men went their separate ways.

As Ravenscroft made his way up the Homend, light flakes of snow began to fall, giving the pavement a wet, slippery appearance. A short walk brought him to an alleyway which bore the words 'Smoke Alley' at its entrance. He made his way down the darkened, uninviting passageway that ran between two buildings, avoiding the piles of rotting vegetables and dog excrement which lay on the cobbles, until he found himself standing in a courtyard where a collection of tall, ramshackle buildings on three sides cast dark shadows over the small, claustrophobic space. For a moment

Ravenscroft thought he was back once more in Whitechapel, until he reminded himself that he was in the country town of Ledbury and that the former darkened world he had previously known was but a distant memory. Nevertheless, a few seconds before he had turned away from the bustle of the Homend with its collection of fine Georgian buildings and half-timbered structures; now he was standing in what appeared to be a darker, more menacing world.

Adjusting his eyes to the darkness, he gradually noticed two small children staring up at him from the floor of the yard.

'Can you tell me where Mrs Leewood lives?' he asked, bending over the children, observing that despite the cold weather, they wore no more than a collection of rags about their persons and that their feet were dirty and blood spattered.

The children remained silent, looking up at his eyes with blank expressions on their faces. Ravenscroft reached into his pocket and brought out a silver coin, which he held out in front of the eldest boy. 'I want to see Mrs Leewood. Tell me where she lives—' he repeated in a louder voice.

The eldest ragged boy reached out to grab the coin but Ravenscroft quickly redrew it towards his chest. 'Mrs Leewood?' he said firmly.

The second, younger boy looked at him with suspicion, and then pointed to the entrance to one of the buildings. Ravenscroft dropped the coin to the floor, and as the two boys scrabbled to retrieve their prize from the debris, he walked over to the old door and banged his fist on the wood.

He waited for a few seconds before knocking once more. The two urchins had recovered the coin and had run off laughing into one of the other buildings, slamming a door behind them.

Receiving no reply, Ravenscroft lifted the latch and pushed open the door. He called out, and strained his eyes to make out anyone or anything in the darkened room. A flickering candle on a table in the centre seemed to be drawing him inwards.

A sudden cough made him turn quickly.

'I'm sorry. I did knock,' he said, closing the door behind him and drawing closer to the flame.

'Who are you?' Again the cough.

'My name is Ravenscroft. I'm an inspector with the local force,' he replied, making out the figure of an elderly, grey-haired woman, who was wearing a dress and shawl and was seated in a wooden armchair.

'What do you want?' said the woman, holding a hand to her face, attempting to stifle the cough.

'I'm looking for Mrs Leewood,' Ravenscroft said hesitantly. As his eyes adjusted to the scene, he noticed that the table was covered with dirty plates and old newspapers. The room had the air of decay and dampness about it.

'You've found her,' replied the hostile voice.

'Mrs Joshua Leewood,' corrected Ravenscroft. He had expected Leewood's wife to have been much younger in years.

'Joshua is my son,' coughed the old woman, drawing her shawl tightly around her shoulders and giving Ravenscroft a cold stare.

'I was given to understand that your son's family lived here,' said Ravenscroft, taking out a handkerchief from his overcoat pocket and bringing it to his nose in an attempt to block out the foul smell that was being emitted from the kitchen sink.

'His wife left two years ago, ran off with a tinker, after babby had died of the pox.'

'I'm sorry.'

'Nothing to be sorry about; he were better out of it.'

'What happened to the other children?'

'Don't know where they went. Somewhere in Ledbury,' replied the old woman, descending into a set of more prolonged coughs.

Something cold brushed against Ravenscroft's leg. He looked down quickly and was relieved to find it was only a black and white cat of a hungry, bedraggled appearance. 'Where is your son, Mrs Leewood?' asked Ravenscroft, recovering his composure but nevertheless anxious to keep his distance from the figure in the armchair.

The old woman laughed. 'You of all people should know that!'

'Hereford gaol?'

Leewood's mother said nothing as she turned her face away towards the empty hearth. Ravenscroft looked down once more at the cat, who hissed loudly at him. 'I understand that your son protested his innocence when he was sent down?' he said, finally breaking the silence.

'What do you want to know for? You going to help him then?' sneered the woman.

'No. I cannot change what has happened in the past.'

'Thought as much,' muttered the old woman, before resuming her coughing.

'You have heard that Mr Nathaniel Montacute is dead? He was the magistrate who sentenced your son.'

'I know who he was.' Ravenscroft thought he could detect a mixture of resignation and bitterness in her voice.

An old clock on the mantelpiece chimed twelve, and he counted the strikes to himself. Neither he nor the old woman spoke.

The cat hissed loudly again at Ravenscroft, before crossing over to the door.

'Did your son ever say anything about Mr Montacute?'

'How do I know!'

The cat began to scratch the door in an angry fashion.

'Cat!' shouted the old woman.

Ravenscroft opened the door, and the animal gave him a venomous look before it quit the room. 'Do you visit your son in prison?' he said, returning to the table.

'How can I afford the fare to Hereford?' laughed the old woman.

'Does your son write to you?' asked Ravenscroft, knowing that his line of questioning was going nowhere.

'Can't read nor write, nor can Joshua,' coughed the woman.

'Should your son return in the near future—' began Ravenscroft.

'My son is still in gaol, where he has no cause to be!' shouted out the old woman, before being convulsed by a fit of coughing.

'Can I get you anything?' he offered, knowing that he could do little to relieve her suffering.

The woman made an angry gesture with her arm, indicating that Ravenscroft should leave.

'Perhaps I could ask Doctor Andrews to call upon you?'

'How do you expect me to be able to pay for some old quack?' growled the old woman.

'I'll pay for Doctor Andrews to call on you, and to give you something for that cough.'

'Nothing can cure me once the fluck has taken hold. Save your money – and get out!'

'I'm sorry,' said Ravenscroft, feeling helpless as he moved back towards the door.

'Get out!'

Ravenscroft realized that it was futile to remain any longer. Opening the door, he stepped out into the courtyard before making his way past the two dirty, shoeless children who had returned to witness his departure.

'Found her then, mister?' asked the eldest of the two boys, looking up at him.

Ravenscroft said nothing but made his way quickly down the alleyway, to where he hoped a brighter, more genteel, welcoming world would be waiting to greet him.

A sudden blast of cold air blew into his face, however, as he turned back into the Homend, reminding him that it was the first day of January and that he could expect little better at this time of the year. He turned up the collar of his coat and made his way through the swirling snowstorm.

As he came down towards the market hall he could hear the sound of dogs yelping and people shouting. Drawing nearer to the Feathers, he saw a group of a dozen or so men on horses, surrounded by a pack of hunting dogs.

'Ah, Ravenscroft, come to see the hunt off, have you?' said the voice of Major Onslow, who was seated on a large white horse.

'Not exactly, Major.'

'Damn snow! Can't see more than five feet in front of me,' snapped Onslow, reaching down to grasp a small glass of liquid from a silver tray, which a shivering waiter from the Feathers was holding out towards him.

'Not a good day for the hunt,' shouted Ravenscroft through the driving snow.

'Eh? What's that you say? Speak up, man,' demanded the master of the hunt before swallowing the contents of his glass in one gulp.

'I said, it's not a good day for hunting!'

'Soon clear. Should get two or three of the blighters before dark. Caught who killed poor old Montacute yet?' asked Onslow, taking another glass from the outstretched tray.

'Our investigations are still at an early stage.'

'Suppose so. Bloody awful thing to happen! Who the devil would want to kill old Montacute?'

'Who indeed, Major?'

'Snow seems to be dying down a bit. Best be on our way, we can't keep the foxes waiting. Good day to you, Ravenscroft,' shouted

Onslow, banging his empty glass down on the tray and signalling to one of the huntsmen to sound the horn.

Ravenscroft stepped back towards the wall of the Feathers as the riders in their bright red coats, black breeches and hunting caps rode away from the old coaching inn, a pack of black and white dogs barking behind them and a collection of some thirty or forty retainers and townsmen bringing up the rear of the procession.

'Rather them than me on a day like this,' said Crabb, walking over the road and joining his superior officer.

'Rather them than me on any day of the year, Crabb. Hunting is a pastime which has never held any appeal for me. You look cold. Let's go inside,' said Ravenscroft, opening the door to the inn.

The two men made their way to the snug, where a welcoming fire spluttered loudly in the hearth.

'Just the thing,' said Ravenscroft, removing his overcoat and rubbing his hands in front of the flames.

'Good day to you, gentlemen. Can I get you something to eat and drink? We've some nice venison pie left over from the festivities,' said a cheery-faced barman.

'Excellent – and two tankards as well, if you please,' instructed Ravenscroft.

'I sent off the telegram, sir, with instructions that they are to reply as soon as possible,' said Crabb, seating himself on one of the stools.

'Good man. It will be interesting to see what the prison authorities can tell us about Leewood.'

'How did you get on with the family, sir?'

'The Leewoods live off the Homend, in a miserable place in Smoke Alley. If I said it was as bad as some of the places I used to visit in Whitechapel, I would not be far off the mark. Even the rats appeared to have left last year.'

'I know what you mean, sir,' sympathized Crabb.

'I spoke with an old woman, who appears to be dying from some form of consumption, who said she was the mother of our Joshua Leewood. She told me that her daughter-in-law had run off with a tinker some two years ago, and that her grandchildren were living she knew not where in some other part of Ledbury. Apparently she has neither seen nor heard anything concerning her son since he was sent down,' said Ravenscroft, standing before the fire and feeling the heat beginning to make its way up his back.

'Bit of a blank there then, sir.'

'At least there was no sign that Leewood was there, so one can only assume that he is still locked up in Hereford gaol.'

'We won't know that until we receive the reply,' replied Crabb, accepting two plates of food from the barman. 'This looks mighty good.'

'Ah, you won't be disappointed there. Best venison pie in the whole of Herefordshire. I'll just get your ale, gentlemen.'

'Thank you, my man. Have one yourself at our expense,' said Ravenscroft, looking down at the plate before him.

'That's uncommonly good of you, sir, I don't mind if I do.'

'Eat up, Crabb. Hopefully the snow will have eased after our lunch and we can go and pay a visit on Mr Catherwood and attempt to discover what part, if any, he plays in this affair.'


An hour later Ravenscroft and Crabb left the Feathers Hotel. A thin layer of snow had settled over the ground and a hesitant sun was attempting to appear from beneath a dark-looking cloud as the two men made their way on foot up a narrow lane that ran off the marketplace.

'I thought it best if we walk in this weather, Crabb. Catherwood's place can't be more than ten-minute's away from here,' said Ravenscroft.

Their journey took them away from the town as they began to climb steadily upwards, past a wood on their right and some fields stretching away downwards on their left-hand side. Eventually a large, rambling, black and white house came into view, the grounds of which were surrounded by a forbidding wooden fence. As they drew near they could hear the sound of dogs barking.

'That would seem to be the main gate over there,' said Ravenscroft, pointing to one side.

'I don't like the look of those animals,' said Crabb, observing that their approach was being heralded by two large dogs intent on preventing any intruders from entering the grounds of their domain.

'Perhaps if we wait here for a minute or two their owner may appear and give us safe passage,' suggested Ravenscroft.

'What do you two want on my land?' called out a voice suddenly.

Ravenscroft and Crabb turned to see a middle-aged man of stocky, rugged appearance walking towards them.

'Mr Catherwood?' enquired Ravenscroft.

'Depends who wants him.'

'Inspector Ravenscroft from the local constabulary, and this is my associate Constable Crabb.'

'And what do you want with me?' said the man in an offhand manner.

'We are investigating the death of Mr Montacute. I believe you may be able to assist us in our enquiries, if we might have a few moments of your time?'

The man stared at the two detectives for a few seconds and then said, 'You best come in then.'

'Thank you,' replied Ravenscroft.

'Mind the dogs,' instructed Catherwood, opening the gate.

One of the animals leapt up to greet its master, while the other growled at a nervous Crabb and seemed intent on trying to jump upwards on to the constable.

'Down, you brute!' shouted Catherwood.

The two dogs instantly obeyed.

'Dogs won't hurt you unless you startle or threaten them. Follow me, gentlemen.'

Crabb gave Ravenscroft a look of relief as the two men followed the owner and his dogs along the path towards the main door of the residence.

'You are not originally from these parts then, Mr Catherwood?' asked Ravenscroft.

'Yorkshire.'

'How long have you been resident in Ledbury?'

'Twenty-one years,' replied Catherwood, opening the door and indicating that they should enter.

Ravenscroft and Crabb found themselves standing on the quarry-tiled floor of a large room of rustic appearance, which was dominated by a great oak table and chairs in its centre, and a roaring log fire blazing forth from a stone hearth at the far end.

'Take a seat, gentlemen,' said their host, throwing his hat down on the table. 'I thought it would not be long before you arrived.'

'Oh, why do you say that, sir?' said Ravenscroft, pulling out one of the chairs from the table and seating himself as the two dogs stretched out before the fire.

'You know perfectly well, Ravenscroft, that Montacute and myself were once business partners and that we had a severe falling out. You no doubt see me as your main suspect,' replied Catherwood without hesitation.

'I would not say that, Mr Catherwood. At this stage we are merely making enquiries. The more we can discover about the late gentleman's affairs, the more information we can obtain which may help us to eventually make an arrest,' said Ravenscroft, sensing that his host was a man who liked to come quickly to the main point of an argument, and that he would need to tread carefully so as not to give offence.

'Don't mince your words, Ravenscroft,' said Catherwood.

'Tell me why you and Montacute fell out,' said Ravenscroft.

'The man cheated on me.'

'Can you elaborate further, Mr Catherwood?'

'Shortly after I arrived in Ledbury, Montacute got me to invest a large portion of my savings in some old cottages and land at the bottom of New Street, telling me all kinds of fanciful stories about how their value would double in five years. Then after two years he said the council – of which he was the mayor of at that time – would need to acquire the land in order to widen the road and that we would have to sell for a fraction of the price we had paid. There was nothing I could do but comply with the demand, or face the courts. Montacute then said that if I invested the sale proceeds, I would soon double my investment, as he knew of a good company in the city that was involved in shipping and was sure to do very well. I, like a fool, believed him. The following year, Montacute sold his share of the New Street properties to the Ledbury Gas Coke and Coal Company for the new gas works and made a pretty pile in the process – seemed as though he had not sold his share of the original investment after all. At the same time the company I had speculated in became bankrupt after one of their ships was lost at sea.'

'Unfortunate,' muttered Crabb, writing in his notebook.

'Not unfortunate at all! I sold out my share of the investment to Montacute, only to learn later that the company had been resurrected and had doubled its profits the following year. I call that sharp practice,' added Catherwood.

'I can see why you disliked Mr Montacute,' said Ravenscroft, trying to sound sympathetic.

'Dislike is putting it mildly. I hated the man at the time, Ravenscroft, but I soon realized I was powerless to do anything about it. Montacute had nearly ruined me, but he had such a strong hold on the affairs of the town that I could see little opportunity for redress,' replied Catherwood, throwing another log on the fire.

'And do you still hate Mr Montacute?'

'No point. At the time I could have killed him quite easily, but as the years go by you soon realize it does you little good to think about the past. No amount of bitterness on my part will bring back my money. I had no time for the man, but I certainly did not kill him. I would not soil my hands with his death.'

'I see,' said Ravenscroft, looking sideways at Crabb. 'Can you tell me where you were last night, Mr Catherwood?'

'Here, as I am most nights.'

'You live alone?'

'I prefer it that way. People in Ledbury say I am a recluse, and that I keep to myself. Who am I to correct them in their assumptions?' said Catherwood, bending down and patting one of his dogs on its head.

'So there is no one who can prove that you were here at your house last night?' asked Ravenscroft.

'Only my dogs. I keep no servants – only an old woman from the town who comes up here to keep the house clean and cook me a meal in the middle of the day. That serves me well enough. I have little cause to go into the town.'

'You have not seen Mr Montacute recently?'

'Last time I saw Montacute was three years ago on the other side of the street. He barely noticed my existence.'

'Do you have cause to still invest with Cocks and Biddulph?'

'After all that has happened? I keep what little money I have left over to myself,' laughed Catherwood.

'Well, sir, you have been most informative. Before we go, can you recall anyone else who may have lost money through dealings with Montacute?' asked Ravenscroft, getting to his feet.

'None that I can name, though I'm sure there must have been others. Men like Montacute don't increase their wealth by doing large favours for those less fortunate than themselves,' said

Catherwood, motioning to the dogs that they were to remain where they were as the two policemen prepared to leave.

'So you can think of no one who would have wanted Montacute dead?'

'As I said, Inspector, there are almost certainly others out there whose dislike of the man may well have been greater than my own.'

'Does the name Leewood mean anything to you? Joshua Leewood?'

'Leewood? No, the name means nothing to me.'

'Thank you, Mr Catherwood. If you remember anything that could assist us in our enquiries, I would be obliged if you would let us know,' said Ravenscroft, shaking the large, rough hand.

'Let me see you out.'

As Ravenscroft and Crabb walked back towards the centre of the town, the former paused for a moment to turn round and look back at the building in the distance. 'A strange kind of existence, living day after day with only two dogs and a visiting domestic for company. If Montacute had ruined Catherwood and caused him to become a recluse, you would have thought that Catherwood would have displayed more anger and bitterness towards the banker. Instead he seemed almost resigned to his fate, accepting that he could do little to alter circumstances.'

'Perhaps, as he said, he has long forgotten the wrong that was done to him?' suggested Crabb as the two men resumed their walk.

'In my experience, Crabb, men who have been financially ruined by another neither forgive nor feign indifference with the passage of time. Catherwood was far too accommodating for my liking. His calm, down-to-earth exterior may well be hiding an intense anger beneath. Either we are dealing with a man who really did not care what happened to Montacute, or with a very clever man who is more than capable of murder.'

'Trouble is, sir, if no one saw him enter the Feathers in the dark, then we won't be able to prove that he is our murderer.'

'Exactly, Crabb. Also, that inn has far too many entrances and exits for my liking. I wonder if there are others in the town who might have fallen out with Montacute over the years? Or was Catherwood just implying that there were others who hated the old banker in an attempt to deflect suspicion away from himself?' said Ravenscroft, quickening his pace.

'If Catherwood did not kill Montacute, then who did? Rivers? Leewood? Both must be strong suspects, sir.'

'Talking of Leewood, let us call in the mail office and see if we have had a reply to your telegram.'

A few minutes later the two men entered the mail office in the centre of the town.

'Ah, Inspector Ravenscroft. I have a telegram from Hereford for you,' said the clerk, handing over the piece of paper.

'Thank you, my good man,' said Ravenscroft, reading the message.

'Well, Crabb, this looks interesting. It appears that Leewood managed to escape from Hereford gaol last week – and that no one has seen or heard of him since!'

# CHAPTER FIVE

## LEDBURY, 2 JANUARY 1889

The following morning, Ravenscroft stepped out of his cottage in Church Lane to discover that more snow had fallen during the night, and that the ground had become frozen by the late frost.

'Need to be careful, sir,' said Crabb, as the two men met up outside the police station.

'Any news of the escaped convict, Leewood?'

'None, sir. The Hereford police have posters up all over the town, and I have informed the stations in Malvern and Worcester to keep a lookout in case he shows up there. It seems he escaped two days before Christmas.'

'Well done, Crabb. I wonder where the fellow is now? He can't have got far in this weather, without any food or money.'

'I suppose some former associate could be sheltering him? I went to Smoke Alley earlier this morning with a couple of the men but there was no sign of him there. I see what you mean when you said it resembled your old haunts in Whitechapel,' said Crabb, stamping his feet on the ground in an attempt to keep warm.

'I suppose that is probably the last place he would go to, knowing that it would be the first place we would go looking for him.'

'So you think Leewood could be our killer, sir?'

'He certainly had cause to seek his revenge on the old man, and he was certainly at large on New Year's Eve. However, it would have been extremely difficult for him to have obtained a poisonous liquid, and even more difficult for him to have slipped into the Feathers unnoticed. By coming back to Ledbury, where he was known, he would be sure to be seen and arrested sooner or later. If I had been Leewood, I would have put a great distance between the county and myself after my escape,' said Ravenscroft, turning up the collar of his coat and pulling his hat further down his head.

'He could have travelled west into Wales?' suggested Crabb.

'Possibly. Of course, we are assuming that Leewood would have behaved in a rational manner, whereas in fact his intense bitterness towards Montacute might have overridden common sense. Either way, we won't know if he did kill Montacute until we've caught him.'

'Where are we going today, sir?'

'I sent word to The Gables, earlier this morning, saying that we would be calling on Mrs Montacute and would be desirous of speaking with her.'

'Right, sir.'

The two men made their way from the high street and towards The Gables.

'Thinking back to yesterday, Crabb, I find it strange that Catherwood remained in Ledbury after the end of his financial involvement with Montacute. You would have thought he would have sold up and gone back to Yorkshire. There was nothing to keep him here in Ledbury – so why did he not leave?' said Ravenscroft, treading carefully on the frozen road.

'Perhaps he could not afford to move?'

'I would have thought the sale of his home and grounds would have netted a tidy sum. No. There has to be another reason why Catherwood has remained here all these years.'

'Waiting for his time to kill Montacute?'

'Rather a long time to wait to extract his revenge, don't you think? He could have killed Montacute years ago – no need to wait until now.'

'Perhaps he is wanted in Yorkshire for some previous crime he committed long ago, and was afraid to go back there?'

'Whatever the reason, it does not seem to add up. Why stay in a town where you are regarded as some kind of strange recluse, and where your greatest enemy lives just down the road? We will need to enquire further into the affairs of Mr Catherwood.'

A voice interrupted their conversation. 'Good day to you, gentlemen!'

'Good morning, Mr Rivers. We were just on our way to The Gables to see Mrs Montacute,' said Ravenscroft, observing that the gamekeeper was carrying a shotgun under his arm.

'You don't want me, then? I'm off to the woods, shooting pheasants,' Rivers told them.

'No, we have no need to question you at the present. Mrs Chambers has confirmed that you were in the kitchen between eleven thirty and a quarter to twelve last night. Why did you not remain in the kitchens to see in the New Year, Mr Rivers?' asked Ravenscroft, looking the gamekeeper full in the face.

'Thought I told you – I was out looking for poachers.'

'So you did, Mr Rivers, so you did,' said Ravenscroft, smiling.

The gamekeeper gave a shrug of his shoulders before striding away in the direction of the woods.

'You still suspect him, sir?' enquired Crabb.

'At the present time I don't know who is the more likely suspect – Leewood, Catherwood or Rivers. Ah, here we are at The Gables. Let us see whether Mrs Montacute is well enough to see us today.'

Ravenscroft rang the bell and the maid opened the door.

'Good morning. It is Inspector Ravenscroft and Constable Crabb to see Mrs Montacute, if you please. I believe we may be expected.'

'If you will just wait here, sir,' said the maid, showing the two men into the hall.

After a few moments she returned and instructed them to follow her into the drawing-room. 'Inspector Ravenscroft and Constable Cribb, my lady.'

'Crabb. Constable Crabb,' corrected the policeman.

'Ravenscroft.' Maurice Montacute was standing by the fire.

'Good morning, Mr Montacute,' replied Ravenscroft, shaking hands with the banker.

'Mrs Montacute has agreed to answer your questions, Ravenscroft.'

'Good morning, madam. Please accept my sincere condolences for your loss,' said Ravenscroft, stepping forward and giving a slight bow in the direction of the lady who was sitting on a chair before the fire.

'You were there at the Lamplighters' Ball, when my husband . . .' said Mrs Montacute, her voice trailing away, the red eyes indicating the symptoms of her grief.

'I thought it best if I were present, Ravenscroft,' said Maurice.

'Of course, sir.'

'Do take a seat, man. How are your investigations proceeding?'

'Slowly, but with thoroughness, sir,' replied Ravenscroft, accepting the chair and trusting that he had given the answer that had been expected of him.

'I hear that you suspect some man whom my husband sent to prison some years ago?' enquired the lady, looking directly at Ravenscroft.

'We have discovered that a certain Joshua Leewood was indeed sentenced to a term of imprisonment by your late husband, and that this man absconded from Hereford gaol shortly before Christmas. Does the name Leewood seem in any way familiar to you, Mrs Montacute?' asked Ravenscroft.

'I hardly think that Mrs Montacute would have had any recollection of this Leewood. After all, the incident occurred before Mrs Montacute met my father,' interjected Maurice.

'Of course. I just wondered whether your husband ever mentioned his name, in conversation, at some later date?'

'No, Inspector. The name is unfamiliar to me.'

'Did your husband ever mention anyone whom he thought might have been his enemy?'

'No. My husband always kept his business affairs to himself. He very rarely discussed his financial undertakings with me,' replied the young widow, looking down at her neatly folded hands.

'So you cannot think of anyone who would have wanted to kill your husband?' asked Ravenscroft, noticing that tears were beginning to form in the reddened eyes.

'Look, Ravenscroft, you can see how distressed Mrs Montacute is. Could we not leave this until another day?' said Maurice anxiously.

'No, Maurice, it will be quite all right. The inspector must do his duty if my husband's killer is to be brought to account. Please proceed with your questions, Mr Ravenscroft.'

'Thank you, Mrs Montacute. Can I take you back to the ball at the Feathers? I know this must be rather difficult for you, and I will try and be as brief as possible. When the lamplighters came into the room, you were standing next to your husband?'

'Yes.'

'Can you describe what happened next?' asked Ravenscroft, leaning forward.

'Well, my husband raised his glass and toasted the lamplighters, that is all.'

'Did your husband drink from the glass?'

'Yes, we all drank from our glasses.'

'And what happened next?'

'My husband and I watched the lamplighters go round the room as they extinguished the lights.'

'I want you to think very carefully now, Mrs Montacute, before you answer my next question. You and your husband were standing at the head of the room, near the entrance, I believe?'

'That is correct.'

'Can you remember if you were talking with anyone in particular at the time? Was there anyone close to you when the lights went out?' asked Ravenscroft, beginning to feel that he was coming nearer to obtaining the vital information he sought.

'I can't recall anyone in particular. I remember we had just been talking with Major Onslow, shortly before.'

'Major Onslow,' repeated Ravenscroft, looking across at Crabb, who was taking notes in his pocket book. 'You say you had just been speaking with Major Onslow?'

'Yes, I believe that was so.'

'Then what happened, Mrs Montacute?'

'We all listened for the clock to finish striking, then everyone said Happy New Year to one another as the lights came back on.'

'When the lights came on, was Major Onslow still with you, or had he moved away? This is very important.'

'I cannot remember. I am so sorry.'

'Come now, Ravenscroft, you can see that Mrs Montacute is distressed,' interrupted Maurice Montacute.

'When your husband reached out for his glass, can you recall whether it was on the table or whether he took it from perhaps a waiter?' asked Ravenscroft, ignoring the interjection.

Mrs Montacute thought deeply for a moment. 'I think my husband's glass was on the table. Yes, I am sure of it – he picked up the glass from off the table.'

'The same glass he had been using only a minute or so before?' asked Ravenscroft, pressing home his point.

'Yes.'

'When you stood there in the darkness, listening to the chimes, were you aware of anyone brushing past you, or anyone leaving or entering the room? Think carefully, Mrs Montacute.'

'No. I don't think there was . . .' replied the widow hesitantly.

'But you are not sure?'

'Come now, Ravenscroft—' protested Maurice.

'But there was someone?'

'I don't know. Yes, I suppose so – in the dark, I thought someone brushed past me, but I could not see who it was,' replied Edith, a strained expression on her face.

'Do you think it was a man or a woman?' enquired Ravenscroft.

'I'm sorry, I don't know. That's all I can recall. It just felt as though someone had moved in front of us and had then left the room.'

'Thank you, Mrs Montacute. I promise that I will not detain you for much longer. I wonder if you could tell me how you and Mr Montacute first met?'

'It was in Rome, nearly two years ago. Nathaniel, my late husband, had just lost his second wife. He was travelling alone around Europe. On the "Grand Tour", you might say. I was staying at the same hotel, near the Vatican City.'

'And you were married shortly afterwards, I hear?' said Ravenscroft.

'Dear me, Inspector, you make it all sound so—'

'Forgive me. I had not intended to suggest that there was anything unusual in your marriage,' said Ravenscroft, leaning back in his chair and realizing that he had been less tactful than he had intended.

'I acknowledge that there is – was – quite an age difference between my husband and myself, and I realize that my arrival here must have caused a few people to think that perhaps I had married Nathaniel for his money – but I can assure you, Inspector, that despite our age difference, we married for love and for love alone,' explained Edith Montacute, becoming increasingly agitated.

'I really do think you have overstepped the mark this time, Ravenscroft, and must ask you to leave before any more distress is caused to my stepmother,' said Maurice Montacute, standing up.

'Of course. Thank you, Mrs Montacute, for answering all my

questions. I am sorry to have questioned you at a time like this, but I am sure you will agree that if we are to discover who killed your husband we must pursue all possible lines of enquiry,' said Ravenscroft, observing that the young widow had already turned away.

'Ravenscroft, I'll see you both out,' said Maurice.

'That won't be necessary, sir. We can find our own way. Thank you once again, Mrs Montacute,' said Ravenscroft, giving a short bow before walking across to the door. He noticed that Edith Montacute did not look up as he and Crabb left the room.

In the hallway, he paused to look upwards again at the fine portraits which hung on the wall overlooking the sweeping staircase.

'Rather a miserable, pathetic collection, I think you would agree?'

Ravenscroft turned to see that the speaker was young Rupert Montacute, who had just entered the front of the building.

'Good day to you, Mr Montacute.'

'Spoke with you at the ball, didn't I? Ravenswood, isn't it?'

'Ravenscroft,' corrected the detective. 'I was just admiring the portraits.'

'Six generations of upstanding noble Montacutes. Every one of them pillars of society; dull, crusty old sticks. That's the old man at the bottom, painted some twenty years ago when he was better looking. God, I suppose there will now have to be a new one, now that Maurice has become the head of the clan.'

'But not one of yourself, sir?' asked Ravenscroft.

'God forbid! No room for second, dissolute sons on the grand staircase,' laughed Rupert.

'Your brother is the last of the line?'

'I suppose he is. He'd better get on with it, and marry some dull, boring woman and produce some ghastly urchins, or there won't be any more Montacutes to carry on after him.'

'Unless you marry, sir,' suggested Ravenscroft.

'God forbid, Ravenswood! No woman of any importance is going to saddle up to me,' replied Rupert, giving a casual laugh.

'And what will you do now, sir?'

'What do you mean, what will I do now?'

'I mean, sir, what will you do now that your father is dead?'

'Lord knows. Not given the matter much thought. Carry on as before, I suppose, if my wonderful stepbrother will indulge my profligate ways.'

'Can you think of anyone who would have wanted your father dead?' asked Ravenscroft, seeking to steer the conversation in another direction.

'Half the town, Inspector, half the town,' laughed Rupert.

'Anyone in particular, Mr Montacute?'

'Can't think of anyone special. Look here, Ravenswood, how can you expect such a silly fellow as myself to remember important things like that?'

'No, sir, I suppose not,' said Ravenscroft, smiling and giving Crabb a sideways glance. 'Can you remember, sir, where you were exactly in the room when your father collapsed?'

'Fireplace. Yes, I remember, I was having a drink and talking to a pretty young lady by the fireplace when the lights went out.'

'Who was that, sir?' asked Crabb.

'So your assistant does speak!' said Rupert sarcastically.

'Who was the young lady, sir?' asked Ravenscroft firmly.

'How the devil should I know? I've never seen her before. Wore a pink dress and had crooked teeth – that's all I can remember.'

'Thank you, Mr Montacute. We won't detain you any longer,' said Ravenscroft, moving towards the door.

'Glad to have been of help, Inspector Ravenswood,' said Rupert, beginning to make his unsteady way up the staircase.

'Well, those two brothers are certainly different from one another,' said Crabb as the two men walked away from The Gables.

'Same father, different mothers.'

'You could smell the drink on Rupert.'

'Yes, he is rather "fond of the bottle", as they say. I find it interesting that although Rupert was clearly the worse for wear at the Lamplighters' Ball, and appears to remember little about everyday events, he was very quick to tell us exactly where he was standing when his father was poisoned – yet he can't remember the name of the person who he was talking with,' said Ravenscroft, deep in thought.

'Very convenient, if you ask me,' added Crabb.

'Did you also notice, Crabb, how protective Mr Maurice Montacute was of his stepmother? On three separate occasions, he interrupted my line of questioning when he thought I was being too bold with my enquiries.'

'Could be something going on there, between Maurice and his stepmother?' suggested Crabb.

'You think Maurice might have killed his own father so he could inherit both the bank and his wife? That is a fascinating possibility, Crabb. So far in this case, the more people we question, the longer our list of suspects becomes—'

'I think I can see one of the men from the station running in our direction, sir,' interrupted Crabb.

'Glad to have caught you, sir,' said the breathless constable, coming to a halt. 'Urgent message from Mr Catherwood. Can you come as quickly as you can, sir, to Dog Hill.'

'Did Mr Catherwood say what he wanted?' asked Ravenscroft.

'No, sir – only that I was to find you as quickly as possible and bring you in the direction of the hill, and that Doctor Andrews was to come as well.'

'Then you best lead on, Constable.'

The three men made their way quickly towards the church. After walking through the churchyard, they turned the corner and joined the old trackway that gradually took them upwards, away from the town.

'There's Mr Catherwood, sir,' indicated the constable, pointing ahead of them. As they drew near, one of Catherwood's dogs began to bark at the group, until its master shouted the command for the animal to sit.

'Good morning to you, Mr Catherwood,' called out Ravenscroft.

'Over here, man!' Ravenscroft could see that Catherwood was standing near some of the undergrowth at the side of the track.

'Found him not half an hour ago – or rather the dog did,' said Catherwood, standing back.

Ravenscroft stepped into the snow-covered bracken and looked down at the ground.

'What is it, sir?' asked an inquisitive Crabb.

'It appears to be the body of a man, lying face downwards!' replied Ravenscroft. 'You say the dog found him?'

'Yes, we were out for a walk. Dog went off into the undergrowth and started barking and pawing at the ground. I came over and discovered the body.'

'Did you touch anything?' asked Ravenscroft, surveying the deceased.

'No. I came straight to the station.'

'You did right, Mr Catherwood.'

'I told the constable to fetch Andrews as well,' said Catherwood.

'Thank you, sir, you acted correctly. Well, whoever he is, he has been here for quite a while, I would say. The fact that there is a thin layer of earth on top of him rules out death from any natural causes, and I would say that he died several days ago.'

'Could be Leewood?' suggested Crabb.

'Maybe, but this fellow looks as though he was too well dressed, in this long overcoat, to be Leewood – and, anyway, why would anyone want to kill Leewood?' replied Ravenscroft.

'Sir, I think Doctor Andrews has arrived,' interrupted the constable.

'Good morning, Ravenscroft, Catherwood. What have we got here?' said Andrews, hurrying over to where the body lay.

'He was uncovered by Mr Catherwood's dog, Doctor Andrews,' said Ravenscroft.

'I see,' said Andrews, crouching down by the side of the body. 'Can you give me a hand to turn him over?'

'Constable, go to the station, get the cart and return with some men. We will need to move the body,' instructed Ravenscroft, before he and Crabb knelt down by the side of the corpse.

The three men eased the body on to its back. 'My God, he must have been here for quite a while!' exclaimed Ravenscroft, taking a step backwards and bringing his handkerchief to his nose.

Crabb took one glance at the dead man and turned away quickly.

'It looks as though he was hit on the forehead by something hard. Part of the skull and face have caved in,' said Andrews, bending over the body. 'By the state of him, I would say that he has been here for at least a week, possibly longer. The intense cold weather and snow have helped to preserve the body to a certain extent, though I see that some animal has been gnawing at his ears and nose. One eye has completely gone.'

'What description do we have of Leewood?' said Ravenscroft, addressing Crabb and quickly distancing himself from the body.

'Approximately five feet two inches tall, stocky build, rugged appearance, deep scar on right cheek,' replied Crabb, consulting his pocket book.

'What can you tell us about this man, Doctor?' asked Ravenscroft.

'Not much without a proper examination, but I can at least tell you that this is not your escaped convict. This man must be over six feet in length, quite slender build, no sign of any scar on the face, and he looks far too well dressed to be an escaped prisoner,' replied Andrews.

'Have you ever seen the man before?' asked Ravenscroft.

'If you mean was he one of my patients, then the answer is no. I have never seen him before. I would guess that he is probably not from around these parts.'

'Thank you, Doctor. We'll take him to the mortuary for a closer examination.'

Later that afternoon, Ravenscroft and Crabb stood in a cold, colourless room, staring down at the contours of the body that lay beneath a grey sheet.

'Well, Doctor, now that you have completed your examination, what else can you tell me about the man?' asked Ravenscroft, eager to know more about the mysterious stranger.

'I don't think I can add much to my initial examination. I would conclude that the age of the deceased was approximately forty years, fairly healthy for his years, no previous injuries – and that he was not a gentleman,' replied Andrews, washing his hands in a bowl of red-coloured water.

'Oh, why do you say that, sir?' enquired Ravenscroft.

'Although the deceased was well dressed, his attire, I would say, was more suited to the weather at this time of the year than due to any degree of wealth. In other words, although he dressed well, there was no show or display. His hands are quite rough but not unduly so, suggesting that although he was used to performing some manual labour he was not a common labourer. I would think that your unknown corpse was either a tradesman or servant, but someone of reasonable standing. The nature of the wound was quite severe, indicating that whoever struck him undoubtedly wanted to kill him. He certainly did not die as the result of a fall and hitting himself on a rock. Such was the force of the blow, he must have died straightaway. Your killer then dragged the body into the undergrowth, but because of the nature of the terrain could only partially cover the body with some loose earth. He might have remained undiscovered for several weeks had the dog not uncovered him. I'm sorry I cannot tell you any more.'

'Thank you, Doctor Andrews. You have been most helpful and informative. So, Crabb, who do you think our mystery man is?'

'Not Leewood, that is for certain. Although I suppose the convict might have killed him? There are no papers or money in the pockets except for a few coppers.'

'I don't think this is the work of Leewood. Had the escaped convict come across this man and struck him on the head with the intention of robbing him, he would have taken the coins in his pockets. He would also have taken the overcoat in order to keep warm and to conceal his own appearance. No, I don't think Leewood had a hand in this,' said Ravenscroft.

'I can see your reasoning, sir.'

'There are no papers or documents of any kind on his person?'

'No, sir. I've searched every pocket of his clothes. There is nothing at all.'

'That is interesting. I would say that after our killer struck the victim on the head, and before his crude attempt to conceal the body, he must have gone through all the poor man's pockets, making sure that anything that could possibly help us to identify the body was removed. Our killer wanted to make sure that nothing could be traced back to him. Robbery does not appear to have been the motive for the killing, as otherwise all the coins would have been taken along with the coat. No, our murderer meant to kill this man, not steal his valuables.'

'What a way to die – struck on the head and then left out in the wild for the animals to feed on,' muttered Crabb.

'At least we can be certain of one thing. This man has been dead for at least a week. He cannot therefore have anything to do with old Montacute's murder.'

'Strange that it has been quiet for several weeks, sir, since your arrival in the town, then we have two bodies in two days!'

'Too much of a coincidence, you think? Perhaps Montacute had something to do with this man's death? I wonder. However, we cannot proceed further until we have found out more about the victim. Who was he – and why did he come to Ledbury?' said

Ravenscroft, removing his spectacles and polishing them on his handkerchief.

'If you'll excuse me, gentlemen, I'll leave you to your deliberations,' interrupted Andrews, putting on his coat.

'Thank you, Doctor.'

Andrews left the room and closed the door behind him.

'Why did he come to Ledbury? At Christmas as well,' added Crabb.

'Yes. Why Christmas? That is the intriguing thing.'

'Coming home for the festive season to be reunited with friends and relations?'

'But we have no reports of any missing persons at present.'

'He could have been meeting someone important in the town?'

'Yes, but why at Christmas?'

'Perhaps he was not working over the holiday?' suggested Crabb.

'I think you have it, Crabb! This man came to Ledbury at Christmas because he was not employed over the festive season. Now, who could be given time off at Christmas?' wondered Ravenscroft.

'Schoolteachers?'

'That is a possibility, although the coarse nature of his hands suggest that he was engaged in some light manual employment.'

'Not tradesmen, or clergymen – it's their busy time of the year.'

'I agree. Servant? Andrews thought the man might have been a servant. Sometimes domestics are given a few days off at Christmas to visit relatives, although many are retained over the festive season by their employees. Then we have this coat. He was wearing a long, thick, expensive overcoat. That suggests to me that perhaps our mystery man was a servant who worked mainly out of doors.'

'Like a coachman?'

'Exactly! Our mystery man could have been a coachman. But all this is conjecture, of course, until we find out who he really is. Let's go through his clothes again. There might just be something that our killer overlooked and forgot to take away with him. You take his trousers while I have another look at this expensive overcoat.'

'There is nothing in the trousers, sir. I'll go through his waistcoat pockets again,' said Crabb.

'This is interesting. There is a small hole in this pocket of the overcoat. I wonder if anything could have slipped through into the lining? Give me those scissors, Crabb. Now, you hold the coat while I enlarge the hole. Right, that should do. Now let us see whether there's anything inside,' said Ravenscroft, running his hand between the lining and the outer layer of the coat. 'Yes, I can feel something here. Feels like a small piece of paper. Ah, here we are. Damp and screwed up. Lay it on the table and we will see if we can unravel it.'

'Looks like a ticket of some kind,' offered Crabb.

Ravenscroft gently prised the coloured paper apart and then held it up to the light. 'See here, Crabb – we have what looks like the remaining portion of a return railway ticket from London Paddington to Ledbury. So that is where he originated from. Our victim came from London, and had every intention of returning there, but was unfortunately murdered before he could undertake the return journey.'

'At least we now know where he came from.'

'Yes, Crabb, but we are really no further forward. London is a big place. We still don't know who he was and what he was doing here. I suppose there is nothing else in his other pockets?'

'Nothing,' sighed Crabb.

'Then we are at a loss again. All we can do now is make enquiries at the railway station, to see if anyone can remember him arriving in the town.'

'Right, sir.'

'Well, Tom, I think that is all we can usefully gain from this gentleman. Let's be on our way.'

'Snowing again, sir,' said Crabb, looking out of the window. 'Good job we have our coats to keep us warm on a day like this.'

'What was that you said?' said Ravenscroft suddenly. 'Yes. The coat! Of course. Look at this coat. What does it tell you, Crabb?'

'Well, it's an expensive coat, and well made. I wish I had an overcoat as good as this,' replied Crabb, picking up the garment and examining it closely.

'Precisely. If this man was a servant, possibly a coachman, the coat may have been bought for him. His employer bought the coachman not just any coat to keep his servant warm, but a special coat that would add to his own importance. In other words, he wanted to show London society that his coachman was well turned out.'

'I'm with you, sir. Forrating, we call it, in Worcestershire.'

'Let us see who made the coat. The label is quite worn but I think I can just make it out,' said Ravenscroft, taking the coat nearer the window. 'Yes, here we are. Gambit and Ashbury.'

'Who are they, sir?' asked a puzzled Crabb.

'Gambit and Ashbury are one of the finest tailors in London. I believe their premises are located somewhere in the vicinity of St James's. Only the very rich can afford to be fitted out by them.'

'I knew that coat was worth a lot of money when I first saw it.'

'I have a feeling that if we can find out the identity of the deceased, and why he came to Ledbury, we may then be able to discover whether there is any connection between the death of this man and the murder of Nathaniel Montacute.'

'However are we going to do that, sir?'

Ravenscroft remained deep in thought for a few seconds before finally speaking. 'Get your notebook out, Crabb, and make a note of the size, then cut a small portion off the bottom of the coat.'

'Whatever for, sir?'

'Tomorrow I intend returning to London to pay a visit on Messrs Gambit and Ashbury!'

# INTERLUDE

## LONDON, 2 JANUARY 1889

Late in the afternoon, on the second day of the New Year, a tall, well dressed gentleman alighted from a cab in a quiet suburb of London. To the casual observer it might be supposed that the man in question had been in the army in his younger days, for such was his bearing: precise moustache, neatly combed-back black hair and upright stature. Others would have agreed that he was indeed a gentleman of some wealth and standing, for his overcoat, gloves and cane were all evidence to that fact.

The man reached into his coat pocket and gave the driver of the cab a silver shilling, with instructions that he was to keep the change.

'Thank you, governor,' replied the cabman, touching the side of his cap before urging the horse forward.

The gentleman watched as the vehicle turned the corner and disappeared from view, then withdrew into the shadow of one of the tall buildings so that he could ascertain whether his arrival had been noticed.

'Only two pence tonight, darling. Special rate for the New Year!'

The voice made him turn suddenly. The speaker was a middle-aged woman, scantily clad despite the cold weather, who seemed intent in flaunting herself before him.

The man raised his walking cane and threatened to bring it down upon the woman's head. ''Ere, no offence,' she said, backing away quickly. 'There's no need for that. We've all got to make a living, ain't we?'

'Here's your money. Now go away!' he replied, flinging a coin down on to the pavement before quickly moving on. The last thing he wanted was to draw attention to himself.

'Bless you, sir, may God look after you.'

He turned the corner and found himself in a square of fashionable Georgian houses, then made his way past the dimly lit gas lamps until he reached an insignificant-looking brick-built building at the end of the street, which bore the words West Kensington Freemasons Society on a brass plaque.

He stood still, listening and watching for any sign which would suggest that he might have been followed, then after a few seconds rang the bell at the front entrance to the building.

The heavy oak door was opened by a grey-haired servant in livery uniform. 'Good evening, sir. How can I help you?'

'My name is Major Monk,' he replied.

'Of course, sir. You are expected. Please step inside. If you would care to take a seat in the hall, I will inform the gentlemen of your arrival.'

'I would prefer to stand,' he replied, gazing at the old portraits that hung down one side of the hallway.

The servant disappeared from view, leaving him alone with only the sound of a ticking clock for company. As the minutes passed and the servant did not return, he grew uneasy, took out his pocket watch and examined its hands, and paced up and down the uneven floor. He had not wanted this. He was not used to being at such a disadvantage. Then he reminded himself that carrying out someone else's wishes always contained an element of undue risk. That was the price he had to pay for being at another's service.

The door opened and the servant finally returned. 'We are so sorry to have kept you waiting, sir. If you would care to follow me, the gentlemen are ready to see you now.'

Monk followed the servant down the drab-looking corridor, some part of his mind telling him that he should withdraw now before he became further involved, but he also knew that some new challenge would be awaiting him and that some financial gain would be his. He had carried out his mission as he had been instructed. They would not be able to fault him on its execution.

Evidently they would not have called him back if there was not further work to be undertaken.

'Major Monk, gentlemen,' said the servant, opening the door at the bottom end of the passageway. He entered the room, and sought to adjust his eyes to the dim light which struggled to escape from the partially lit oil lamp in the centre of a large table.

'Ah, Major Monk, we are so sorry to have kept you waiting. Do please take a seat,' instructed an elderly, quiet voice.

Monk said nothing and accepted the empty chair that had been left for him at the bottom of the table, placed his gloves and cane before him, and strained to see the half dozen or so faces that were seated before him in the half light of the room.

'For the sake of my fellow Brothers, I would be obliged if you would inform us of your progress concerning the man Robertson,' asked the elderly gentleman who had spoken previously.

Monk cleared his throat. He hated giving any account of himself and his movements to anyone else, but he realized the importance of the occasion. The fact that he could not clearly see the faces of the figures at the other end of the table, however, disturbed him. He had been used to carrying out work for singular individuals and upon his own territory. He distrusted organizations, and despised the affluence and power of the gentlemen who now wanted him to do their bidding. 'After being informed about the man Robertson, I kept watch on the said person at his lodgings and at his place of work for two days without discovering anything of an untoward nature. Early on the morning of 24 December I found that the gentleman had not returned to his rooms the previous evening, and upon further enquiry I learnt that he had purchased a return railway ticket to the market town of Ledbury.'

'Where is Ledbury?' interrupted one of the faces.

'I believe it lies in the county of Herefordshire,' replied the main speaker. 'Please proceed if you would, Major.'

'I journeyed to Ledbury, where I discovered that Robertson had arrived three hours previously. Nevertheless I was able to prevent his return to the railway station later that evening – and was able to carry out your instructions. I can report that he will not be returning to the capital, as you so wished,' reported Monk in his usual, unemotional manner.

'Excellent,' said another voice from the far end of the table.

'You were careful to remove all traces from his person, as to his identity?' enquired a fourth speaker. 'It is important that the trail should not lead back to us in any way.'

'I can assure you, gentlemen, that should the body be found, there would be no way in which an identification could be made,' replied Monk, brushing his moustache with the side of one of his fingers.

The main speaker whispered a few words with one or two of his companions. Monk looked down at the floor uneasily. He had fulfilled his task. They would not be able to complain that he had not been efficient in his work.

'You have done well, Monk. You will find an envelope before you on the table. That is the remainder of your fee,' said the first voice.

Monk reached out for the envelope.

'However, we have further need of your services. It has now come to our attention that Robertson was in the possession of certain documents. A search has been made of both his place of work and his lodgings, but the papers have not been found. We can only conclude therefore that Robertson took the papers with him to Ledbury,' continued the first voice.

'I can assure you that I made a thorough search of his person. They were not upon him.'

'You state that Robertson arrived in Ledbury three hours before yourself?'

'I believe that to be the case.'

'Then clearly it can be assumed that he has left these papers, documents, with someone in the town, you would agree?' interjected a new voice.

'That must have been so.'

'It is important, Monk, that these papers are recovered as soon as possible. They are of the utmost importance and must be returned to us,' said another, more solemn voice from the end of the table. 'We want you to return to Ledbury tomorrow and locate the documents. You will be paid well. Three times your previous fee, payable when we receive the papers.'

'May I enquire as to the nature of these papers?' enquired Monk.

A long silence followed, until eventually the last speaker resumed. 'The papers are of a highly sensitive nature. They must not fall into another's hands. The very safety of the realm depends on their return. That is all you need to know. Suffice it to say that should these papers ever be made public, the lives and careers of certain prominent political and royalist persons could be put at risk. I trust we have made ourselves clear?'

'I see,' replied Monk, casually brushing a hair off the knee of his finely pressed trousers.

'You will undertake this assignment not just for the good of the Brotherhood, but for the security of your country as well,' continued the speaker.

'I will be pleased to carry out your request, gentlemen.'

'Excellent. I knew that we could depend on you, Monk.'

'We must remind you, Major, that nothing must be disclosed, to anyone, either about your mission, or about this meeting here tonight – which of course did not take place,' said the main speaker in a firm manner, leaning forwards across the table so that Monk could see the reflection of the flickering flame in the lenses of his glasses.

'You have my assurance, gentlemen.'

'Then there is nothing more to be said. At all costs recover those papers. We wish you well, Major,' said the main speaker, sitting back in his chair and indicating that the meeting was at an end.

Monk rose from his chair, picked up his gloves and cane and made his way out of the room. The manservant conducted him to the main entrance of the building.

'A cold night, sir,' remarked the servant as he opened the outer door.

Monk said nothing as he stepped outside, and retraced his steps quickly back along the tree-lined square.

Back in the room he had just left, the senior figure was addressing the rest of the group. 'I do not feel that we can entirely trust Major Monk. He knows far too much about our affairs.'

'What do you suggest?' asked one of the speakers.

'Should he recover the documents, we would have little further need of his services. It would then be of the utmost importance that he should never be traced back to us. We should ensure that this last remaining loophole be closed.'

'I agree, Brother,' concurred the speaker.

'Our Major Monk might be tempted to take the papers elsewhere. I saw the greed in his eyes. We cannot afford to let that happen. Fortunately, Brother 127 resides in Ledbury. I will contact him by letter tonight, with instructions that he is to keep us fully informed as to the major's progress.'

# CHAPTER SIX

## LEDBURY AND LONDON,
## 3 JANUARY 1889

The early morning sun shone brightly on the snow-covered road as Ravenscroft and his wife walked arm in arm up the Homend towards the railway station.

'Now, you are sure you have everything, Samuel?'

'You have asked me that same question twice already, my dear,' replied Ravenscroft.

'I'm sorry,' said Lucy, somewhat crestfallen.

'No, it is I that should apologize. I am not used to having such an attractive wife who takes such great pleasure in organizing me. I am a fortunate man indeed,' replied Ravenscroft, squeezing his wife's hand.

'How long do you think you will be away for?'

'At this stage I cannot tell. Hopefully, Gambit and Ashbury may be able to provide me with some information regarding the unfortunate owner of the coat. Once I have learnt his identity, I can then find out as much as I can about him. Then we might be able to discover eventually why he came to Ledbury, and who killed him.'

'The poor, unfortunate man. Fancy coming all this way to Ledbury just to die like that, and at Christmas as well.'

'That is the biggest mystery of all.'

'What happens if your Gambit and Ashbury have no knowledge

of the owner of the coat?'

'Then all I can do is see if the Yard has any information on the man and ensure that his description is circulated to all the stations in London. I am sure that someone somewhere must know who he is. Either way, I hope to be back by tomorrow.'

'Do you think that this man's murder has anything to do with poor Mr Montacute's death?' asked Lucy as they approached the station.

'In all honesty, I just don't know at this time. I have instructed Tom Crabb to continue with the investigation whilst I am away. He will interview some more of the guests at the ball to see if anyone can remember seeing anything.'

'Good morning to you, sir,' said the ticket collector at the station.

'Good morning to you as well. I would like a ticket to London, please.'

'First or second class, sir?'

'Oh, I don't think the police authorities would allow me the indulgence of first-class rail travel,' said Ravenscroft, smiling.

After purchasing his ticket, Ravenscroft and his wife walked on to the platform. 'It seems very quiet today,' said Lucy, looking round at the near-empty platform, where only two gentlemen could be seen conversing with one another.

'I suppose not that many people want to travel at this time of year.'

'Spare us a halfpenny, governor!'

Ravenscroft turned. He had not noticed the old, bearded beggar sitting on one of the seats near the entrance. He reached into his pocket, took out a coin and gave it to the man, before moving his wife away down the platform.

'Samuel, you should not encourage these people,' whispered Lucy.

'The man looked in need of a good wash and some food. It was the least I could do, considering this cold weather,' replied Ravenscroft. He looked across once more to where the beggar had been sitting, but found that the occupant of the seat had quickly departed.

'You have a soft heart, Samuel Ravenscroft, and I love you for it,' said Lucy, laughing.

'Strange, but I thought I had seen that fellow before.'

'Probably loitering around the streets of Ledbury?'

'I expect you are correct, my dear. No matter. Now please take care of yourself and little Richard whilst I am away,' said Ravenscroft, stepping back from the edge of the platform as the noise of the approaching train could be heard. 'Do you know, I have only been away from London for a few weeks, and yet it seems that I have always lived here in Ledbury.'

'That is because you are content – and happy,' said Lucy, smiling.

'And may it long be so.'

The train drew into the station, and Ravenscroft opened the door of one of the carriages.

'Take care, Samuel. I could not bear it if you never returned,' said Lucy, gripping her husband's arm and quickly planting a kiss on his cheek.

'Do not worry, Lucy. I have every intention of returning to Ledbury, I can assure you.'

Lucy waved as the train slowly pulled away from the station, and it was not until it finally disappeared from view that she moved away from the edge of the platform and made her way out of the building.

No passengers from Hereford had alighted from the train, and she began to make her solitary way back towards the town. Only the old ragged beggar seemed to have noticed the passage of her journey. . . .

Later that day, Ravenscroft found himself standing outside the opulent premises of Gambit and Ashbury, situated in the area of London known as St James's. He glanced at the expensive coats and suits displayed in the windows with some degree of envy, acknowledging that he would never be able to afford any of the items on offer with his insignificant salary.

'Good morning to you, sir,' said the doorman, ushering him into the shop. Ravenscroft found himself in a large room lined with rows of glass-fronted cabinets. Two or three assistants were occupied serving customers; at the far end of the room another client stood with outstretched arms, having his measurements taken.

'Good morning, sir,' said a middle-aged assistant, coming

forward to meet him. 'How may I be of assistance to you?'

Ravenscroft observed that the man was running his eyes over his drab coat with a slight look of disapproval, and felt uneasy in such austere surroundings. 'I would like some information.'

'Of course, sir – a new overcoat, perhaps?'

'Not exactly.'

'Ah, a new suit might be more to your liking. Or perhaps sir is about to undertake a journey to the country?'

'No, I have come up from the country today.'

'Evening wear – yes, of course.'

'No. I require some information regarding one of your clients.'

'I'm afraid we cannot disclose any information regarding our clientele. Our customers come to us in the full knowledge that they are being dealt with in the strictest confidence,' said the assistant, adopting a more defensive tone and giving Ravenscroft a cautious look out of the corner of his eye.

'My name is Ravenscroft, Inspector Ravenscroft. I am making enquiries concerning the death of one of your clients.'

'I think it would be expedient if we were to step into the back room, sir,' replied the assistant in a low tone of voice.

'I understand.'

Ravenscroft followed the assistant through the door at the rear of the shop and soon found himself in a large office.

'As I said, Inspector, all our clients come to us in the strictest confidence.'

'I appreciate that, sir, but unfortunately the client I am particularly interested in met with an untimely end in the town of Ledbury, and therefore the issue of confidentiality no longer applies in this case. There was nothing on his person to enable us to identify him. He was, however, wearing a long overcoat with your name inside.'

'We sell many overcoats. All of them are, of course, hand made individually to fit the requirements of our customers,' said the assistant, forcing a brief smile and clearly feeling uncomfortable.

'The deceased was wearing an overcoat of this design,' said Ravenscroft, reaching into his pocket and laying the piece of material on the desk.

'Ah yes, that would be from our Moncrief range, individually crafted by our tailors, on the premises, for the discerning gentleman. It is one of our most expensive cloths,' replied the assistant, picking up the material and running it through his fingers.

'Have you sold one recently? Say in the last year or so? The coat was practically new,' said Ravenscroft.

'A number, I would expect.'

'How many is a number, sir?'

'We usually sell six or seven a year.'

'This gentleman in question was tall and thin, probably just over six feet in height, and size 36. Do you keep records?'

'Certainly,' said the assistant, replacing the cloth on the desk and consulting a large open ledger. 'I will need to go through our records.'

Ravenscroft watched as the assistant turned back the pages, running his fingers down the neat copperplate writing. 'Ah, here we are, Inspector. This would seem to fulfil your requirements – Moncrief overcoat, size 36, height of client six feet one inch. Sold just over one year ago.'

'And the name of the client?'

'I don't really—'

'I must remind you, sir, that this is a murder enquiry. The name, if you please.'

'Robertson,' replied the assistant somewhat reluctantly after a few moments silence.

'Can you remember anything at all about the gentleman? Was he one of your regular clients?'

The assistant thought deeply for a moment or two. 'No, he was not one of our regular customers. In fact, he was not a gentleman at all. He was a coachman, if I remember correctly,' he continued, a note of disapproval in his voice.

'I knew it!' exclaimed Ravenscroft. 'Tell me, Mr—'

'Webster.'

'Mr Webster. How much would the coat have cost? It would surely have been out of range for a humble coachman to have afforded?'

'You are correct in that assumption, Inspector.'

'Perhaps his employer purchased the coat for his coachman?' suggested Ravenscroft.

'That was indeed the case in this instance.'

'It would be helpful, sir, to our inquiries, if you could provide me with the name and address of Mr Robertson's employer.'

'I'm afraid I am not at liberty to disclose such information,' replied Webster, adopting his former defensive posture.

'And I have to remind you, sir, that this is a murder enquiry,' said Ravenscroft, trying to sound as assertive as he could.

'That may be true, Inspector, but if it was learnt that I had violated the confidentiality of a client's trust, our business would suffer the gravest consequences.'

'If I have to return later this afternoon with a warrant and twenty policemen to search these premises, I think we would agree that your clients would withdraw their patronage once they had received news of our visit,' said Ravenscroft firmly, becoming increasingly impatient at the salesman's intransigence.

The two men looked at one another. Finally the assistant turned away. 'I cannot provide you with the information you require, Inspector. If it was discovered that I had divulged the name of Robertson's employer to you, then the integrity of the business and my position would be severely called into question. However, if I was to be called away into the shop urgently to deal with a customer, I could not be held responsible for any action an individual might carry out in my absence,' remarked Webster, tapping the ledger with his forefinger.

Ravenscroft smiled and took out his notebook as the assistant walked back into the shop.

Ravenscroft walked up the two steps and rang the bell of the elegant townhouse. 'I would like to speak with Sir James Stanhope,' he said, addressing the maid who opened the door.

'I'm sorry, sir, but Sir James is not at home at present. Who shall I say has called?'

'Who is that, Simpson?' called a man's voice from inside the house.

'A gentleman to see Sir James, Mr Saunders,' replied the maid, moving to one side of the entrance doorway.

'Good day to you, sir, I had hoped for a few words with your master,' said Ravenscroft, addressing the butler.

'Sir James is visiting his club at present,' replied Saunders in a superior tone, casting a wayward glance in Ravenscroft's direction and indicating that the maid should close the door.

'Then perhaps I might have a word with you, Mr Saunders,' said Ravenscroft quickly, anxious that he should not be excluded now that he had come so far. 'It is concerning Robertson, your coachman.'

'You have news of Robertson?' asked the butler anxiously, returning to face him.

'My name is Ravenscroft, Inspector Ravenscroft. Perhaps you will allow me to enter? I have some very important news regarding your coachman.'

'Yes, yes, of course – if you would care to follow me, Inspector.'

Ravenscroft followed the butler into the hallway, down a flight of stairs and into a small room situated at the rear of the kitchens.

'Please take a seat, Inspector,' said Saunders, indicating a chair. 'You say you have news of Robertson?'

'Yes, Mr Saunders. But tell me first, when was the last time you saw Robertson?'

'The day before Christmas – he was given two days leave for the Christmas season by Sir James.'

'Did Mr Robertson say where he was going?'

'I don't think so. We all assumed that he was visiting relatives or friends for Christmas.'

'Would it surprise you to learn, Mr Saunders, that he travelled to Ledbury?'

'Ledbury? I am sorry, where is Ledbury?' asked the butler, a puzzled expression on his face.

'In Herefordshire,' said Ravenscroft. 'Did he say when he would be returning?'

'On the twenty-sixth, I believe.'

'I'm afraid I have some very bad news for you. Mr Robertson was unfortunately killed in Ledbury.'

'Oh, dear me! What a terrible thing to happen! That would explain why he did not return. Sir James – indeed the whole staff – have been most concerned over his absence. You say he was killed? Was it a coach or a railway accident?'

'Mr Robertson was in fact murdered. Someone struck him on the head with a heavy object, probably a stone,' replied Ravenscroft, looking down at the floor.

'How dreadful!' replied the butler, visibly shaken.

'So you can see, Mr Saunders, why it is important that we learn as much as we can about Mr Robertson,' said Ravenscroft, trying to sound as sympathetic as he could.

'Yes. I see. What would you like to know?'

'How long had Robertson been in your master's employ?'

'Four years. Yes, just over four years.'

'And he was Sir James's coachman, I believe?'

'Yes.'

'Tell me, what was the nature of his duties?'

'He conveyed Sir James round town in his carriage.'

'Did Sir James purchase an expensive new coat for his coachman, about a year ago?'

'Yes. Sir James always likes to see his servants have the best attire. But how do you know about the coat?' asked a baffled Saunders.

'It was just that Robertson was wearing the coat when he was killed. Did Robertson ever mention the town of Ledbury to you in any conversation you had with him?' asked Ravenscroft.

'No.'

'Did Mr Robertson have any relatives that you know of?'

'No. He was a single gentleman, I believe.'

'So he never mentioned any relations or acquaintances?'

'No. He appeared to be quite alone in the world.'

'I wonder if I might have a look at his room?' asked Ravenscroft, rising from his seat.

'Yes, of course, but I don't see what use that will be to you, Inspector.'

'I believe that Mr Robertson went to Ledbury for a specific purpose. There may be something in his room which may help us to determine the reason for his visit.'

The butler led the way up three flights of stairs at the rear of the house, and through a door which opened out on to a landing. 'Mr Robertson's room was there,' indicated Saunders, pointing to one of the rooms.

'Thank you. You mentioned that Mr Robertson appeared quite alone in the world. There must have been someone in the house whom he confided in?' asked Ravenscroft, opening the door to the coachman's room.

'There was no one in particular. There was perhaps Simpson, the maid. They walked out once or twice, that's all, nothing serious. She opened the door to you when you arrived.'

'Mr Saunders, you have been more than helpful. I wonder if I might speak with Simpson?'

'Yes, I suppose so. I'll ask her to come up here.'

'That would be most kind of you. Before you go, however, there is one more thing you could do for me.'

'Anything, Inspector.'

'What did Robertson do in his spare time?'

'Nothing really. He usually kept to his room.'

'So the only time he went out was when he was performing his duties with Sir James?'

'Yes.'

'It may be useful to our enquiries if we could build up a picture of the dead man's activities. I wonder if it would be possible for you to make a list of the places where Robertson used to take Sir James?'

'That may be difficult, Inspector. Robertson was used to taking Sir James to a great many places in London.'

'I appreciate that. A list of perhaps the most frequent places would be useful.'

Ravenscroft listened to the butler's footsteps making their way down the stairs and then turned his attention to the coachman's living quarters. The room was simply furnished – a brass bed, wash stand, chest of drawers, bedside cabinet, small bookcase and a chair – and a mahogany-framed cracked mirror hung on one of the walls, while a thin, plain rug lay on the floor. Clearly Sir James Stanhope's fashionable concerns for the appearance of his servants did not extend to their rooms. He opened the chest of drawers and went through them one at a time, but found only various items of clothing, then took down the five or six books from the bookcase and examined them in detail for any loose papers or inscriptions. A search of the wardrobe and its contents proved equally futile. Finally he opened the top drawer of the bedside cabinet, and lifted out a small framed print which he found there.

He walked over to the window so that he might obtain a better view of the contents of the frame. The print was an early nineteenth-century view of the exterior of an unnamed church, similar to many thousands of others that had been produced at that time to illustrate topographic books. Ravenscroft studied the print, and the more he looked at it the more it seemed to be familiar to him. He began to wonder why Robertson had kept such an insignificant framed print in his bedside cabinet. He turned the frame over but found no writing on the back to indicate the name of the church, but then, observing that it was loose, he lifted up the one rusty tack that was holding the frame together and removed the print from its housing. There in faded writing on the back of the print were the words 'Ledbury Church, Herefordshire. 1805'. So that was why the print had looked so familiar to Ravenscroft – and that was why Robertson had journeyed to Ledbury! He had not chosen to travel to Ledbury at random – the town obviously had some appeal or fascination for the coachman. Robertson had kept the print in the cabinet by the side of his bed because of its strong associations. Perhaps Robertson had once lived in Ledbury?

The door opened. Simpson the maid entered. Ravenscroft noticed that she had been crying. 'You asked to see me, sir?'

'Yes. I'm sorry to be the bringer of such bad news.'

The maid said nothing and looked down at the floor.

'Please take a seat, Miss Simpson' said Ravenscroft, pointing to the only chair in the room.

'You say Mr Robertson has been killed?' asked Simpson, seating herself. 'Murdered, so Mr Saunders said.'

'I'm afraid so. I understand that Mr Robertson was used to confiding in you?'

'Not really, sir.'

'Oh, I was given to understand from Mr Saunders that you and Mr Robertson went out together upon a number of occasions?'

'Yes, sir. But there was never anything in it, if you take my meaning. It was only once or twice.'

'I see, so you and Mr Robertson were not in any way close to one another?' asked Ravenscroft, trying to put the matter as delicately as he could.

'No. There was nothing at all like that.'

'Nevertheless, you and Mr Robertson were used to conversing with one another?'

'Yes, sir.'

'Did he ever mention any relatives or friends at all?'

'No, sir. I think he was alone in the world, sir.'

'Do you happen to know where he was going for Christmas?'

'No, sir.'

'Did he ever mention a place called Ledbury to you?' asked Ravenscroft, beginning to think that he was clutching at straws.

'No, sir. I have never heard of Ledbury.'

'So you don't know why Mr Robertson was going there at Christmas?'

'No, sir.'

'I want you to think very carefully now, Miss Simpson, before you answer my next question. Did you speak with Mr Robertson on the morning of his departure?'

'No, sir. I did not see Mr Robertson at all on the morning he left.'

'I see,' said Ravenscroft, feeling somewhat dejected by the failure of his questions.

'I did speak with Mr Robertson the night before.'

'Can you recall what Mr Robertson said?' asked Ravenscroft hopefully.

'He said he had some important papers to dispose of in a safe place, and that he needed to get away from London as soon as possible.'

'I see. How did he seem when he spoke with you?'

'How do you mean, sir?'

'Did Mr Robertson seem anxious in any way? Did he appear frightened, or did he say those words in a lighthearted way?'

'Oh no, sir, he wasn't making a joke or anything like that. He was quite serious, and yes I suppose he did seem a little anxious, now you mention it.'

'Did he tell you what the papers were?' asked Ravenscroft, believing that at last he might be on the verge of gaining some important information from the maid.

'No, sir. I do remember that the papers were in a large envelope, like a packet. Brown, it was.'

'Did you see inside the packet?'

'No, sir. It was sealed.'

'When Mr Robertson said he had to get away from London, did he say anything else?'

'He said that if he did not leave soon, there would be others who would prevent him from going.'

'Can you remember his exact words?'

The maid thought deeply for a moment. 'Yes, sir. He said, "There are some people who would stop at nothing to get their hands on that packet."'

'Some people who would stop at nothing to get their hands on that packet,' repeated Ravenscroft. 'Did he say anything else?'

'No, sir – nothing else.'

'He never said who those people were?'

'No, sir.'

'Thank you, Miss Simpson. You have been most helpful. One final question before you go. Does the name Montacute mean anything to you? Did Mr Robertson ever mention the name Montacute to you?'

'No, sir. Can I go now?' asked the maid, standing up.

'Yes – and thank you.'

'Will you catch the person who killed poor Mr Robertson?'

'I sincerely hope so,' said Ravenscroft as the maid left the room.

He stood for some minutes looking down at the print. So Robertson had left London in a hurry, taking a packet of important papers with him – and had chosen to travel to Ledbury because he knew the town. Did he travel to Ledbury to meet someone? Someone he could trust with the envelope? 'There would be others who would prevent him', that is what the maid had said. Who were these 'others' and what was so important about the contents of the envelope that had caused Robertson to leave quickly and travel to Ledbury? No packet had been found on the dead man. Had he been robbed of the packet when he had been killed – or had Robertson managed to pass over the envelope and its contents to someone else in the town before his death?

Ravenscroft returned the print to its frame and replaced it inside the drawer of the cabinet, knowing that its owner would never be returning to reclaim it. Then, closing the door of the room behind him, he made his way down the three flights of stairs until he reached the kitchens.

'Ah, Mr Ravenscroft,' said Saunders the butler, coming forward to meet him. 'I have tried to compile a list of the places that Robertson and Sir James visited. It is quite long, I'm afraid, and perhaps not comprehensive enough to be of use to you.'

'Thank you,' said Ravenscroft, taking the paper and reading down the list of places. 'Sir James is quite a man about town.'

'Whites, that is the name of Sir James's club, and those are a list of Sir James's friends. Lord Arthur Somerset is a particular friend – he is, I believe, an equerry to the Prince of Wales,' said Saunders, pointing to the paper.

'Sir James is used to socializing in important social circles, I can see,' said Ravenscroft, recognizing the names of two or three cabinet ministers and several prominent churchmen.

'That is Sir James's tailors, and a jewellers in Mayfair that he frequents to buy presents for his friends, and that is a gaming club in Pall Mall.'

'I'm impressed by your diligence and assistance, Mr Saunders,' said Ravenscroft.

'Oh, I realize I have missed off one other place that Sir James often visits. I don't know the exact address, but I believe it is in Cleveland Street.'

'Cleveland Street,' said Ravenscroft, looking up. 'Do you know why Robertson and Sir James went there?'

'No, sir, I cannot help you.'

'Thank you, Mr Saunders. This list may prove very useful,' said Ravenscroft, folding up the piece of paper and placing it in his pocket.

'Shall I inform Sir James that you called?'

'By all means. Should you or Sir James have any further information regarding Robertson, I would be grateful if you would send a message to the police station in Ledbury.'

'Certainly, sir.'

Ravenscroft shook hands with the butler on the doorstep of the house, and strode away down the street, his mind busily considering all that he had uncovered at the coachman's residence. When he had entered the building, not thirty minutes previous, he had been unsure what he expected to gain. He now knew why Robertson had been killed, and perhaps why he had gone to Ledbury – but he was as far away as ever from finding out who had killed him and what connection the coachman's death had with the demise of Nathaniel Montacute.

Then there was Cleveland Street. He had heard the name of that street mentioned before, but could not remember when, or by whom. If only he could recall. . . . The name intrigued him. What was so special about Cleveland Street? Finally he gave up trying to remember – Cleveland Street was after all only one place on a very long list.

# CHAPTER SEVEN

## LEDBURY, 5 JANUARY 1889

Ravenscroft looked out of his compartment window at the snow-covered fields. In another hour he would be returning to Ledbury, and after two days of following the deceased coachman's trail around London, he was now somewhat relieved that his weary search had been halted. The arrival of Crabb's telegram informing him that he was needed to give evidence at the inquests of Montacute and Robertson had necessitated his leaving the capital. Two days of investigations had revealed very little. Certainly he had discovered the coachman's name, found out where he resided, and uncovered his possible reasons for visiting Ledbury on Christmas Eve and the motive behind his death, but he was no further forward in ascertaining who had killed the man or what the mysterious package might have contained. However, as he had walked the streets of London, he had become more and more convinced that the answers to his questions would be found not there but in Ledbury. The murderer and the package were more likely to be there than in some tree-lined square or gaming club in London, and if he could only discover the dead man's association with the town then all might be revealed. The rest of the places that Sir James Stanhope and his coachman were in the habit of frequenting could wait for another day.

Then there was Nathaniel Montacute's murder to be solved. It seemed more than a coincidence that both men had been murdered within a few days of each other, but at present he could see no connection between the two. His investigations into the banker's poisoning had thrown up a number of suspects: Catherwood, Rivers, Onslow, Leewood and the two Montacute brothers all came to mind and he would not be surprised if Crabb had come up with yet more during his absence. The trouble was that although he could see any one of these men killing Montacute, he could find no possible reason why any of them should have wanted to murder the stranger Robertson. And yet the coachman had kept the old print of Ledbury church in his bedside cabinet, as a kind of keepsake or memory, so he must have had some connection with the town. He knew now that when he returned to Ledbury his first priority would be to try and find out Robertson's connection with the market town – there had to be someone he had met on the day he had visited Ledbury, or perhaps even someone he had known previously.

The sound of the door to his compartment being opened broke into his deliberations.

'I say, it's Ravenswood, isn't it?' said the unmistakable tones of Rupert Montacute, throwing himself down on one of the seats.

'Ravenscroft. Good day to you, Mr Montacute.'

'Caught the old man's killer yet?'

'We are proceeding with our investigations,' replied Ravenscroft, able to smell the drink on the young man's breath despite the distance between them.

'That means no, then.'

'These things take time, Mr Montacute.'

'Suppose so. Miss the old man, you know. Damned shame for someone to go and poison him like that. He was a bit stingy and frightfully dull, but that was no excuse for someone to go and kill him.'

'Your stepmother seems very upset,' suggested Ravenscroft.

'Yes, shame for her as well. Marrying Papa like that just two years ago, and then he goes and gets himself murdered! Still, I suppose she'll be all right.'

'Oh, why do you say that?'

'Well, he'll have left her all his money, won't he? Stands to sense that he would look after her, what with her being much younger than he was. Fancy a drink, Ravenswood?' said Montacute, taking out a hipflask from his pocket and attempting to pass it over to the detective.

'Er, not for me, thank you.'

'Please yourself then. Don't mind if I do?' asked the young man, taking a swig from the flask.

'It must have been hard for you when your mother died,' said Ravenscroft, hoping that Rupert might provide him with additional information.

'Yes, Mama, the blessed Enid Montacute! Do you know, she was a saint, my mother. Saint Enid of Ledbury, that's what we used to call her. Saint Enid of Ledbury! On all the local welfare committees, was my mother – local hospital, relief for the poor – you know the sort of thing. Never refused a request from a needy soul, did my mother. Worked tirelessly for the good of the community,' explained young Montacute, lying back in his seat and adopting a reflective, melancholic tone.

'I understand that she died quite suddenly?'

'Got some infection or picked up some fever or other. Nothing anyone could do for her. Went down very quickly. All of us were put out by her death. Saint Enid, poor old Enid Montacute. Old Catherwood never got over her death.'

'Oh, why Mr Catherwood?' asked Ravenscroft, wondering why Rupert had singled him out in particular.

'Oh, you don't know about my mother and Mr Catherwood?' enquired Rupert, leaning forward and speaking in a quiet, slurred voice. 'My mother and old Catherwood, they were once lovers! Many years ago, of course, when I was a young minnow. Caught them kissing in the garden once – the saintly Enid and that Yorkshire terrier! No one knew about it but me – and of course my mother. She knew that I knew. That would explain why she always gave me a wide berth after that. Left me to go my own way. Now look at me. God, it's all a mess!'

Ravenscroft said nothing, and looked out of the window. So that was why Catherwood had never left the town – he and Enid Montacute had been lovers. He wondered whether the old banker had discovered his wife's infidelity and whether it had been Enid that had caused the rift between the two former business partners all those years ago? If so, that would explain a great deal.

He turned back in Rupert's direction but found that the young man had fallen asleep, his head slumped to one side, the hipflask lying on his lap. He could not help but feel sympathetic towards young Rupert. No wonder the youth had turned into the sorry specimen he now saw before him, after being shunned by his father and ignored by his mother.

A few minutes later, as the train entered the Colwall tunnel, Ravenscroft leaned over and shook the young man's shoulder.

'God, I must have dropped off. Sorry about that, old man.'

'The train is just coming into Colwall station. Next stop Ledbury,' said Ravenscroft.

'Good job you woke me up, or I'd have ended up in Hereford. Look, I hope I did not say anything silly just now? I'm inclined to ramble on a bit at times. Take no notice. It's only the drink, you know.'

'Not to worry.'

'We're a bad lot, us Montacutes. Brother against brother and all that!'

Ravenscroft smiled.

A few minutes later the train drew into Ledbury station. Ravenscroft and his fellow passenger alighted from their compartment and went their separate ways.

'Good morning to you, sir. I trust your visit to London bore fruit?' asked Crabb, joining Ravenscroft at the entrance to the station.

'I discovered the dead man's identity. He was a coachman, as we suspected, who worked for a young aristocrat by the name of Sir James Stanhope in a fashionable part of London. I also found that the man had some previous connection with Ledbury, and that he left London in a hurry on Christmas Eve.'

As the two men walked down towards the town, Ravenscroft recounted his investigations in London. 'I must admit that your telegram came as a welcome relief. I was becoming tired of visiting all those clubs in London and calling upon Sir James's associates. But tell me, Crabb, have you made any progress with the investigation here?' asked Ravenscroft, relieved that the snow had at least melted from the roads during his absence.

'I must have interviewed quite a good number of the people who were at the Lamplighters' Ball, but not one of them can remember either anyone leaving the room when the lights came back on, or indeed seeing anything unusual at all,' replied Crabb.

'I'm not surprised. Our killer was very skilled.'

'Oh, and there have been two or three possible sightings of the escaped convict, Leewood, in various places such as Stoke Edith and Mathon, but nothing definite.'

'People often imagine something which they want to see,' muttered Ravenscroft.

'No one has come forward with any information about the dead coachman. I checked the local hotels and boarding establishments in both Ledbury and Malvern but no one can remember him making a booking. The clerk at the station can recall him arriving about midday on Christmas Eve, but that's all.'

'You have been very busy, Tom.'

'The inquest opens in about two hours' time, sir.'

'Then there is just time for me to go home, see my wife, and change out of these clothes.'


'Thank you, Inspector Ravenscroft. You may step down.'

Ravenscroft made his way back to his seat in the crowded courtroom as the coroner began his summing up.

'It would appear that Nathaniel Montacute was poisoned by a person, or persons, unknown. I will therefore enter a verdict of unlawful killing. I appreciate that the police are conducting further enquiries. The court offers its sincere condolences to Mrs Montacute and to other members of the Montacute family. Turning now to the stranger, Robertson, who was killed in such a brutal fashion out on Dog Hill. From what Inspector Ravenscroft has told the court, the stranger worked as a coachman in the city of London. As further enquiries are still taking place, both in London and in Ledbury, I will record an open verdict until further information is forthcoming as to the deceased's purpose in visiting the town and the reasons for his untimely demise.'

'Excuse me, your honour. I am Doctor Andrews. I have been appointed by the Montacute family to make a formal request for the release of Nathaniel Montacute's body, so that he may be buried as soon as possible,' asked the medical man, rising to his feet.

'Thank you, Doctor Andrews. I see no reason why the court should not accede to such a request, unless of course, Inspector Ravenscroft, you have any objections?'

'None that I can think of, your honour.'

'Very well. Court is adjourned.'

Ravenscroft and Crabb made their way through the departing throng. 'Ah, there is someone over there I need to speak with. Major Onslow, if I could just have a few words with you?'

'Better make it snappy, Ravenscroft. Got important meeting with me solicitor in ten minutes,' replied the master of the Ledbury hunt.

'I won't detain you long, sir. If you would step outside where it is quieter?'

'Right, Ravenscroft, ask away,' demanded Onslow, once the three men had moved away from the departing crowds.

'Major Onslow, can you remember where you were just before the lights went out at the Lamplighters' Ball?' asked Ravenscroft.

'Good God, man, how the deuce can you expect me to remember something so mundane?' snapped Onslow.

'It is very important, sir.'

'Well, I suppose I was helping myself to one of those sausage rolls from off the table. Just about to pour meself another glass of wine, when those blasted fellows came in and put out all the lights.'

'You're sure about that, sir?' asked Ravenscroft.

'Course I'm sure. Would not have said so had it not been true,' growled the major, who was clearly anxious to be on his way to his appointment.

'I only ask because Mrs Montacute remembers that you were speaking with her and her husband just as the lights went out,' said Ravenscroft, attempting to placate the major by speaking in a calm manner.

'Hmm,' replied Onslow, scratching his ear and looking deep in thought. 'Can't remember that. Might have spoken to them earlier in the evening, I suppose. Look, got to be on my way. Yer knows where I live if you've got any more questions.'

'There is just one more thing, Major. When the lights went out and then when they came back on again, were you aware of anyone suddenly leaving or entering the room?'

'No. Don't believe I was. Must dash,' said Onslow, striding away and quickly making his way down the Homend.

'Well, that's interesting, sir,' said Crabb. 'Mrs Montacute says that the major was talking with her when the lights went out, but he says he was helping himself to some of the food and pouring himself a drink at the time.'

'Yes, Tom, which leads us to suppose that either Major Onslow is telling us an untruth, or that Mrs Montacute is at fault when she says she was speaking with Onslow just before her husband was murdered,' said Ravenscroft.

'Maybe the two of them did speak with one another earlier, as the Major said?'

'You could be right.'

'Where to next, sir?' asked Crabb.

'I think we should pay another visit to Mr Catherwood. When I spoke with Rupert Montacute on the train, he indicated that his late mother and Catherwood were lovers at one time, which would explain why his business partnership broke up with Montacute and why he has remained in the town for all these years. If we are quick, we can be there before nightfall.'

As Crabb and Ravenscroft made their way out of Ledbury, the lamplighters were busy about their work, lighting the streets and lanes of the town in preparation for the dark, cold evening ahead. Groups of townspeople passed by the two policemen, anxious to be home, their coats buttoned up tight against the chilly night air. A stray cat ran across the path in front of them, seeking the warmth and privacy of the undergrowth, and as they neared Catherwood's house they could hear the sound of the dogs alerted by their impending arrival.

'Good evening to you, Mr Catherwood. Could we have a few words with you?' called out Ravenscroft, observing that the landowner was standing at the entrance to his home.

'Best come in then.'

They followed Catherwood into his house, as the dogs' owner ordered his restless animals to sit still before the hearth.

'You were not at the inquest, Mr Catherwood. Why was that?' asked Ravenscroft.

'Saw no reason to go. I have no interest in Montacute's death. I was not there the night he died, so why should I be there now? I can see the appeal of such an inquest to idle, inquisitive folk, but I had more important things to do,' replied Catherwood, throwing another log on the blazing fire.

'Mr Catherwood, when I visited you the other day, you said that the reason for the animosity between you and Mr Montacute was the failure of your business partnership some years ago,' began Ravenscroft, sitting down on one of the chairs.

'That's what I said,' replied his host in his usual blunt manner.

'With all due respect, Mr Catherwood, that was not the only reason for your poor relationship with Montacute, was it?'

'What are you getting at, Ravenscroft? If you've something to say, why don't you come out with it straight away?' said Catherwood, clearly becoming annoyed.

'Very well. I have reason to believe that you and Mr Montacute's second wife, Enid, were at one time romantically attached.'

'Nonsense, man, you've been listening to idle gossip!' laughed Catherwood, reaching for another log.

'We have it on good authority—'

'Good authority! What good authority?'

'Rupert Montacute. He said that you and his mother were lovers.'

'And you believe that drunken wastrel?' growled Catherwood.

'He seemed quite assured on that point.'

'Then he were lying.'

'So there was never anything between you and Enid Montacute?'

'I spoke with the lady on one or two occasions, in the early days when I dined at The Gables. That is all.'

'You see, Mr Catherwood, if you were having an affair with Mrs Montacute, it would explain a great deal,' said Ravenscroft, seeking to engage the other's eyes.

'What are you getting at, Ravenscroft?' asked Catherwood.

'Did Nathaniel Montacute discover that you and his wife were on intimate terms, and was that the real reason behind the breakdown of your business relationship?'

'I've had enough of this nonsense, Ravenscroft. I think it's time you left.'

'Is that why you stayed on here in Ledbury, long after the break-up of your business relationship with Montacute, so that you could be near Enid Montacute?' asked Ravenscroft, warming to his subject and keeping one eye on the dog that was beginning to growl at the side of the hearth.

'Enough, man!' snapped Catherwood angrily.

'It would assist us a great deal in our enquiries, Mr Catherwood, if you were to be frank and honest with us. Were you and Enid

Montacute lovers?'

A long pause followed as the two men stared at one another, each testing the other's mettle.

'All right, man! Yes, if you must know, Enid and I formed a strong relationship shortly after I came to the town,' sighed Catherwood, throwing himself down on the old faded leather armchair before the fire. 'Enid – Mrs Montacute – was dreadfully unhappy, married to that dull old skinflint. As her husband's business partner, she confided in me – but we were never lovers, Ravenscroft. I would never have done anything that would have caused her ruin.'

'Nevertheless, Nathaniel Montacute found out about your relationship?' asked Ravenscroft, leaning back in his chair and trying to sound as understanding as possible.

'Yes,' admitted Catherwood after a brief pause. 'Then he set about ruining me. He made believe that he knew nothing about our affair until he had involved me in all his dubious business concerns. It was not until much later, when it was too late to cancel my investments, that I learnt that he had known about our association all along. He was not happy until he had seen me financially ruined. It was his way of getting back at me.'

'And afterwards you remained in the town because of Enid Montacute?' asked Ravenscroft.

'I could not bear to leave her alone with that awful man. I thought that if I remained here, I could see that no harm would befall her. That may be difficult for you to understand, Ravenscroft. We had to be discreet, meeting as if by accident, on the hills, never in the town. She had a reputation to uphold. We hoped that eventually old Montacute would die, and we would be reunited.'

'You waited a very long time,' said Crabb, looking up from his notebook.

'But Enid died before Nathaniel,' added Ravenscroft.

'Yes, her death came quite suddenly. I was not invited to the funeral, and paid my own private respects later. The old man had his revenge on me in the end, I suppose. Now he too is dead, and of course you suspect me of his death – but I tell you one thing, Ravenscroft, if I had wanted to kill him, I would have thought of a more ingenious way and I would have done it a long time ago,' said

Catherwood with bitterness.

'Thank you, Mr Catherwood. It would have helped if you had told us all this before, but I appreciate your reticence in admitting the truth. We won't take up any more of your time. Tell me one thing before we go. Why did you not leave after Enid's death? Surely there was nothing to keep you here after that?' asked Ravenscroft, standing up.

'You understand nothing, Ravenscroft. Enid Montacute lies buried in the churchyard here at Ledbury. That is why I remain in this awful town.'

Ravenscroft allowed himself a brief smile before he and Crabb made their way outside.

'Do you think he killed Montacute?' asked Crabb as the two men walked back down the narrow, winding lane towards the distant lights of the town.

'Possibly. Of all our suspects, he had perhaps the strongest reason to see Montacute dead. It must have been frustrating for him to know that the woman he clearly loved was forced to live every day with his arch enemy, and that he was powerless to do anything about it. As he said, though, he could have killed Montacute years ago, so why wait until now?'

'Could not bring himself to do the fatal deed?' suggested Crabb.

'You may be right. Either way, I find it strange that Catherwood still remained here after Enid's death. I don't really accept that he had no desire to move because he simply wanted to continue visiting Enid's grave every day. In fact, I don't believe that Mr Catherwood is as heartbroken as he makes out.'

'We could bring him into the station for further questioning. It was Catherwood, after all, who discovered Robertson's body. Very convenient, if he killed the coachman as well.'

'You are forgetting one thing, Crabb – although Catherwood had every reason to kill Montacute, he does not appear to have had any reason to see off the coachman.'

'Why did that fellow come to Ledbury? On Christmas Eve as well?'

'That is what we need to find out tomorrow. There has to be someone in this town who met up with him, who knows what brought Robertson here.'

Suddenly, Ravenscroft pulled up sharply. 'Do you hear that,

Crabb?' The two men stood still, listening in the cold night air. 'I thought I heard something moving in the undergrowth just behind us!'

'Could be an animal of some kind?' suggested Crabb.

'I don't think so. I've had the distinct impression that we have been followed ever since we left Catherwood's house,' said Ravenscroft, looking quickly around him.

'Could be one of Catherwood's dogs got loose?'

'Unlikely – the animal would have attacked us by now. Come out, my man, and show yourself!' shouted Ravenscroft. 'It's no good, we know you are there!'

'I'll double back, sir, and see if I can see anyone in the wood on our left,' said Crabb, setting off at a brisk pace.

'Be careful – these woods can be treacherous in the dark. I'll look in the undergrowth on this side. Don't go far, and try and keep the path in sight at all times, if you can.'

'Right, sir,' said Crabb.

'Show yourself!' shouted Ravenscroft again, straining to see any kind of movement in the darkened wood. 'Step forward and show your face!'

The two men continued with their separate searches for a full minute or more.

'Anything, Tom?' asked Ravenscroft as the two men were reunited once more on the path.

'Nothing, sir, although I thought I did hear something moving deeper into the wood. Nothing on your side, sir?' asked a breathless Crabb.

'No. Whoever it was has made a quick exit once he realized that we had discovered his presence. Someone had evidently taken it into his head to follow us. I wonder why, Crabb? What possible reason could anyone have to be following us on such a night as this? It does not make sense. I suppose it could have been a poacher, or even an animal, as you suggested. Nevertheless, we will need to be on our guard,' said Ravenscroft, resuming their journey back towards the town.

'Whoever he was, I don't envy him being out here in this cold,' said Crabb, shivering.

'I think we have done enough for today. Time you and I, Tom, returned to our respective homes. We have two good wives awaiting our return, and I must say I'm particularly looking forward to a good supper and a quiet, relaxing evening in front of my warm fire!'

# CHAPTER EIGHT

## LEDBURY, 6 JANUARY 1889

The church clock struck the hour of eleven as they buried the old banker, Nathaniel Montacute. Ravenscroft and Crabb positioned themselves in the corner of the churchyard, and watched as the coffin was placed in the old family vault.

'It's interesting to see who's attending the old man's funeral,' said Ravenscroft. 'Obviously the family are all here – Edith the grieving widow being supported by Maurice Montacute, Rupert standing alone. There's Doctor Andrews, and I think I can see Onslow, Chambers the cook, Rivers – and yes, Midwinter the solicitor.'

'Quite a few others as well,' added Crabb, looking at the thirty or forty figures who were busy filing out of the church and taking up their positions at a respectable distance from the main party.

'Montacute was quite an important figure in the community. Besides being the town's banker, he had twice been mayor. There are no doubt many prominent people here today who are anxious to pay their respects, and who wish to be seen to do so.'

'Can't see Catherwood amongst them,' said Crabb.

'I would not have expected the man to have attended. After all, he has his reputation as a recluse to uphold. I find it sad that everything eventually comes to this – a few minutes of orderly grief in a cold churchyard whilst the world continues with its unremitting progress. Montacute's place has no doubt been waiting for him all these years, next to his two wives and alongside all the other Montacutes, but I wonder who will remember him in a hundred years time?' said Ravenscroft in a reflective mood.

'Who will remember any of us?' said Crabb.

'Only our families, it is to be hoped. The future lies with your son, and with Lucy's son, and with their children, who are as yet unborn. I wonder what kind of world they will create, what kind of problems they will encounter?'

'Don't like funerals, sir,' muttered Crabb.

Ravenscroft allowed himself a brief smile. The vicar was uttering the last words of farewell. Edith Montacute placed a wreath on top of the family vault and then cried on Maurice's shoulder. Rupert held back, looking lost and forlorn.

'Look over there, Crabb!' said Ravenscroft, suddenly pointing across to the other side of the churchyard. 'Do you see that figure standing just by the trees?'

'That tall gentleman wearing a long black coat and hat?'

'Yes. He seems to be taking an interest in observing the funeral. He is too far away for us to identify him. Look, he has noticed that we are looking in his direction and has moved out of view. Quickly, Crabb, move as discreetly as you can and see if you can catch up with him and ask him to return. I'll continue to watch here.'

Ravenscroft watched as his constable set off across the churchyard, but he knew that the figure had gone and that Crabb would be fortunate indeed to catch him. Edith, Maurice and Rupert began to make their slow way back to the waiting coach, as the other mourners began to pay their respects one by one. As he moved nearer, Anthony Midwinter, the solicitor, came forward to meet him.

'A cold morning, Ravenscroft.'

'It is indeed, Mr Midwinter.'

'You asked me, Inspector, to let you know when the will was about to be read.'

'I did indeed.'

'I will shortly be making my way back to The Gables. After some refreshment, I will undertake the reading of the will. I have explained to the family that you will be present – as an observer only, of course.'

'I thank you, Mr Midwinter. I will join you presently.'

The old solicitor nodded and began to make his way out of the churchyard as a breathless Crabb rejoined Ravenscroft. 'I'm afraid

I was too late, sir. The fellow was gone by the time I got there. I looked down Church Street and back the other way but he was nowhere to be seen.'

'Don't worry, Tom, you did your best. Whoever it was disappeared quickly enough as soon as he noticed that we had observed him. It seems as though we were not the only ones who had an interest in attending the funeral today.'

'Could have been our murderer, sir?'

'Who knows? I wished we could have got a better look at him. Under that long coat and hat he could have been anyone. I had a strange feeling, though, that I had seen that man somewhere before. . . .'

Later that morning, Ravenscroft and Crabb stood in the corner of the dining-room at The Gables, observing the people who had arrived for the reading of the old banker's will. In addition to the Montacute family – Edith, Maurice and Rupert – and a number of their servants, including Rivers the gamekeeper and Chambers the cook, the two policemen also noted that Andrews and Onslow were present. Anthony Midwinter, the family solicitor, had already taken his seat at the head of the table and was busily engaged in reading through some of the papers that lay before him.

'Don't think much of this sherry,' muttered Crabb.

'I think I'm inclined to agree with you,' replied Ravenscroft, discreetly returning his glass to the table. 'I don't know what it is but they always seem to serve the poorest kind of sherry at funerals.'

'Eats are not too bad though,' whispered Crabb, helping himself to another sandwich.

'I think it best if we occupy these two chairs in the corner, where we won't be in the way and where we can observe the behaviour of the people as the will is read. I must say that I am very intrigued to see what the documents says, and to find out more from Mr Midwinter later as to why the old man drew up this latest document not more than six months ago.'

'You think the new will might give us some clues as to who might have murdered Montacute?' asked Crabb.

'You never know. People have often been known to kill off their relations in a desperate attempt to acquire their wealth. There is nothing like the prospect of a handsome legacy to stir the crooked church mouse into direct action. Ah, I think Mr Midwinter is about to begin.'

'Ladies and gentlemen,' said the solicitor, clearing his throat, 'if you would care to be seated for the reading of the will.'

One by one the assembled group seated themselves round the large mahogany dining table.

'Before we begin, I should perhaps explain that Inspector Ravenscroft and his assistant are with us today as observers. As you know, the inspector is investigating the untimely demise of Mr Montacute—' began Midwinter.

'Damned interference, I call it!' growled Onslow, giving the detective a severe look.

'I have no objections to Mr Ravenscroft's presence,' said Maurice, 'and I am sure that Mrs Montacute does not mind either.'

Edith Montacute gave a brief nod of her head.

'Now we come to the reading of the will—'

'Excuse me, sir,' said the maid suddenly entering the room, 'but there is a gentleman who is at the door and insists that he is present for the reading.'

'Who on earth—' began Maurice, but before he could complete the sentence, Catherwood strode into the room.

'What the deuce!' protested Onslow.

'Good morning to you all,' said Catherwood, walking quickly over to one of the chairs and seating himself.

'Look here, Catherwood, this is most irregular. You have no business being here,' said Maurice, standing up from the table.

'I have every right to be here, Mr Montacute. Your father was my business partner for a number of years, and as such I have every intention of hearing the reading of his will.'

'My father dissolved the partnership many years ago,' protested Maurice.

'That's as may be, but I still have an interest in the hearing of the will,' replied Catherwood, leaning back in his chair.

'This looks to be fun!' interjected Rupert, smiling.

'Be quiet, Rupert! Mr Midwinter?' said Maurice, turning to the solicitor for assistance.

'I agree, it is somewhat unusual, but as a will is a public document, I cannot see that we can prevent Mr Catherwood from being present.'

'Very well,' sighed Maurice, regaining his seat. 'Please proceed, Mr Midwinter.'

'Interesting, sir,' whispered Crabb in the corner of the room.

Midwinter adjusted his spectacles and after clearing his throat, looked down at the document before him and began to read. '"This is the Last Will and Testament of me, Nathaniel Jacob Montacute, banker and owner of The Gables in Ledbury, in the county of Herefordshire, made this day August 1, in the year 1888, the fifty-first year of the reign of our sovereign Queen Victoria. I give my soul to Almighty God and desire that my body be placed inside the Montacute family vault situated in the churchyard of Ledbury chuch in the county of Herefordshire. Firstly, I do appoint my good friend, Major Charles Onslow, and my solicitor, Anthony Midwinter, as executors of my will – and I give (free of duty) to the said Charles Onslow and Anthony Midwinter the sum of fifty pounds each in friendship and for their duties, as executors of this, my will. Secondly, I give the sum of twenty-five pounds each to Philip Rivers and Agnes Chambers, in gratitude for their many years of loyal and faithful service. Thirdly, I leave the sum of one hundred pounds to the almshouses of St Katherine in the town of Ledbury, the money to be invested in South African securities and the interest to be shared between the inmates on Easter Day of each year. Fourthly, to my former business partner, James Catherwood of Ledbury, I leave the sum of one pound exactly—"

'Serves you right, Catherwood!' interrupted Onslow, giving a hearty laugh.

Catherwood said nothing but Ravenscroft thought he detected the flicker of a brief, sarcastic smile across the Yorkshireman's face.

'"... James Catherwood of Ledbury I leave the sum of one pound exactly, in recognition of the disservice he has caused me. Fifthly, to my son, Maurice Montacute, I leave my partnership in Cocks and Biddulph, the bank of Ledbury, as I know that he will carry on the traditions of the said bank with his usual diligence and fortitude. Finally, I leave the rest of my estate, including my house The Gables in Ledbury, my stocks and shares and all my worldly possessions to my wife, Edith Montacute née Henshaw, to hold the same absolutely for her own sole and separate use. Signed this first day of August, eighteen eighty-eight, Nathaniel Jacob Montacute."'

A long silence followed as Anthony Midwinter looked up from his reading and began to wipe his glasses on a large pocket handkerchief.

'Thank you, Mr Midwinter. Gentlemen, if you will excuse me,' said Maurice, suddenly standing up from his seat and beginning to leave the room, his face strained and ashen.

'Maurice!' called out Edith, but Maurice had already closed the door behind him.

'Gentlemen, Mrs Montacute. I bid you good day,' said Catherwood, also standing up and about to make his departure. 'I thank you, Mr Midwinter.'

'Well, that's a fine kettle of fish,' whispered Crabb, as the other members rose from the table.

'Lord bless the master!' exclaimed Chambers the cook, beginning to cry. 'I knew he would always remember us.'

'Come now, Mrs Chambers,' said Rivers the gamekeeper, placing his arm round the cook's shoulders. 'That won't do. Let us go down to the kitchens and toast the master's health.'

'If you will excuse me, I must go and see if I can find Maurice,' said Edith, quickly leaving the room.

'Major, if you would care to accompany me back to the town?' said Andrews.

'Yes. Right, could do with a walk. Clear the air and all that. Good day to ye,' replied the major as he and the doctor departed.

'Bloody old skinflint, left me nothing!' said Rupert, banging his fist down on the table. 'Nothing! His son. I tell you, Midwinter, it is not to be borne!'

'I'm sorry, Rupert. There was nothing I could do for you. I tried to reason with your father—' began the solicitor.

'For God's sake!' exclaimed Rupert, striding out of the room, his face red with anger.

Ravenscroft and Crabb rose from their seats and joined Midwinter.

'Poor Rupert. He seems to have taken it quite hard. He is the second son, though, I suppose,' said the solicitor, gathering up his papers.

'I thought Maurice took it hard as well,' said Ravenscroft.

116

'Yes, one would have thought that his father would have provided more for his first son, although he will want for nothing as he has inherited his father's share in the bank.'

'Looks as though Mrs Montacute gets practically everything,' said Crabb, replacing his notebook in the top pocket of his tunic.

'Mr Midwinter, you say that Nathaniel Montacute drew up the will last August, only a few months ago. Did he give any reason as to why he was making a new will?' asked Ravenscroft.

'None. He just asked me to call upon him one day, and requested that I draw up the new will. I think he was anxious that his new wife would be provided for in the unexpected early eventuality of his own death.'

'The will seems particularly harsh in its treatment of both Maurice and Rupert. Rupert is obviously the younger son and was not on good terms with his father, but Maurice has been left only the partnership in the bank.'

Midwinter said nothing as he replaced the will inside his briefcase.

'Mr Midwinter, Nathaniel Montacute obviously made an earlier will. Can I ask how this present will differs from any former document?' asked Ravenscroft.

'Mr Montacute drew up his previous will some ten or twelve years ago. In that document he provided for his then wife, Enid, should she outlive him – and I believe he was more generous towards Maurice, leaving both The Gables and his investments to his son on condition that he looked after Enid during her lifetime.'

'That is very interesting. And Rupert, how did he fare in this earlier will?'

'I believe he was again left nothing. I think the rest of the terms of the will were the same, with bequests to Onslow, myself, Rivers and Chambers – and of course the bequest to the St Katherine almshouses.'

'Thank you, Mr Midwinter. You have been most helpful. I think my constable and I will be on our way now. Thank you for allowing us to attend the reading,' said Ravenscroft, beginning to leave the room.

'Glad to have been of some assistance, although I fail to see how Nathaniel's will can assist you in your enquiries into his murder.'

'We will see. Good day, Mr Midwinter.'

'Er, there is just one more thing before you go, Inspector. Something has been lying upon my conscience and disturbing me for a few days now. I wonder whether you could find the time to call upon me at my offices this afternoon, gentlemen?'

'Yes, certainly, Mr Midwinter.'

'It is rather difficult to talk here, you understand. Would two o'clock be convenient?'

'Well, sir, and what did you make of the old banker's will?' asked Crabb, helping himself to another piece of cheese in the snug at the Feathers.

'It was certainly a most interesting document. The only one who stands to benefit substantially from the will is Mrs Montacute. Maurice was quite clearly upset when he learnt that he had acquired neither The Gables nor his father's money, although his share of the bank must amount to something. Poor Rupert stood to gain nothing from either the new will or the old will – and I wonder why his father treated him so harshly?' replied Ravenscroft, warming his hands in front of the roaring fire.

'Probably his father thought that Rupert would only drink away any monies left to him.'

'Possibly but it was unusual for him not to have been provided for in some small way. It was almost as though the old man was punishing him for being his son.'

'As neither of the two sons stood to gain by old Montacute's death, there would have been no reason for either of them to have killed him,' suggested Crabb, before taking a drink of his ale.

'And likewise we can discount Rivers, Mrs Chambers and Major Onslow, as they only received small sums and had nothing to gain by Montacute's death. Then there was Catherwood. Why the devil did he turn up for the reading? He surely cannot have expected anything from his old enemy. The pound he was left was clearly meant as an insult. No, as I said, the only person who stood to gain by Montacute's death was his wife,' said Ravenscroft, sitting down at the table and breaking a piece of bread.

'You think she killed him?'

'If she did, she would not have been the first wife who poisoned her husband in order to obtain his wealth – but she was clearly well situated and provided for by her husband and seems genuinely

118

saddened by his death. One can understand why the old banker changed his will so that his new young bride would be taken care of when he died. After all, Montacute was over sixty. No, I think you could say that none of the people present at the reading today would have killed old Montacute in the expectation of becoming richer as a result.'

'With the exception of Catherwood,' interjected Crabb.

'Yes, I agree with you, Tom, but although Catherwood stood to gain nothing financially by the old man's death, he could still have acted out or revenge or hatred.'

'There is still Leewood.'

'Indeed, yes, Leewood. Although I cannot see Leewood resorting to poison, he nevertheless cannot be ruled out until he has been secured and questioned. I had hoped that the reading of the will would have provided us with some indication as to who murdered old Nathaniel Montacute, but I have to confess that the mystery appears to grow cloudier with each hour that passes. We seem to be no further forward in our investigations than when we first began,' said Ravenscroft, sighing and looking into the flames of the fire.

'What I can't understand, sir, is what has this man Robertson to do with all this business?'

'If I knew the answer to that question, I'm sure I would be halfway to solving Montacute's murder.'

'I wonder what old Midwinter the solicitor wants with us?' asked Crabb.

'Perhaps he has some knowledge about the Montacutes to impart to us? Let us hope so. We could do with any assistance in this case. Anyway, it is not quite two yet – still time for another tankard, and that leg of cold lamb looks inviting!'

'Do come in, gentlemen, out of the cold,' said Anthony Midwinter, ushering his two guests into his office. 'That will be all, Perkins, you may go now. See that we are not disturbed.'

'Very well, Mr Midwinter,' said the clerk, leaving the room and closing the door behind him.

'You have a good view of the main street,' said Ravenscroft, crossing over to the window and surveying the scene before him.

'Do you know, I never look out of the window. I suppose I have been here for so many years I have long ago taken the view for granted. Do please be seated, gentlemen,' said the solicitor, seating himself behind his large desk.

'Thank you, Mr Midwinter. You implied this morning that you had something to tell us – something which you said was troubling you?' asked Ravenscroft, as he and Crabb each drew up a chair.

'Yes indeed. I have been wrestling with my conscience for several days now.'

'You have some information regarding the poisoning of Mr Montacute?' said Ravenscroft hopefully.

'Oh no, it is nothing to do with Nathaniel's death. I am referring to the stranger, Robertson,' said Midwinter, scratching his head.

'You knew the man?'

'Well, I may – or may not. I'm very sorry, Inspector. This is all rather confusing.'

'Perhaps you should start at the beginning,' suggested Ravenscroft, trying to put the troubled solicitor at his ease.

'It was on Christmas Eve. Rather late in the afternoon. Perkins, my clerk, and I were just about to finish work when a gentleman, who was previously unknown to us, entered our office and asked if he might have a few words with me.'

'Did this gentleman give a name, sir?' asked Crabb, taking out his notebook.

'No, I'm afraid not. In fact, he was rather anxious that he should not disclose his identity.'

'Can you describe the gentleman to us, sir?' asked Ravenscroft.

'Well, he was about forty years of age, I would say. Quite tall, slim build and he spoke with a London accent.'

'How was he dressed?'

'He was dressed in a long overcoat and hat, much the same as many other people at this time of the year.'

'Can you tell us what this stranger wanted with you?' asked Ravenscroft.

'He was most desirous of leaving a large packet of papers with me for safekeeping,' said Anthony, leaning back in his chair and pausing for his words to take effect.

'Please go on, sir,' said Ravenscroft, giving Crabb a sideways glance.

'He said I was to look after the envelope until his return on 1

May, when I would be rewarded for my trouble, and that if he did not return by that date, I was to take the envelope to the bank – Cocks and Biddulph – and give it to the senior partner there. I remember he was quite insistent on this latter point. I was to give the envelope to the senior partner, and to no one else.'

'The senior partner in this case being Mr Nathaniel Montacute?'

'Exactly.'

'Did the gentleman say anything else, or give any other instructions?' asked Ravenscroft, becoming more and more interested as the narrative unfolded.

'That was all. Oh, he mentioned something about the papers being very important.'

'Can you recall his exact words? They could prove important to our investigations.'

The old solicitor thought deeply for a moment or two. 'I think his exact words were that the papers were of a private and sensitive nature, and that if their contents were revealed the very fabric of our society would be put at risk. Yes, I think that was what he said – or something very much like it.'

'Thank you, Mr Midwinter, this is proving most interesting. May I ask where you have kept the envelope?'

'In my safe, over there, gentlemen,' replied Midwinter hesitantly.

'I wonder whether we might examine the envelope?'

The solicitor rose from his desk, walked over to the safe, turned his key in the lock and swung open the heavy door. 'Here we are, on the shelf, where I left it on Christmas Eve.'

'May I examine the envelope?' asked Ravenscroft, rising from his chair.

'You may examine the outside of the envelope, Inspector, but at this time I cannot permit you to open the packet unless you can prove to me that the dead man Robertson was indeed the stranger that called on me. Without that confirmation, I am still bound to carry out my client's instructions.'

'Begging your pardon, Mr Midwinter, but your client is presently lying on a mortuary slab,' said Crabb, looking up from his notebook.

'Nevertheless, Crabb, at this stage we must appreciate Mr Midwinter's caution. We have not yet proven that Robertson and the gentleman who called here are indeed both the same man,' said Ravenscroft.

'Thank you, Inspector. If we establish that they are indeed the same man, then I would be bound to see that the dead man's instructions are carried out.'

'But Mr Montacute is dead,' protested Crabb.

'That is so, Constable, but Mr Maurice Montacute is now the senior partner, and as such we cannot open the envelope unless he is present,' said Midwinter, giving Crabb a stern look. 'My instructions in this case were made quite clear to me – the envelope was to be given to the senior partner of the bank, and to no one else.'

'Of course, Mr Midwinter, we appreciate your predicament. It would not contravene your ethical code, however, if I was to just examine the outside of the packet?' asked Ravenscroft.

'No, I suppose that would be in order, Inspector,' replied the solicitor, handing the large brown envelope to Ravenscroft.

'I wonder if you would mind if I took it over to the window? The light is better there,' requested Ravenscroft.

'I see no problem in that.'

Ravenscroft walked across to the window and held the package up to the light. He turned it over two or three times in his hands as a bewildered Crabb looked on. 'I see there are two initials written in the corner: A and V. You have no idea what these letters mean, Mr Midwinter?'

'I'm afraid not, Inspector. My client offered no inclination as to their origin.'

'Perhaps the package was originally owned by someone with the initials A.V.?' suggested Crabb, trying to sound helpful.

'Or the papers in this envelope relate to someone whose name is A.V.?' said Ravenscroft, crossing back to the solicitor. 'Thank you, Mr Midwinter. I would secure the envelope again in your safe.'

'I will indeed, Inspector.'

Ravenscroft regained his seat and waited for the solicitor to lock the papers back inside his safe and resume his place behind his desk.

'Mr Midwinter, I have no doubt that the man Robertson was indeed the stranger who called upon you on Christmas Eve, but I also acknowledge your caution in this matter given that you would be unable to give a positive identification of the deceased due to his decayed condition. I have recently returned from London, where I made enquiries regarding the man Robertson. I learnt that he was employed as a coachman in the service of Sir James Stanhope. I also learnt that he had left the capital suddenly on the morning of Christmas Eve, taking a large packet with him. As yet, I have been unable to discover why the gentleman chose to come to our town or why he should have selected yourself as the custodian of such a package – but I do believe that he was anxious that the contents of the envelope should not fall into the wrong hands. I also believe that Robertson was killed because his assailant believed the envelope was still upon his person, and wanted to take possession of it.'

'Dear me, this is all rather serious and mysterious,' said Midwinter, looking perplexed and adjusting his spectacles.

'A serious matter indeed, Mr Midwinter. Since my return from London, I have had the distinct impression that my every move has been observed. Yesterday evening my constable and I thought we detected someone following us in the wood near Mr Catherwood's residence, and this morning I am sure that someone unknown to us was watching the burial of Nathaniel Montacute. On both occasions when we sought to apprehend the person, he proved too quick for us. When we entered this room today, I was anxious to look out of your window. Before we visited you here today, opposite your premises, on the other side of the street, I observed an old beggar slumped on the pavement, although I am sure if you looked now you would find him gone.'

'This is terrible, Inspector,' said the solicitor, breaking into Ravenscroft's narrative.

'You think this beggar is following us in the hope that we can lead him to the missing packet?' suggested Crabb, looking up anxiously.

'I do indeed.'

'But you took the envelope over to the window, where he would—' began Crabb.

'Exactly! As soon as you told us about the packet, Mr Midwinter, the idea took root in my mind that we might set a little trap for our murderer,' replied Ravenscroft.

'I'm afraid I don't quite understand, Inspector,' said Midwinter, a puzzled expression on his face.

'By going over to the window on the pretext of obtaining more light with which to examine the packet, I was able to show the beggar that we were in possession of the very documents he had been searching for. We will also have ensured that he has seen the package being replaced within your safe.'

'Good heavens!' exclaimed the solicitor.

'Now that he knows that you are in possession of the documents, I have no doubt that Robertson's killer will attempt to break into your premises tonight in the hope of being able to retrieve the papers from your safe.'

'What are we to do?' asked the worried solicitor.

'Mr Midwinter, is there a back entrance to your premises?' asked Ravenscroft.

'Why, yes, there is a small kitchen and storeroom at the back of the property, which leads directly out into the courtyard.'

'Excellent. Perhaps you would be kind enough to show us this yard before we leave and furnish us with a key. Constable Crabb and I will then leave by the front entrance in the normal way. You would then oblige us by continuing with your usual work. I have no doubt that our killer will be watching our every move. You should lock up your premises at your usual time and return home, Mr Midwinter. Shortly afterwards my constable and I will let ourselves in the back way, and with your permission will lie in wait for our man to make his move. I trust that you would not object if we were to make use of your office for the evening?'

'Well, no, I suppose that would be in order – anything I can do to assist you in the apprehension of this man.'

'Good. Don't worry, Mr Midwinter, we will see that your safe and its contents remain untouched. Now, if you would be so kind as to show us the rear entrance to your rooms, Constable Crabb and I will leave you to continue with your work. Before the day is out, we will have our killer under arrest! Of that I am sure.'

The town clock struck the hour of eleven.

'I wish this fellow would hurry up and show himself,' said Crabb irritably, stretching out his legs in the darkness of Midwinter's office.

'I do not think we will have much longer to wait. The town

seems almost at sleep,' replied Ravenscroft, looking towards the corner of the window to where a solitary shimmer of light could be seen on the wet pavement lower down the street.

'I wish old Midwinter had stoked up his fire before he left. It's decidedly chilly in here,' continued Crabb, drawing his coat closer around him and breathing on his cold hands in an attempt to bring back some warmth into his limbs.

'The flames would have created too much light for our purpose. It is important that we remain still and quiet here in the dark so that our murderer believes that the office is empty, and is reassured in his resolution.'

'Don't see why we could not have opened the envelope, then we could have found out what all this is about.'

'We have to respect Mr Midwinter's position. He is under a legal and moral obligation to see that his client's wishes are fulfilled, even if he believes that his client is deceased. Robertson was clearly running away from someone whom he believed was anxious to steal the contents of his envelope, which now lies in Midwinter's safe. I still don't see why the coachman came to Ledbury, and why he decided to leave the envelope with Midwinter of all people?' said Ravenscroft, thrusting his hands once more into the pockets of his overcoat.

'Why not just take it to Montacute?'

'That was only his last resort. Robertson gave Midwinter instructions that the package should only be taken to the banker should he himself fail to return by 1 May. Clearly he hoped to return some time before that date and recover the envelope.'

'It's all a mystery to me, sir.'

'I hope that things will become a little clearer once we have caught our man and taken the envelope to Maurice Montacute to open. Perhaps we might then also learn why the old banker was poisoned, and what part his death plays in all this affair.'

'Which way in do you think our intruder will use, sir?'

'The front entrance faces directly on to the street, and although there appears to be no one about, there is always the chance that he would be observed. No, I think he will break in through the back door. The yard there leads off a dark alleyway. I doubt that anyone would see him come in that way.'

'Just wish he would get on with it,' muttered Crabb, watching his warm breath drifting up towards the ceiling through the cold air.

'Here, Tom, take a sip of this to keep you warm,' said Ravenscroft, passing over a small metal flask in the dark.

'Bless you, sir,' said Crabb, gratefully accepting the offering.

'Shush! I think I heard something.'

'What, sir?'

'A door! I think I heard the sound of a door being forced,' whispered Ravenscroft. 'Keep absolutely still, Crabb, until I give the word.'

The two men stood in silence as Ravenscroft strained to hear the almost inaudible sound of approaching footsteps drawing nearer towards the room. The only thing he could see in the darkness was the dim outline of his constable.

As the footsteps appeared to draw closer, he was aware of the rapid beating of his heart. His chest began to tighten and he fought to suppress the beginning of an irritable cough which threatened to break the silence.

Slowly the old oak door opened, inch by inch, creaking as it did so.

A tall, dark figure emerged into the room. Ravenscroft strained to catch a glimpse of the intruder but could see nothing of the man's face underneath the hat that was pulled down low, obscuring his features. The man stood on the threshold of the office, then paused for a moment before crossing over to the window. Confident that there was no one in the street outside, he began to make his way across the room.

Ravenscroft watched as the intruder knelt before the safe and began to force open the lock.

'Now, Tom. Grab him!' shouted Ravenscroft, rushing towards the intruder.

'I've got him, sir!' replied Crabb.

In his haste to assist his constable, Ravenscroft collided with a chair in the dark of the room and fell to the floor. When he looked up he saw the outlines of Crabb and another figure locked in combat. 'Keep hold of him, Tom!' yelled Ravenscroft, attempting to get to his feet.

Suddenly a shot rang out in the darkened room.

Then Ravenscroft felt himself being violently thrust up against the desk as the blackened figure darted quickly past him and out of the room. He struggled quickly to his feet and called out, 'Tom! Tom! Where the devil are you? Are you all right?'

But there was no reply from his constable.

# CHAPTER NINE

## MALVERN WELLS AND LEDBURY,
## 7 JANUARY 1889

Shortly after eleven o'clock on the morning following the dramatic events at Midwinter's offices, Ravenscroft made his slow way along Westminster Road in the area known as Malvern Wells, situated some seven or eight miles from the town of Ledbury. Pausing for a while to steady his breathing after the climb up on to the upper road, the detective shaded his eyes from the bright winter sun that shone down on the white fields that stretched out from the easterly range of the hills. The overnight fall of snow and the resulting early morning frost had made the roads treacherous, and Ravenscroft had abandoned his cab down on the Wells Road, giving instructions to the cabman that he was to return and collect him within one hour. Now, as he stood looking out at the snowy landscape, at the stillness and quiet of the scene, feelings of despair and loneliness seemed to overwhelm him. Apprehending Robertson's killer and being able to solve the murder of Nathaniel Montacute had all been within his grasp. Today he and Crabb should have had the man safely behind bars. The mystery would have been solved. The case put to rest. But in his haste he had tripped over that damn chair, and their intruder had escaped in the ensuing struggle. Now he was no further forward with his investigations than he had been a few days previously. The killer was out there somewhere, and Ravenscroft still had no idea who he was and where he could be found. He was more than aware, however, that he had been negligent in his duty. He should have made better precautions to see that the man had been secured. Worst of all, he had let Crabb down.

The envelope now seemed the only way forward. The intruder had risked everything in a desperate attempt to retrieve the package. At least he had not been successful in his endeavour. The envelope still lay within the solicitor's safe, and Ravenscroft had posted two of his men within Midwinter's office to deter any future raid, before he had left earlier that morning. At least he had been able to convince the old solicitor that the contents of the envelope should be revealed as soon as possible and had urged him to make an appointment with Maurice Montacute at the bank so that they might all open the package together – but even here, he had been frustrated, for he had learnt that the banker had left the town on the early London train and would not be returning until the following day.

Reluctantly, he continued his steady progress along the road, the noise of his boots bearing down on the crisp snow being the only sound to accompany him. After passing by several buildings, he opened the gate of a small white-painted cottage and paused for a brief moment before bringing his hand down on the front door.

'Oh, Mr Ravenscroft, you best come in out of the cold,' said a young rosy-cheeked woman, opening the door.

'Thank you, Jennie. How is Tom this morning?' he said, stepping into the hallway.

'Is that you, sir?' called a voice from the inner room. Ravenscroft handed his coat and hat to the woman, relieved to hear the sound of his constable's familiar tones.

'Do please go in,' said Jennie.

Ravenscroft walked into the inner room. A blazing fire in the hearth welcomed him. Crabb, wearing night attire under a large dressing gown, and sporting a bandage secured round the top part of his head, was seated in an old chair before the fire.

'My dear Tom, you do not know how pleased I am to see you again this morning,' said Ravenscroft, eagerly shaking his constable's hand. 'For one dreadful moment last night, I thought that blaggard had killed you!'

'Take more than a stray bullet to see me off, sir. We Crabbs are made of sterner stuff.'

'And how are you feeling this morning?' asked Ravenscroft, accepting the chair that Crabb's wife offered to him.

'Head feels a bit sore sir, but other than a slight headache, doctor says I should be fine in a day or so.'

'You had a lucky escape, Tom. Another inch and the result could have been entirely different. I'm so sorry, Tom. I should have had him but in my haste I fell over that damned chair.'

'Not your fault, sir. It was very dark in that room.'

'Nevertheless, I feel responsible. I should have realized the chair was there. I didn't know the fellow would come armed. He was evidently quite desperate to recover those papers. I don't suppose you got a look at him at all?' asked Ravenscroft, stretching out his hands towards the fire and rubbing them together.

'I'm afraid not, sir. It was so dark in there and his face was partially covered by his hat. I would say he was fairly tall and of thin stature, probably around forty years or so.'

'I didn't catch much of a look at him, but I am inclined to agree with you, Tom.'

'There was something though, sir. Although the villain did not seem like any of our suspects in this case, he did remind me of someone.'

'Go on Tom,' said Ravenscroft eagerly.

'Well, sir, there was just something about the fellow which kind of reminded me of someone we have encountered in the past – but I'm afraid I can't for the life of me remember who.'

'Don't worry, Tom. It may come back to you,' said Ravenscroft, leaning forward and patting Crabb on the shoulder. 'I have no doubt that the intruder was the same man we encountered in the wood near Catherwood's place and the man we saw at Montacute's funeral. He seems a very slippery customer, as well as being a master of disguise. I have instructed the men in both Ledbury and Malvern to keep a sharp lookout for anyone of his description or anyone acting suspiciously, but I would not be surprised if he has gone to ground. We are evidently dealing with a very dangerous and clever individual.'

'All the more reason to see what is inside that envelope,' suggested Crabb.

'Indeed, Tom. Unfortunately Maurice Montacute is in London until tomorrow, and Midwinter, quite correctly, won't open the packet until he returns, so I'm afraid we will have to wait for a day or so more before the envelope yields up its secrets.'

'What will we do now, sir?'

'You, Tom, will do nothing but rest in front of this warm fire, for the next two days at least. I will not allow you back on duty until the doctor says you are well enough to resume work.'

'I feel fine now, sir,' protested Crabb, attempting to move from his seat.

'That's as may be, but you have had a very nasty shock and come within an inch of your life. Tell him, Jennie, that he is to stay indoors.'

'I've done that already, Mr Ravenscroft. I have done everything within my power to get him to sit in that chair but he keeps saying he must be about his duty,' said Jennie Crabb, shaking her head.

'Constable Crabb, I am ordering you to at least obey your wife, even if you will not accept the advice of a colleague. You should listen to your wife. Wives always know what is best for us, even if we are not prepared to acknowledge such a fact.'

'Very well, sir,' replied Crabb somewhat reluctantly.

'Good,' said Ravenscroft, rising from his chair.

'You will take a drink with us, sir, before you leave?' enquired Jennie.

'I have a cab returning for me down on the Wells Road at twelve,' said Ravenscroft, consulting his pocket watch. 'A warm drink will be more than welcome on such a cold day as this.'

Two hours later, Ravenscroft walked up the long drive towards The Gables, deep in thought, his mind going over the events of the previous two days, and not knowing why he had decided on his present course of action. As he neared the house, a familiar figure came towards him.

'Good afternoon, Doctor Andrews.'

'Good day to you, Ravenscroft. How is Constable Crabb today?'

'I visited him this morning and he seems in remarkably good spirits, thank you,' replied Ravenscroft.

'The man is lucky to be alive. A good job the bullet just grazed the side of his head. He should be fine in a day or so.'

'It was fortunate that you were able to attend to him.'

'Glad to have been of service. What brings you to The Gables on such a day?'

'I was hoping to have another word with Mrs Montacute. How is your other patient?'

'She is bearing up, under the circumstances. All this has been rather a shock for her, as I'm sure you will appreciate. Now if you will excuse me.'

'Of course, Doctor – and thank you once again.'

The two men went their separate ways. Ravenscroft rang the bell at the side of the door.

'Good morning, sir. Can I help you?' said the maid, opening the door.

'Inspector Ravenscroft. I would like a few words with your mistress, if you please.'

'Yes, sir. If you would care to wait here, sir, in the hall, I will see whether Mrs Montacute is able to see you.'

'Thank you,' said Ravenscroft, handing his overcoat and hat to the servant.

After a minute, the maid returned. 'If you would follow me, sir, Mrs Montacute will see you now.'

Ravenscroft followed the maid into the drawing-room. Edith Montacute rose from one of the chairs as he entered. Ravenscroft observed that the widow was still wearing the same mourning clothes she had worn the previous day. 'Mr Ravenscroft, do take a seat. You have news of my husband's murderer?' she asked anxiously.

'Our investigations are still continuing. Last night my constable and I attempted to make an arrest concerning the murder of the man Robertson, but I'm afraid the villain absconded before we could apprehend him,' replied Ravenscroft, looking down at the floor.

'You think the death of my husband and this man Robertson are connected in some way, Inspector?'

'We believe that is a strong possibility, Mrs Montacute. Your husband never mentioned to you that he had any dealings with a man called Robertson?'

'I do not believe so. The name is unfamiliar to me.'

'Of course. Your late husband has provided well for you under the terms of his will?' said Ravenscroft, tentatively changing the subject.

'He has been most generous, yes, but I would rather that he was still with us,' replied Edith, forcing a brief smile.

'I assure you that you have our deepest sympathy in this matter. However, do you not find it somewhat strange, Mrs Montacute, that Nathaniel should have left you everything in his will, almost to the total exclusion of his two sons?' said Ravenscroft, coming straight to the point and anxious to observe the widow's reaction to his question.

'If you are implying that I influenced my husband in some way to draw up a new will in my favour then I can assure you that you are incorrect in that assumption. I was not even aware that my husband had drawn up a new will,' replied Edith firmly.

'Nevertheless, you would agree that the terms of the will were particularly unfavourable to your late husband's two sons?'

'I much regret that. Had I known that Nathaniel was drawing up his will, I would have urged him to have made better provision for his sons.'

'Mr Maurice Montacute has been left his father's share of the bank, that is all,' stated Ravenscroft, observing that his hostess was becoming unsettled by his questions.

'Indeed so, but I would have wished that Nathaniel had left this house and his investments to Maurice. It is more than his right. I know that he was very upset when the will was read yesterday, and I tried to speak with him afterwards, and indeed before he left for London this morning, but he was not available to see me.'

'And Rupert has been ill provided for,' added Ravenscroft.

'You are no doubt aware, Inspector, that my late husband and his youngest son were not on the best of terms. I know that Nathaniel was greatly concerned over the welfare of Rupert.'

'Yet he made no provision?'

'As I said, Inspector, had I known at the time of my husband's intention, I would have urged him on a different course of action. I will see that Rupert will want for nothing, you have my assurance on that point.'

'Can you tell me how you and Mr Montacute first met?' asked Ravenscroft, changing his line of questioning yet again.

'We met at a hotel in Rome. But you know this already,' replied Edith.

Ravenscroft thought he could detect a note of irritation creeping into her voice. 'You were alone there at the time?' he asked.

'I was with my mother. My father had recently died, leaving my mother and myself quite alone in the world. He left us well provided for, so you see I have no need of Nathaniel's money. I have no other brothers or sisters. My mother and I had decided to visit Rome to see the antiquities – it had always been a particular wish on my mother's part.'

'You lived in Cheshire, I believe? Your mother still lives there now?'

'The Henshaws of Nantwich in Cheshire have always been a prominent family in the county. Unfortunately my mother died last year,' replied Edith, tears beginning to form in her eyes.

'I am sorry.'

'So you see, Inspector, I am now quite alone in this world – first my parents and now Nathaniel. There is no one that I can turn to for consolation,' she said, looking deep into Ravenscroft's eyes.

'Forgive me, my dear lady,' said Ravenscroft, feeling uncomfortable and realizing that his questions were beginning to cause distress. 'I am sure that in time—'

'You are going to say, Mr Ravenscroft, that I am still young, that I have my whole life ahead of me, and that I might well marry again at some future date – but I can assure you that Nathaniel was the great love of my life. I would not seek anyone else to take his place.'

'I understand,' said Ravenscroft, rising from his seat, leaning forward and kissing the outstretched hand. 'Thank you for answering my questions. Rest assured, my lady, that our investigations will continue until the murderer of your husband is brought to justice.'

'That is some comfort, Inspector,' replied Edith, wiping away a tear.

Ravenscroft left the room and made his way along the hallway towards the front door.

'Begging your pardon, sir, before you go Mrs Chambers would like a word with you – if you would care to come with me, sir?'

Ravenscroft followed the maid down the steps to the kitchens, where he found the cook pacing up and down. 'Oh, Mr Ravenscroft, it's Master Rupert!' she said in an agitated state, coming forward to meet him.

'Calm yourself, Mrs Chambers, and tell me what it is that

concerns you,' said Ravenscroft.

'It's Master Rupert. No one has seen him since yesterday afternoon. He went off after the reading of the will. His bed has not been slept in. I'm afeared that something terrible has happened to the young gentleman.'

'Have any of the other servants seen him?'

'No sir.'

'Is Master Rupert in the habit of going off on his own for days at a time?' asked Ravenscroft.

'He sometimes goes into Worcester, and comes home late – but nothing like this.'

'You have made a search of the house?'

'Yes sir.'

'You say you saw him after the reading of the will?'

'Yes, sir. He came down here and took a bottle of wine from the cellars.'

'How did he seem?'

'Very upset, sir. I think he had been crying. After taking the bottle, he banged the kitchen door behind him, and that was the last I saw of him,' replied the cook, becoming more and more distressed.

'Don't worry, Mrs Chambers. I'm sure there is a good reason for Master Rupert absenting himself for so long. No doubt he will soon return.'

'I don't think so, sir.'

'Oh, why do you say that?' enquired Ravenscroft.

'Before he walked out of the kitchen he shouted that no one in his family cared for him, that he was all alone in the world, and that he wished himself and all of them dead!'

'I see,' said Ravenscroft, showing concern.

'I thought nothing of it at the time. The lad was obviously upset at being cut out of his father's will. It was cruel of the master to have treated him in that way. Cruel, I say. It is only now that I realize the importance of his words. Sir, I think something terrible has happened to him. He could be lying injured somewhere, outside, all alone, in all this awful weather,' said the cook, giving a loud sob and drying her eyes on a large cloth.

The outer door to the kitchens suddenly opened.

'Master Rupert?' called out the cook hopefully.

'It's only me, Mrs Chambers. Ravenscroft, good day to you,' said Rivers, noticing the policeman's presence as he strode into the room.

'Mr Rivers,' acknowledged Ravenscroft.

'Mrs Chambers has no doubt been telling you about Master Rupert going off on his own,' said the gamekeeper, crossing over to the fire and warming his hands.

'Indeed.'

'I have just been making a search of the grounds. No sign of him there.'

'Can you think of any places that Master Rupert could have visited? Perhaps there is a particular favourite place that he is in the habit of frequenting?' asked Ravenscroft.

'I sent one or two of the servants to check on the local ale houses but no one had seen him there. One of the farm lads said he saw the young master walking off in the direction of Coneygree Wood early yesterday afternoon,' replied Rivers.

'Can you think of any reason why Master Rupert would have gone there?'

'None that I can think of – although I remember I did take the lad up there with me once, some years ago, when he were young. We were shooting birds. It's a wild place.'

'Mr Rivers, I think we should organize a search party at once. If Rupert has gone into the wood and met with an accident, that would explain why he did not return home last night. He may have spent the night out in the open air. The weather is very cold. He may not survive for a second night in such conditions,' said Ravenscroft urgently.

'Oh, my Lord!' exclaimed the cook, bursting into tears.

'Now, Mrs Chambers, don't distress yourself. I'm sure we will be able to find Master Rupert,' said Ravenscroft, realizing that he'd said too much.

'It's a big wood. There are acres of it. All the way over to Eastnor,' said Rivers.

'There are paths through the wood?'

'In some places, yes.'

'Mr Rivers, we only have another two hours of daylight left. Get as many men as you can together. I'll return to the station and collect the two constables and anyone else I can find. Meet me by the entrance to the wood in fifteen minutes. Bring some torches with you.'

'Right, sir.'

'And see that the men are properly attired. We may be out there for some time, and it could be a very long, cold night!'

Ravenscroft stood, addressing the dozen or so men that stood at the side of the road. 'We are looking for Mr Rupert Montacute, who I am sure is well known to you all. He was last seen entering the wood early yesterday afternoon. We believe that he could have met with an accident, in which case he may well be seriously injured. It is important that we find him as soon as possible. Mr Rivers knows the wood well and will guide us up through the paths. Whilst there is still some daylight, we should spread out on both sides, but always keep the path and the next man in view at all times. We don't want to lose anyone. Do you all understand?'

'Aye, sir,' shouted out one or two of the farm labourers, as the rest of the group expressed their agreement.

'Doctor Andrews has agreed to accompany us so that Mr Montacute can be attended to when he is found. Right, Mr Rivers, we are all in your hands.'

'Heard the news, Ravenscroft, and thought you could do with another pair of hands,' shouted a breathless Catherwood, suddenly appearing along the side of the road, holding one of his dogs on the end of a lead.

'Indeed so, Mr Catherwood. Your assistance would be much appreciated. Lead on, Mr Rivers!' said Ravenscroft, urging the party onwards.

The group made their way in single file, up the steep winding path that led from the road into the start of the wood, before Rivers divided the men into two groups, sending them out to the left and right, whilst he and Ravenscroft kept to the centre path. Slowly their search took them upwards, until eventually they arrived at a clearing on the upper reaches of the wood.

'After here the wood becomes much thicker for the next two or three miles, before it drops down towards Eastnor,' said Rivers, addressing the group. 'Before we go on, I think we should search more of the slopes we have just climbed to make sure Master Rupert has not fallen there. If everyone spreads out and meets back here in fifteen minutes, before it becomes dark.'

The men went their separate ways, leaving Ravenscroft and Catherwood alone on the path. 'I'll take the dog along the path this way, Ravenscroft. He might be able to pick up something,' said Catherwood, striding away. Ravenscroft took the opposite side of the path and set off at a brisk pace. The disappearance of Rupert Montacute had put a new complexion on the case. At first sight, it appeared that Rupert had been so angered and distressed by his father's failure to recognize him in his will that he had taken off into the woods and now lay injured somewhere, but another possibility now presented itself to Ravenscroft. What if it had been Rupert who had killed his father, and he was now so overcome with remorse that he had fled the family home with the intention of doing away with himself in some isolated spot? Ravenscroft knew, however, that whatever the true reason for Rupert's disappearance, it would have to wait. His duty now was to find the young man before the weather closed in again for the night. It was doubtful that an injured man could survive a second night in such inhospitable terrain, unless he had been fortunate enough to have found some form of shelter.

Ravenscroft retraced his steps and watched as one by one the men returned empty-handed to the chosen place. The last to arrive was Catherwood with his large dog. 'Nothing that way,' he muttered as he rejoined the others.

'What next then, Mr Rivers?' asked Ravenscroft.

'We will need to go deeper into the wood. Keep close to the path. Light the torches!' replied Rivers, leading the way along the path that led into the upper reaches of the wood. 'Look on the ground. There may be tracks.'

'Let me go first, Mr Rivers,' said Catherwood. 'The dog may be of assistance to us.'

As the group moved into the wood, the last minutes of daylight faded. The men lit their way with three or four burning torches, and a full moon bore down on the white snowy landscape, aiding their progress. To Ravenscroft, as the minutes passed slowly by and became an hour, the futility of the search became more and more apparent. He knew that if Rupert Montacute had wandered away from the path, deeper into the wood, and had fallen, it would be almost impossible to find him, and that his body might not be discovered until the snow melted. He also knew that they were duty bound to continue the search, to try and save the young man.

Suddenly Rivers brought the group to a halt. 'Quiet! Everyone stay still!' he instructed, holding the blazing torch up high before lowering it to the ground. 'Look, there are some footmarks in the snow leading off that way. If my memory serves me correctly, there is an old hut in a clearing just over to the right. Whoever made these prints may have taken shelter there. Keep behind me.'

The group followed the gamekeeper, in single file, as he led them forward. Ravenscroft strained to see what lay ahead, hoping that at last their endeavours would be rewarded, that they had not arrived too late.

'Over there!' shouted Rivers. 'There's the hut!'

The men ran ahead. The hut lay in the centre of the clearing. Catherwood and his dog were first to arrive at the building. He pushed open the door.

'Good God!' he exclaimed.

Ravenscroft quickly entered the hut behind Catherwood. He could just make out the body of a man, covered in an old overcoat, lying stretched out in one corner of the timber-framed building. 'Is it Montacute?' he asked. 'Bring the light nearer.'

Suddenly a loud groan was heard from beneath the coat.

'My God, he's alive!' exclaimed one of Ravenscroft's constables.

Catherwood drew back the coat.

'Is it Master Rupert?' asked one of the men.

'I don't think so, gentlemen,' said Catherwood, standing back so that the rest of the group could see the man.

'Then who the devil is it?' asked Doctor Andrews, approaching the sleeping body.

'I know who it is,' said one of the farm labourers, coming forward. 'That's Leewood – the escaped criminal! I'd recognize him anywhere.'

'Leewood! So this is where he has been hiding out,' said Ravenscroft. 'Is he injured, Doctor?'

Suddenly the man woke with a start and stared up wildly at the group of men who were looking down on him.

'It's all right, my man. We mean you no harm. Are you hurt in any way?' asked Andrews, kneeling down at his side.

The dishevelled man suddenly leapt to his feet and began to run towards the entrance of the hut.

'Quickly men, secure him. Don't let him get away!' shouted Ravenscroft.

The criminal uttered a strong oath as three or four of the men grabbed him by the arms. 'Bring him over here, men,' instructed Ravenscroft. 'Now then, Mr Leewood, we have been looking for you for a very long time.'

'Who the devil are you?' growled Leewood.

'I am Inspector Ravenscroft of the Ledbury Constabulary, and you, sir, are Joshua Leewood, if I am not mistaken, recently absconded from Hereford gaol.'

'Damn you!'

'Watch your language, man!' snapped Rivers.

'How long have you been out here?' asked Ravenscroft.

'What's it to you?' replied the convict, attempting to break free from his captors.

'Have a civil tongue in your head, Leewood. I'll deal with you later. At present we have more pressing things to attend to. We are looking for a young man who is lost in this wood. Have you seen anyone in the wood in the last day or two?' asked Ravenscroft.

'Seen no one,' muttered Leewood.

'I don't think you are telling us the truth, Leewood. It will go bad for you if you don't tell us what we need to know and we find the gentleman lying dead in the wood tomorrow morning, knowing that we could have saved him if we had reached him tonight. Think carefully before you answer, Leewood. Have you seen anyone else in the wood during the last day or so?' said a determined Ravenscroft, staring into the grizzled, unshaven face of the felon.

'I might have caught sight of someone late yesterday afternoon,' replied Leewood.

'What did he look like?'

'I don't know, do I.'

'I said, what did he look like?' repeated Ravenscroft angrily.

'Young gent, dressed in long brown coat and hat. That's all I saw.'

'Young master's coat is brown,' said Rivers.

'Where did you see him?' asked Ravenscroft.

'I don't know, do I.'

'I don't believe you. My patience is running out with you,

Leewood. Either you tell me now exactly where you saw the young gentleman or I'll make sure you go down for another ten years,' threatened Ravenscroft.

'You can't do that,' protested Leewood.

'I can do anything I like. I have the law on my side. I won't ask you again, Leewood!'

'I was out near Eastnor. In the other wood on the other side of the hills, near the obelisk, that's where I saw him,' replied Leewood sullenly.

'What's this obelisk?' asked Ravenscroft, turning eagerly towards Rivers.

'It's a tall monument built by the Somers family of Eastnor Castle in commemoration of one of their soldier ancestors,' replied the gamekeeper.

'How far is it from here?'

'About three miles or so. We will need to drop down to the road near the village before we can go up again through the woods up towards the main hills,' said Rivers.

'You better be telling us the truth, Leewood, or it will be the worse for you. Constables, put the cuffs on him, take one of the torches and escort him back to the station, as quickly as you can. Lock him up in the cells for the rest of the night. I'll deal with him in the morning. Then bring some transport and wait for us in the village of Eastnor.'

Ravenscroft watched as the constables led Leewood away.

'It's a wonder he survived for so long out here in these conditions,' said Andrews, using his boot to turn over some of the debris which lay on the floor of the hut.

'There are the remains of a stale loaf and a piece of cheese. I would say that either someone has been feeding him out here or he has stolen these items from somewhere in Ledbury or Eastnor,' said Ravenscroft. 'Anyway, gentlemen, our task is not yet completed. Will you be so good, Mr Rivers, to lead the way down to the village?'

The group continued on their journey through the darkened, overgrown wood, which to Ravenscroft seemed to have no end, but after nearly another hour the search party finally left the wooded area as a gentle path led them steadily downwards across some fields, towards a distant light that signified that they were about to enter the village of Eastnor. Passing by the side of a church, Ravenscroft knocked on the door of a nearby cottage and made enquiries concerning the youth.

'The fellow there says that he saw a young gentleman of Rupert's description late yesterday afternoon crossing the road in the direction of the hills,' said Ravenscroft, returning to rejoin his companions.

'That would seem to confirm what Leewood told us,' said Catherwood.

'Mr Rivers, can you lead us up towards this obelisk? I have asked the man in the cottage to wait for our constables to return and instruct them to remain here.'

'Right, Mr Ravenscroft. Follow me, you men,' instructed the gamekeeper.

The group, although tired and cold, nevertheless set off at a brisk pace across the snowy landscape, knowing that their journey might shortly be reaching its climax. Rivers held the torch high above his head, lighting the way, as Catherwood sought to restrain his dog as it pulled anxiously on its leash. Ravenscroft could feel his chest tightening and his breath coming in short gasps as he fought against a cold wind that seemed to blow directly into his face.

Their journey took them steadily upwards across open parkland until they again entered more woodland. 'Not far now, gentlemen!' shouted Rivers, as Catherwood's dog suddenly slipped its leash and disappeared from view.

'There are some footprints in the snow!' exclaimed Ravenscroft.

'The dog's picked up something!' said Catherwood, breaking into a run, the rest of the group following suit.

Ravenscroft and his companions quickly found themselves on a piece of high, open ground, as a tall obelisk gradually came into view, silhouetted by the moon's glow against the whitened landscape.

Catherwood's dog began to bark loudly as the men ran towards the edifice. 'The dog's found something!' shouted Catherwood.

The searchers came to a halt as they reached the monument. Ravenscroft could just make out the outline of a figure slumped at the base of the obelisk.

'It's Master Rupert!' exclaimed Rivers, approaching the figure.

'Pray God we are not too late,' said an anxious Catherwood,

pulling back his dog.

Suddenly the figure moved.

'He's alive!' shouted one of the farm labourers.

'Master Rupert, it's Rivers!' called out the gamekeeper.

'Keep back, all of you!' shouted Rupert, lifting up a pistol that had evidently lain at his side and aiming it at the group.

'It's all right, Master Rupert, it's Rivers come to look for you. Don't be afraid, you'll be all right now. We've come to take you home.'

'Stand back, I say,' said the agitated youth. 'One more step and I'll blow my brains out. Leave me alone to die in my own time.'

'He's been out too long in the cold,' whispered Catherwood, moving slowly forward.

'Keep back! I mean it. If you come any closer I'll end it all now,' said Rupert, raising the pistol to his temple.

'You don't want to do that, lad,' said Catherwood in a reassuring tone. 'We are here to help you.'

'I warn you. If you come another step nearer, I'll do it. There's no point in going on. Nobody cares if I live or die. My father hated me!' said Rupert, crying and waving the pistol around his head.

'Come now, lad. There's folk that cares for you. All these people have come out here tonight to look for you. Don't end it all like this. Give me the pistol,' said Catherwood in a sympathetic, reassuring voice as he inched towards him.

'Nobody loves me! Keep back!'

'Come, lad, give it to me. Nothing we can't sort out in the morning,' said Catherwood, extending his hand out towards the weapon.

'Why can't I end it all?' cried the distraught youth.

'Because you know that would be wrong. You're young, you have everything to live for. Give me the pistol, lad,' said Catherwood firmly.

Rupert dropped the pistol to the ground and sobbed uncontrollably. Ravenscroft quickly recovered the weapon as Doctor Andrews placed a comforting arm around the forlorn figure.

A few minutes later, the search party made its slow progress back through the wood and down the path to Eastnor, where Ravenscroft was relieved to see that his men had returned with two horsedrawn vehicles. As they journeyed back to Ledbury, the men, weary and cold after their exertions, sat with bowed heads in silence, the only sounds being that of the wheels on the frozen road and the occasional sob from Rupert Montacute.

Eventually the vehicles came to a halt outside The Gables. 'I'll take Mr Montacute inside and put him to bed. He will no doubt see things differently in the morning,' said Andrews, alighting from one of the conveyances.

'Thank you, Doctor – and, you Mr Rivers, and all you men for your assistance,' said Ravenscroft as the group began to go their separate ways. 'Mr Catherwood, perhaps you would care to accompany me back to the town?'

Ravenscroft and Catherwood walked back in silence for a while before Ravenscroft finally spoke. 'That was a very brave thing you did tonight, Mr Catherwood. The lad could have shot you at any moment.'

'That's as may be.'

'Why did you come with us tonight? You have no obligation towards the Montacute family.'

'I think you know the answer to that question, Ravenscroft – unless of course you are a complete fool, which I very much doubt.'

'That Rupert Montacute . . . is your son?'

Catherwood said nothing but gave a brief smile before turning away and striding purposefully in the direction of his house.

# INTERLUDE

## LONDON, 7 JANUARY 1889

The Brothers of the West Kensington branch of the Freemasons Society took their places around the large oak table, as the flickering light from the oil lamp placed in the centre of the room cast fleeting shadows on the portraits of their illustrious predecessors.

The eldest member, and more senior of the group, cleared his throat. 'Gentlemen, apologies for the brief notice given to you all for the convening of this meeting this evening, but I have just received a report from our Brother in Ledbury which contains some rather disturbing news.'

'Please go on, Brother,' said one of the gathering.

'I received the communication from Brother 127 of Ledbury late this afternoon. In this letter he states that he believes the papers are located in the offices of one Midwinter, Oliphant and Burrows, Solicitors of the town. It seems likely that the man Robertson deposited the package there before his untimely death at the hands of our agent Major Monk.'

'It should be an easy task for Major Monk to retrieve the package and bring it to us,' interjected a high-pitched voice from lower down the table.

'That apparently is what Monk endeavoured to do yesterday evening, but unfortunately he was thwarted in his enterprise by the local constabulary and had to leave empty-handed. A trap had evidently been laid to arrest the good major,' continued the main speaker.

'That is rather unfortunate. Do we know who is in charge of the police there?' asked another of the group.

'A man by the name of Ravenhill or Ravenscroft, I believe,' replied the speaker, looking down at the letter which lay before him on the table.

'Not one of our number, I suppose?'

'Unfortunately not. Furthermore a police guard has been placed in the offices of the solicitors to prevent any further attempts to retrieve the papers.'

'This is most unwelcome news, Brother,' muttered the questioner.

'I have also received a communication from Major Monk in which he acknowledges that the case presents difficulties but stating that he knows of another way to recover the papers and that he is confident that they will be in our hands by the end of the week.'

'I do not like this, Brother. Monk has twice failed us in his attempts to secure the papers. Why should we expect his next attempt to succeed?' wheezed a stout, elderly Brother.

'In the present circumstances there would appear to be little that we can do, Brothers, other than trust that Major Monk is successful in his recovery,' replied the senior member.

'Cannot Brother 127 of Ledbury recover the papers for us?' interjected one of the group who had spoken earlier.

'No one in the town knows the identity of Brother 127. It is important for the Brotherhood that he retains his secrecy. If Brother 127 was to make an attempt to recover the papers then his position would be compromised, and at present there is nothing to suggest that he might be any more successful than our man Monk,' continued the elder.

'What do you propose then, Brother?'

'I suggest that we write back to our Brother in Ledbury tonight instructing him to keep a close watch on our Major Monk. Once Monk has fulfilled his task, then Brother 127 should eliminate the major and destroy the papers at the same time.'

'Would it not be better if the papers were returned to us?'

'We cannot take that risk. Someone else could intercept and acquire the papers between their passage from Ledbury to London. For every hour that those papers survive, the risk becomes greater that they will fall into the wrong hands. Far better that Brother 127 acts. Once he has destroyed the papers, there would be no evidence to support anyone who might seek at some future date to bring the issue into the public domain. No, gentlemen – let our Brother in Ledbury see that the papers are burnt.'

'You can trust Brother 127 to carry out this task?' asked the high-pitched voice.

'I have known the Brother personally for a number of years. He can be entirely trusted to carry out our orders. He shares our beliefs and will do anything to uphold the ambitions of the Brotherhood.'

The six members talked quietly amongst themselves for a few seconds before the senior member spoke once again. 'Gentlemen, do I have your agreement? Does anyone dissent? Then we are all agreed. I will write to our Brother in Ledbury tonight. Let us all hope that this matter can be brought to a quick and satisfactory conclusion.'

# CHAPTER TEN

## LEDBURY, 8 JANUARY 1889

'Gent to see you, sir.'

'Thank you, Constable. Show him in.'

It was the following morning, and Ravenscroft had arrived at the police station to interview Leewood.

The constable opened the door. An elderly gentleman, dressed in working clothes and adorned with a snowy white beard, shuffled into the room.

'Good morning, what can I do for you?' asked Ravenscroft, looking up from his papers.

'The name's Sanderson, Albert Sanderson. I am one of the lamplighters,' replied the visitor.

'Ah yes, Mr Sanderson, I thought I recognized you. You were present at the Lamplighters' Ball if I recall.'

'That's what I've come about. Got something to tell yer.'

'Then you best take a chair, Mr Sanderson,' instructed Ravenscroft.

His elderly visitor accepted the seat. 'Yer must excuse me, sir, if I appears to look at yer in a funny way. It's on account of me being boss-eyed, like.'

'Boss-eyed?'

'Me squint. I were born with it. I comes from a family of squinters. Me dad and his dad before him were all boss-eyed. Me brother, he were a squinter as well. Can't do much about it.'

Ravenscroft wondered what the condition of the man's eyesight had to do with the case he was now investigating. 'Please continue,

Mr Sanderson. You have some information for me?'

'I were there that night that Mr Montacute were done in. I might have seen who done it,' said the old lamplighter, pausing for the effect of his words to register with Ravenscroft.

'Yes, go on,' urged Ravenscroft.

'When we arrived at the Feathers, after putting out lamps, the others went on ahead, I followed them up the stairs shortly after. It were then that I saw her,' said Sanderson, leaning forward and looking in Ravenscroft's direction.

'Her?'

'Standing at the top of the stairs she were, just along from the room.'

'Who was standing outside the room?' asked Ravenscroft, wishing that his visitor would come to the point.

'I didn't get much of a look at her. Her head and face were covered in a long shawl, like. I'd say she were quite old though. Almost bent double she were.'

'And what precisely was this woman doing?'

'She weren't doing nothin'. She were just standing there, like, outside the room.'

'Do you remember anything else about this old woman?'

'No, except she had a nasty bussack.'

'Bussack?' asked a bewildered Ravenscroft.

'Bad cough, like,' replied Sanderson, demonstrating the cough. 'Real bad it were. She must have had it for a long time. Likes it will carry her off real soon. Folks is always getting bussacks in Ledbury.'

'Oh, why is that?' enquired Ravenscroft before realizing that he was encouraging the old man to digress from the matter in hand.

'It be the weather, like. Damp no good for the bussacks. Folk in Hereford don't have so many bussacks as we do here in Ledbury.'

'Tell me, Mr Sanderson, did you notice if this woman, who had the bad cough, actually went into the room where the ball was being held?'

'Don't know. I just passed her and went into the room. Then we went round snuffing out all the lights.'

'So after you entered the room, you did not see her again?'

'That's correct, sir,' replied Sanderson, leaning back in the chair with a look of satisfaction on his face.

'So she may have entered the room when the lights went out or she may have just gone on her way? Perhaps she was intending coming into the room once the New Year was announced, like they do in Scotland?'

'Oh, she wouldn't be doing that, sir.'

'Why not?'

'We has a saying in these parts that it is bad luck to have New Year let in by a woman or child. Has to be a man that do that.'

'So she would not have been loitering around outside the ballroom ready to make some kind of entrance when the New Year began? Perhaps she was hoping that the guests would give her something once they began to leave?' suggested Ravenscroft.

Sanderson nodded his head. Ravenscroft was beginning to feel uneasy trying to look the old lamplighter directly in the face, and turned away. 'Tell me, Mr Sanderson, you know that we have been investigating this case for some days now. Why have you waited all this time to come forward? This information could have helped us a great deal had we learned of it earlier.'

'I been staying with me aunt in Hereford. She's a bit craiky and needs looking after.'

'Craiky?'

'Bit weak, on account of her being old,' said the old man, stroking his long beard and winking one eye. 'Hereford folk live to an old age, but they is always craiky. Her husband he were very craiky. Been like that for years. Could hardly get out of bed in a morning.'

'I see. So you have been away in Hereford for a few days, looking after your aunt, and that is why you have not come forward until now?' said Ravenscroft, anxious to break into the lamplighter's flow of words.

'She been a-faltering of late. Bit giddling on her feet. Not likely to see next Gooding Day.'

'I'm sorry to hear that,' replied Ravenscroft, attempting to suppress a smile.

'Well, that be all, sir. I'd best be on my way,' said the old lamplighter, struggling to his feet.

'Thank you for coming in, Mr Sanderson. It is much appreciated. If you remember anything else unusual about the evening, please don't hesitate to come and see me again,' said

Ravenscroft, standing up and shaking the old man's hand.

'I wish you a heart-well new year, sir.'

'And to you, Mr Sanderson. Mind how you go.'

The old man left the room, leaving Ravenscroft deep in thought. Who had been the mysterious old woman who had been seen by the lamplighter outside the ballroom shortly before Montacute had been killed? Had she played any role in his death? If not, what had she been doing there on that night – and furthermore had she seen anyone either leave or enter the room when the lights had been extinguished? If so, the woman could have valuable evidence to impart. Ravenscroft knew that before any of these questions could be answered, he would have to discover the identity of the woman. Sanderson had mentioned that the elderly woman had been coughing a great deal. He had recently encountered one such person who seemed to fit the bill. After a minute or two of further deliberation, he rang the bell on his desk and instructed the constable to bring Leewood up from the cells.

'Sit down, Leewood,' instructed Ravenscroft.

The prisoner threw Ravenscroft a scowl before seating himself reluctantly on the chair.

'Now then, Leewood, I have a few questions to ask you before I send you back to Hereford gaol. It will be in your best interests to answer them as honestly as you can. I will know if you are lying, and if that is the case you will face further charges of police obstruction. The best thing you can do now is to tell us all you know. If I tell the prison governor that you have been co-operative, then things may not go so badly for you. I trust you understand what I am saying?' said Ravenscroft, speaking slowly and with determination.

'I didn't harm that lad, Mr Ravenscroft,' protested Leewood, leaning forward and eager to accept the offer that had been made to him.

'No one said that you did.'

'I just saw him in the wood. I had nothing to do with him.'

'I believe you. Now, Leewood, when you escaped from prison you decided to make your way back to Ledbury?'

The prisoner nodded and looked down at the floor.

'Why did you return to the town?'

'To see my wife – and me mother. That's why I escaped from Hereford.'

'And did you see them?'

'Saw my mother. Wife had left and gone off with another. Taken babby with her, the ungrateful harlot.'

'That's where you got the bread and cheese from – your mother?'

The convict nodded again.

'You have been living in the hut in the woods since your return to the town?'

'Yes.'

'You couldn't expect to stay there for ever, could you?' asked Ravenscroft, leaning forward.

'No. I just wanted to see my family, Mr Ravenscroft. That's all I wanted to do. I was going to give myself up today anyway. Honest I was. You have to believe me,' replied Leewood in a pleading voice.

'Tell me about Mr Nathaniel Montacute,' said Ravenscroft, ignoring the convict's last remarks.

'What do you want to know about him for? He was the beak that sent me down!'

'You protested your innocence at the time?'

'Yes, and that were right, Mr Ravenscroft. I never did it.'

'Mr Montacute thought otherwise, and when he passed sentence you made a disturbance, and said that one day you would get even with him.'

'I might have said something like that,' admitted Leewood reluctantly.

'I assure you that you were quite vocal in your threats.'

'Yes, well, I suppose I was angry at the time. Wouldn't you be, if you had been sent down for a crime that you didn't commit?'

'And did you get even with him?'

'Who?'

'Nathaniel Montacute. Did you set out to kill him, upon your return to Ledbury?'

'No! No, I never laid a hand on him,' said Leewood, crying out.

'Well, someone did. He was poisoned at the Lamplighters' Ball. Did you poison Mr Montacute?'

'No! I ain't seen him since I were sent to gaol.'

'We only have your word for that.'

'You have to believe me!' protested Leewood. 'I didn't mean no harm to the gent when I said those words. I never hurt anyone in my life. Where could I have got poison from?'

'Perhaps your mother procured the poison for you – and then on the night of the Lamplighters' Ball you slipped into the ballroom of the Feathers and dropped the poison into the old banker's glass when the lights went out, whilst your mother kept watch outside?'

'No. I don't know what you are talking about. My mother has nothing to do with this,' replied the agitated convict, staring into Ravenscroft's eyes. 'I didn't kill anyone. You have to believe me.'

The two men looked at one another in silence; Leewood desperate to express his innocence, Ravenscroft unsure whether the felon was telling him the truth.

Suddenly Ravenscroft sprang to his feet. 'That will be all for now. Constable, will you take the prisoner back to the cells.'

'You have to believe me. I didn't kill Montacute. I'm innocent,' pleaded the convict.

'Constable, escort the prisoner from the room,' instructed Ravenscroft, turning away and staring out of the narrow window.

'I tells you, I didn't do it! Why don't you believe me?'

A few minutes later, Ravenscroft paused at the entrance to Smoke Alley. Now that he had spoken with Leewood, it was time to question the mother again. He was convinced that it had been Mrs Leewood who had been seen by Sanderson the lamplighter, loitering outside the ballroom of the Feathers shortly before the lights had been exstinguished, and he was anxious to learn why she had been there that night, what part she had played in the banker's death and whether she had acted alone or in conjunction with her son. Perhaps the mystery of Montacute's death was at last about to be revealed.

After taking a deep breath, he strode down the darkened passageway.

'Give us another coin, governor!' cried out the boy he had encountered on his previous visit, eagerly running up towards him.

Ravenscroft brushed the lad aside, marched into the courtyard and, after briefly banging his fist on the wood, pushed open the door and entered the room.

'Thought you would be back,' muttered the voice of the old woman somewhere in the darkness. Ravenscroft briefly recoiled from the same damp, fetid smell that assailed his senses.

'Mrs Leewood, I have some news for you,' he said, seeking to adjust his eyes to the gloom of the room, as the cat at his feet let out a loud squawk.

'Suppose you've caught him?' coughed the old woman.

'We found your son up in Coneygree Wood. He was hiding out in an old hut that used to belong to the woodmen,' Ravenscroft answered as he neared the chair and looked down at the old woman. The cat moved to a corner of the room, glaring at the intruder and hissing as it did so.

'You're going to send my boy back to Hereford then?'

'I'm afraid so.'

'My lad has done nothing. He should never have been put away in the first place.'

'Mrs Leewood, what were you doing at the Feathers on New Year's Eve?' said Ravenscroft, ignoring the last remark and anxious to confront her with the knowledge he had just gained that morning.

The old woman let out a loud laugh before being convulsed by a series of deep coughs.

'Can I get you some water?' asked Ravenscroft.

'Don't need no water.'

'Has Doctor Andrews been to see you?'

'Sent him packing! What need have I for a doctor? Nothing any doctor can do for me. I ain't long for this world,' grumbled Mrs Leewood.

'What were you doing at the Feathers on New Year's Eve?' repeated Ravenscroft.

'I heard you the first time!' The woman scowled. 'What would I be doing at the Feathers? Feathers is only for the toffs. What use would I have for such a place?'

'You were seen, standing on the landing, outside the ballroom, shortly before midnight when Mr Montacute was poisoned.'

'It's a lie! Who says I was there?'

'Never mind who saw you. I have a reliable witness who can state quite clearly that he saw you standing outside the ballroom. It will be best for both you and your son if you come right out with the truth. What were you doing there?' asked Ravenscroft, adopting a more forceful tone.

'Curse you!'

'Were you waiting for your son to arrive, so that you could slip him the poison that you had procured?'

'Eh? What are you talking about? I had nothing to do with any poison.'

'Or perhaps you did the deed yourself, creeping into the room when the lights went out, pouring the poison into the glass, before making good your escape?'

The woman began a coughing fit again as Ravenscroft continued with his questioning. 'You certainly had cause to hate Mr Montacute. It was him, after all, who had sent your son to prison for a crime which you believed he had not committed. You must have been waiting for the right opportunity to get your revenge. How you hated Mr Montacute! Planning all the time how you would do the deed. Then you suddenly heard about the Lamplighters' Ball, and you remembered how they extinguished the lights to see in the New Year. What a wonderful opportunity to creep into the room. No one would be sure to see you, and you could be away again before the lights were relit. It must have been quite easy to have committed such a crime?'

'All right! All right!' protested the woman through her coughs. 'Yes, I was there, but I don't know anything about any poisoning.'

'I find that very difficult to believe,' said Ravenscroft.

'Believe what you like!' retorted the old woman.

'If you didn't poison Mr Montacute then what were you doing at the Feathers that night?'

'Curse you damned police! I was outside the room waiting for them to come out, so that they could have charity on such an old woman as myself.'

'You were hoping that the guests would give you money as they left?' asked Ravenscroft, noting the bitterness and anger in her voice.

'What else could I do? How else was I to get money to buy food for my boy?' replied the old woman, coughing before spitting on to the floor.

'So you were there, begging for money. I did not see you in the room.'

'It would have been bad luck to have gone in. Then I heard them cry out that old Montacute had been poisoned, so I left as soon as I could. Got what was coming to him, I say!'

'How long were you standing outside the room?'

'About ten minutes.'

'Mrs Leewood, my next question is a very important one, and I would appreciate an honest reply. When you were standing outside the room, did you see anyone going in, before the lights were put out, other than the lamplighters?' asked Ravenscroft, realizing that the woman was probably telling the truth and adopting a more conciliatory tone in his questioning.

'No.'

'When the lights went out, were you aware of anyone either entering or leaving the room?'

'No one.'

'And as the lights came back on, did you notice if anyone left the room in a hurry?'

'I've just said, there was no one!' growled the old woman, before coughing and spitting once more on to the floor.

'You're absolutely sure on that point?'

'Curse you, listen to what I says!'

Ravenscroft looked away, and suddenly became aware that a large black rat was climbing out of the sink. As it made its way down on to the floor, the cat quickly pounced on the creature, and the noise of the ensuing battle engulfed the room.

'Thank you, Mrs Leewood. I wish you good day,' said the detective, feeling a cold shiver run down his spine and walking swiftly over towards the door, bypassing the two adversaries on the way.

'Here, what about my Joshua? You going to send him back to Hereford then?' called out the old woman – but Ravenscroft had already closed the door securely behind him, and had quickly sought the sanctuary of the Homend.

'Good morning to you, my man.'

'Morning to you as well, sir.'

'I see you are busy at your work.'

'Always busy in my line of work, particularly at this time of year.'

Ravenscroft had just entered the churchyard and had found the stonemason, leaning over and busily engaged in creating a new inscription on the side of the Montacute vault. 'Why, it's Mr Sanderson again, if I am not mistaken. Forgive me, I did not recognize you in your different apparel. So you are a carver by profession as well as having charge of the town's lights.'

'That I am, sir. Has to do something during the day, when it ain't dark,' replied the old man, straightening up his body.

'Your industry does you credit, sir. There must be quite a few Montacutes buried here, inside?' said Ravenscroft, impressed by the man's versatility, and walking round the monument.

'Reckon so. I've done a few of them,' replied the stonemason, chipping away at the stone.

'Oh, which ones?'

'His two wives. Round the other side.'

Ravenscroft knelt down to examine the lettering.

Sacred to the memory of Margaret Montacute (1827-1856)
Beloved Wife of Nathaniel and Mother of Maurice and Elizabeth
And to Elizabeth Montacute (1851-1855)
Daughter of Margaret and Nathaniel
Tragically Taken from us at such a Young Age.
May They Rest in Peace

In Loving Memory of Enid Montacute (1839-1886)
Second Wife of Nathaniel Montacute, and Mother of Rupert
She was held in the Greatest Affection by both her Family
And the Townspeople of Ledbury.

'Died quite suddenly, she did,' said the stonemason, looking over Ravenscroft's shoulder. 'Died of a fever, so they say. She were a real lady. It were a great loss to the town when she passed away.'

'Are there any other Montacutes buried inside?' asked Ravenscroft.

'Oh yes, there's the old master and his wife. They are round the other side. It were my father who did for them. He were mason before me,' replied Sanderson, laying down his tools and lighting a small pipe.

Ravenscroft walked round to the other side of the monument, and strained to read the older lettering.

In Memory of Giles Montacute (1798-1860)
Banker and Benefactor of This Town
And to Jane Montacute (1799-1863)
A Loving Wife and Mother.

'Not much room left after I've done with old Master Nathaniel. Just enough for his third wife, Miss Edith, when she goes,' muttered the stonemason.

'She's younger than both of us,' suggested Ravenscroft.

'She could outlive us all, or be killed tomorrow. Death is a funny thing. Creeps up on you when you are least expecting it. Plenty of fevers always about to carry you off. Six-month-old infant one day, old grandmother tomorrow. You can never tell who's next. Did a stone last year for a gent that fell under the hooves of a horse whilst our hunting. Could not have been much above thirty in years. You from these parts, Mr Ravenscroft?' asked Sanderson, drawing on his pipe.

'I came to Ledbury last year.'

'You planning on staying here then?'

'I would hope so.'

'Could be doing your stone in a few years' time then.'

'I sincerely hope not.'

'Any parents?'

'They died some years ago – and my sister.'

'Got yer own family?'

'Yes, but I must not detain you from your work, Mr Sanderson. I am looking for the vicar,' said Ravenscroft, deciding that he had no wish to continue with the mason's current line of enquiry.

'Inside church. Saw him go inside not ten minutes ago.'

'Thank you.'

'Aye, sir, good day – until we meets again.'

Ravenscroft walked quickly away and pushed open the heavy door that led into the church.

'Good morning to you, Mr Ravenscroft,' said the vicar, coming forward to greet him.

'Good morning to you, Vicar,' replied Ravenscroft, remembering that he had been married but a few months previous in this same church.

'And how is Mrs Ravenscroft?'

'Very well, thank you, Vicar.'

'How can I be of assistance to you?'

'You are probably aware that I am investigating the death of Nathaniel Montacute.'

'Yes indeed. What a sad, tragic business. I was there on the night

158

it happened,' said the clergyman, shaking his head.

'I am trying to find out as much as I can about the Montacute family. I wonder if I might go through your parish registers?'

'Of course, if you think they might prove of value to you in your enquiries.'

'I'm not really sure at this stage, but the more I can learn about the family, the closer I may be towards finding out who killed Nathaniel Montacute.'

'The registers are kept in the vestry, if you would care to follow me.'

Ravenscroft followed the clergyman into the side room, where his guide placed a large key in an ancient oak coffer. 'Ah, here we are. How far do you want to go back? The smaller volumes cover the years before the beginning of our present century, the later larger volumes, still in current use, commence with the year 1812,' said the vicar, peering into the interior of the chest.

'I think those that come after 1812 would suffice,' replied Ravenscroft.

The clergyman lifted a number of volumes out of the chest and placed them on a small table in the centre of the room. 'This one covers the marriages that took place in the church – that one is for burials – and yes, this one records baptisms. I'm sure you will find many of the Montacutes in there. Of course, Nathaniel married his third wife, Edith, elsewhere, so you won't find that event recorded. I believe they married somewhere in Italy. Rome, I believe.'

'I think that was the case.'

'I'll leave you to your investigations if you don't mind. I have a few things to do in the church. I'll come back and see how you are progressing in a little while.'

'Thank you, Vicar,' replied Ravenscroft, drawing up a chair towards the desk as the clergyman left the room, and taking out a small notebook and pencil from his coat pocket.

He opened the Register of Marriages and turned to the last few pages of entries, where he was reassured to discover his own marriage and signature. Then turning over the pages of the volume, he worked steadily backwards from the recent entries towards the beginning of the book. Finding the first and second marriages of Nathaniel Montacute, he jotted down the information in his pocket book, before continuing with his search until he found the marriage of Giles and Jane Montacute in 1827.

Placing the volume aside, he opened the next register, which contained details of the burials of Ledbury since the year 1812. The last entry recorded the burial of Nathaniel Montacute on 6 January, two days previously. For the next few minutes Ravenscroft turned back the pages, looking down the columns of surnames and noting down any occurrences of the Montacute name, starting with Enid in 1886 until he reached the burials of the earlier members of the family in the second decade of the century. Finally he turned to the Register of Baptisms, and opening the volume at the page headed 1812 began to work forward in time. After some minutes he found an entry for the baptism of the old banker:

1828. Nov 3rd. Nathaniel. Son of Giles and Jane Montacute. The Cedars Father's Profession – Banker.

After writing down the details, Ravenscroft continued to turn over the pages.

'Ah, and how is your search progressing?' asked the vicar, returning to the vestry.

'Very well, thank you. I have found a number of entries for the family in regard to their marriages and burials,' replied Ravenscroft.

'I see you have found Nathaniel's baptism,' said the clergyman, looking down at Ravenscroft's last written entry in his pocket book.

'Yes, interestingly Giles and Jane don't appear to have given birth to any other children.'

'I think there was another son, born much later. If you keep turning over the pages, I'm sure we will find him. Yes, there we are. "1843. Robert. Son of Giles and Jane Montacute. The Cedars. Father's Profession – Banker."'

'A fifteen-year age gap between the two brothers,' remarked Ravenscroft, recording the entry down in his book.

'A not uncommon occurrence, I can assure you. Some families in the parish have been known to produce as many as eight or nine children or more in as many years, whilst others wait for much longer periods before the birth of second and third children. Some years ago I came across a family whose second child did not appear until the couple had been married for nearly twenty years. Such are the laws of nature.'

'Do we know what happened to this Robert?' asked Ravenscroft.

'Perhaps he died in infancy?'

'There is no entry for his burial in the registers,' said Ravenscroft, consulting his pocket book.

'Then I suppose he must have left Ledbury when he was quite young.'

'Did Nathaniel ever mention him at all?'

'I don't recall that he ever did.'

'Thank you, Vicar, you have been most helpful. Let me give you some assistance in returning the volumes to the coffer.'

'Good afternoon to you, sir.'

It was later that afternoon when Ravenscroft looked up at the old lamplighter who was busily engaged in lighting the lamps of the town. 'Why, Mr Sanderson, we meet yet again!' he exclaimed, wondering how many more times he would encounter the versatile artisan before the day was over.

'Be a cold one tonight.'

'I think you are correct,' replied Ravenscroft, turning up the collar of his coat.

'Mind how you goes, bit slippery under foot,' called out the old man as Ravenscroft continued on his way along the street and on past the ancient market hall. Shortly he would be entering the confines of Cocks and Biddulph, where he had arranged to meet Anthony Midwinter and Maurice Montacute, and where he hoped that the mysterious envelope would at last yield up its secrets. Since his visit to Smoke Alley earlier in the day and his questioning of the old woman, he had now established that the old banker's murderer had been present in the room when the lights had been extinguished. According to Mrs Leewood, no one had either entered or left the room during the arrival of the New Year festivities, and he had almost excluded the possibility that either she or her son had committed the crime in an attempt to gain some kind of revenge. Already new possible lines of enquiry had taken root in his mind, but until he had learned the nature of the contents of the envelope, he was still at a loss to see how the murder of Robertson and the poisoning of Nathaniel Montacute could be in any way related to one another. He wondered whether Robertson's murderer was still following his every move, seeking another opportunity to retrieve the envelope when it presented itself, but although he had kept a vigilant lookout for the man on his varied travels during the day, he had not been able to discern any untoward presence.

Ravenscroft pushed open the doors of the bank and was quickly shown into the main office by one of the clerks.

'Good afternoon to you, Ravenscroft. Mr Midwinter has just been informing me about his Christmas visitor,' said Maurice Montacute, rising from his chair and shaking his hand as he entered the room.

'Then Mr Midwinter will also have told you about the desperate attempt that was made to retrieve the envelope.'

'Yes, indeed. Please do take a seat. And how is your constable?'

'He is recovering well and should be back on duty tomorrow, I thank you, sir,' replied Ravenscroft, shaking Midwinter's hand before accepting the seat.

'That is good. I must say this is all rather mysterious. Why a complete stranger would deposit a package with Mr Midwinter, leaving instructions that it should be delivered to my father in the event of his own demise, is certainly baffling,' said the banker, regaining his seat.

'I trust that when we have opened the envelope we may all be wiser on that point. I should point out to you, Mr Montacute, that I journeyed to London, where I discovered that the man Robertson had been employed as a coachman in the employ of Sir James Stanhope,' said Ravenscroft, casting a glance around the room with its fine mahogany furniture, ornate carpet and austere portraits of what he supposed were the bank's former partners.

'Sir James is well known to me. He has an account with our London offices in Mayfair,' interjected Maurice.

'I learnt that the man had left his employ on Christmas Eve with the express purpose of travelling to Ledbury, and that he had been afraid that an attempt would be made to recover the documents from him had he remained in London. I trust, Mr Midwinter, that you have the envelope upon your person?' asked Ravenscroft anxiously.

'I do indeed have it here, Inspector,' replied the solicitor, taking the envelope from his coat pocket and laying in on the desk before him. 'Your constable escorted me from my offices to the bank, in case any further attempts should be made. I must say that I will be somewhat relieved to be rid of the thing.'

'Robertson left clear instructions that the envelope was to be opened only by the senior partner of the bank, namely Mr Nathaniel Montacute. As you have now taken over that position, then it falls to you, sir, to open the envelope,' said Ravenscroft, addressing the banker.

Maurice reached for the paper knife on his desk and slid the blade under the flap of the package. Ravenscroft and Midwinter leaned forward as the banker withdrew the contents from the envelope and placed them on the desk. 'We seem to have a letter, which is addressed to my father, on this piece of paper. The other item would appear to be some kind of handwritten book,' said Maurice.

'Perhaps we should begin with the letter,' suggested the solicitor.

'Yes indeed,' replied the banker, beginning to read the contents of the letter out loud:

*My Dear Nathaniel,*

*No doubt you will be quite surprised to have a communication from me after such a long period of time. It has long been my regret that we parted on such bad terms all those many years ago. Alas, we will never be able to heal the breach which has kept us apart for so long, for I'm afraid if you are reading these words now it is because some misfortune has befallen me and we will only meet again in the life hereafter.*

*You will find enclosed a journal, written by an esteemed personage. I will not seek to name him in this letter – other than to refer to him by the initials 'A.V'. When you have read the enclosed diary, you should be able to identify the author – and furthermore see why the document must never come into the public domain. I will not tell you how I acquired the journal, other than to say it came from a source close to my employer, Sir James Stanhope, who you will see features prominently in the work along with several other names which may be familiar to you. You will also understand why it is important that the document should never fall into the wrong hands.*

*Once you have read the enclosed journal, I would suggest that the work be given to our Illustrious Client, so that he may take the appropriate steps to safeguard the future welfare of our country.*

*I wish you and your family well. Perhaps sometime in the future you may find it in your heart to forgive the wrong I caused you all those years ago.*

'What a strange letter,' said Midwinter after Maurice had laid the letter down on the desk.

'It appears to be unsigned,' said Ravenscroft, staring down at the writing, 'but clearly Nathaniel would have known who the author was. The writer refers to an event which resulted in a rift between the writer and your father many years ago.'

'I must say that I am at a loss. If my father had still been alive, then clearly he would have been able to identify the author,' said a bewildered Maurice.

'I believe I know the identity of the writer. Your father had a brother, Mr Montacute, called Robert, who was born fifteen years after himself, in 1843. The coachman, Robertson, was none other than Robert Montacute!' said Ravenscroft.

'Good heavens!' exclaimed Midwinter. 'How on earth do you know that?'

'This morning I spent some time examining the parish registers at the church here in Ledbury,' replied Ravenscroft. 'You do not recall your uncle, Mr Montacute?

'Yes, I have a distant memory of him. I was born in 1856. When I was six or seven years of age, I can remember him leaving, that is all.'

'Did your father ever mention the cause of the breach between himself and your uncle?'

'He did mention to me upon one occasion that he and his younger brother had fallen out. All he said was that there had been some financial irregularity in the affairs of the bank, and that Robert had left in a hurry to avoid the scandal,' said Maurice, shifting uneasily in his chair.

'So Robert Montacute left the town of his birth, moved to London, where he changed his name to Robertson and gained employment as a coachman. That would explain why he always kept a print of Ledbury church in his bedside cabinet, to remind him of the churchyard where his parents lay buried. Over twenty-five years later he returned to the town, only to be struck down before he could return to the capital. Your uncle clearly feared for his own life while he was in possession of the enclosed book, and in his hour of need turned to the only person he could trust, your father,' said Ravenscroft.

'But if all this is true, why did this Robertson – sorry, Robert Montacute – insist on leaving the book with me instead of giving it directly to his brother here at the bank?' asked Midwinter.

'Because he hoped that he would not need to do so. He hoped that by returning to his employment the matter would die down and that whoever was seeking to obtain the book from him would give up his purpose. By leaving the book with you, Mr Midwinter, he could return again at a later date and recover his package. By instructing you to see that his brother obtained the enclosed book in the event of his own death, he was ensuring that it would fall into the right hands. In the letter he requests that Nathaniel return the book to "your Illustrious Client, who will take the appropriate steps to safeguard the future welfare of our country".'

'We have many illustrious and important clients who come from all walks of life – prominent clergymen, the aristocracy, parliamentarians, even several members of the royal family,' said a bewildered Maurice.

'Perhaps if we read the journal, we might be able to ascertain who this illustrious client is?' suggested Midwinter.

'It would perhaps be better if you were to read it out loud, Inspector?' said the banker, leaning back in his chair and folding his hands.

'Very well, gentlemen,' said Ravenscroft, reaching out for the book and opening it at the first page, after first adjusting his spectacles. 'The book indeed appears to be some kind of journal, written in neat copper plate writing. The initials A and V have been written on the outside of the volume. The first few pages seem to have been torn out. The first entry reads:

*March 3rd. Went to Cleveland Street this evening with Stephen, who was in good form, laughing and joking and insisting I hear his latest literary offering, which is full of his usual descriptive charm.*

*March 5th. Went again to Cleveland Street with Stephen and one or two of his companions from Cambridge, where we remained until three in the morning on account of our enjoying ourselves so much.*

*March 9th. To Cleveland Street, this time with Arthur Somerset, Stephen being away on official duties in Wales. Wonder what Father would say if he could see us both now!*

*March 15th. Cleveland Street with Somerset, where I saw Sir James Stanhope and his followers. We all had a good time.*

*March 23rd. Should have gone to Cleveland Street tonight with Somerset, but remained in my rooms, finding myself in a lethargic frame of mind, not wanting to do anything.*

*March 30th. Good news! Stephen has returned from Wales. We celebrated his return to civilization by dining out at my club, after which Stephen suggested we go on to Cleveland Street to enjoy ourselves. Hammond keeps a respectable house there, I am pleased to say, and no matter how many times we visit his establishment, there is always someone new to encounter.*

*April 7th. How the time passes drearily in York – nothing but official business to conduct; endless meetings with dull, uninteresting people. To think that one day I shall have to do this all the time. I do not know how I will ever manage. How I long to return to London and partake of my old pleasures at Cleveland Street.*

*April 14th. At last I am free of it! How I hate all that pomp and ceremony. Celebrated my release by going to Cleveland Street with Stephen. Saw Somerset and Stanhope there obviously enjoying themselves. Hammond tells us that he has managed to recruit a new group of messenger boys for us from the Post Office—*

'Good God!' exclaimed Midwinter, interrupting Ravenscroft's reading of the diary.

'I do not think we need to hear any more,' said Maurice.

'He seems to be describing some kind of male brothel!' said Midwinter, growing red in the face and becoming increasingly agitated by what he had just heard.

'I think you are correct, gentlemen. I must admit that when I learnt that Robertson was used to taking his master, Sir James Stanhope, to Cleveland Street, the name of the street appeared familiar to me, but I could not recall the reason why. Now I remember that the place had been under observation by the local police force a year or so ago, when it was suspected as being some kind of den of male prostitution, but nothing was proven at the time.'

'This is absolutely appalling,' said the solicitor, turning away. 'Had I known that the packet within my safe contained such a book of degradation I would have removed it instantly and thrown it on the fire!'

'The diary mentions Stephen, Sir James Stanhope, Arthur Somerset and a person by the name of Hammond. We know that Sir James was the employer of Robertson, your uncle, and Hammond would appear to be the owner of the male brothel. I don't know who either Stephen or Arthur Somerset are,' said Ravenscroft, turning over the pages of the handwritten diary.

'I may be able to help you there. Arthur Somerset is probably Lord Arthur Somerset, an equerry to the Prince of Wales,' replied Maurice.

'This is dreadful!' exclaimed Midwinter. 'To think that someone close to the heir of the throne is used to visiting such dens of iniquity.'

'There is worse, gentlemen. It appears that the Cleveland Street brothel was visited by a number of other prominent people, including at least one member of the cabinet and two prominent churchmen,' said Ravenscroft, leafing through the pages of the journal. 'I can see now why this book was so important, and why your uncle took great pains to see that it did not fall into the wrong hands. Such knowledge, if it ever became public, could almost certainly bring down the government as well as inflicting great harm on the royal family.'

'We must burn the wretched book straightaway!' demanded Midwinter.

'I wonder who wrote the journal? You say there are the letters A and V on the front of the work?' asked Maurice.

'I think I can provide us with the answer to that question, gentlemen,' said Ravenscroft. 'Your uncle has already given us a clue in his letter when he says that your father is to give the book to "his Illustrious Client so that the appropriate steps may be taken to safeguard the future welfare of our country". I think I am correct in assuming that your illustrious client is none other than His

Royal Highness the Prince of Wales?'

'You are indeed correct, Mr Ravenscroft. The Prince is indeed one of our most important clients. His account is deposited with our London offices in Mayfair. I have had the pleasure of meeting the Prince once or twice myself, although my father took overall responsibility for the safeguarding of the royal account. But why should my father give the book to the Prince?' asked a puzzled Maurice.

'Because the journal is written by his son! The initials A and V stand for Prince Albert Victor!' said Ravenscroft.

'Good heavens!' exclaimed Midwinter.

'Your uncle was instructing your father, in his letter, to see that the book be given to the Prince of Wales, so that the Prince could learn of his son's deviation, and so that appropriate steps could be taken by the Prince to bring his son back into line and to suppress any attempt to make the matter public,' said Ravenscroft.

'This is all quite dreadful. Prince Albert Victor is the eldest son of His Highness the Prince of Wales. One day, when our beloved Queen has passed on, and the Prince after her, then this depraved person will sit on the throne of England!'

A long silence followed Midwinter's utterance, as each of the three men began to slowly absorb the significance of the book which now lay before them on the banker's desk, and the future implications that could possibly follow.

'If any of this was made public—' began Maurice, eventually breaking the silence.

'Then almost certainly the monarchy would fall,' added Ravenscroft.

'It does not bear thinking about. To think that dreadful man will one day be the ruler of our country! I cannot comprehend such a dreadful situation, gentlemen. I am only glad to know that I shall be long gone by the time that state of affairs comes to fruition. We must destroy the book at once and swear an oath of secrecy never to divulge to anyone what we have learnt in this room today,' suggested the solicitor.

'By all means let us swear together an oath, but to destroy the book would prevent us from discovering who killed both your uncle and your father, Mr Montacute. Robertson was killed because it was thought that the package was still upon his person; later when his killer discovered that the package lay within the safe of your office, Mr Midwinter, he tried to retrieve it, wounding my constable in the attempt. If we destroy this journal tonight, the killer may learn that we have done so, and will abandon his quest, and thereby escape justice for his crimes. If, on the other hand, we are seen returning the package to your office and securing it within the confines of your safe, Mr Midwinter, then our killer will certainly try again to make another attempt to retrieve the document. As long as we have the package with its letter and journal inside, we still have an opportunity to catch the villain. Once we have him safe under lock and key then we can see that your uncle's wishes are carried out and that the book is given to the Prince of Wales for him to do with it as he wishes,' said Ravenscroft.

'But there is a deeper issue involved here,' protested the solicitor. 'Such a depraved work must be consigned to the flames as soon as possible.'

'I am inclined to agree with the inspector, Midwinter. Whilst I sympathize with your views and agree that the book should be eventually destroyed, nevertheless I want the killer of my father and my uncle brought to justice. If that means that we deposit the package within your safe for the time being, then so be it,' said Maurice with determination.

'Then it is agreed, gentlemen,' said Ravenscroft. 'We may not have long to wait until our killer makes his next move!'

# CHAPTER ELEVEN

## LEDBURY, 9 JANUARY 1889. MORNING

'You look deep in thought this morning, my dear,' said Lucy.

'I'm beginning to wonder if this case will ever be concluded,' replied Ravenscroft, buttering another slice of toast.

'Who would have thought that your coachman would turn out to be Nathaniel Montacute's younger brother?'

'That fact explains a great deal. Two brothers killed within a few days of each other and all for the sake of a packet of papers – or so it would appear.'

'Excuse me, sir, but Constable Crabb has just arrived,' said the maid, peering round the side of the door frame.

'Then show the good fellow in!' said Ravenscroft, jumping up from the table and shaking his associate's hand as he entered the room. 'Good to see you again, Tom. I trust you are fully recovered?'

'Indeed, sir, I am well, thank you. Mrs Ravenscroft,' replied a beaming Tom Crabb.

'I am so glad you did not sustain any great injury. Do take a seat, Tom, and have some breakfast with us,' said Lucy.

'Thank you, Mrs Ravenscroft. I don't mind if I do. It's a bit chilly out this morning and a warm drink would not go amiss, thank you,' said Tom, accepting the seat at the table.

'Sally, would you bring another plate, and a cup and saucer for Mr Crabb, and make some fresh tea and some more toast. And how is Jennie and your little Samuel?' asked Lucy.

'Both in excellent spirits, thank you, ma'am.'

'My husband has been missing your valuable assistance these last few days.'

'Indeed I have, Tom. I have been at quite a loss without you.'

'And how is the case progressing, sir?'

'Slowly. Your attacker is still at large, I'm afraid, but I believe he will soon make another attempt to recover the package, and then we will have him. Since I saw you the other day, there have been a few developments in the case.'

Ravenscroft recounted the events of the previous few days as Crabb enjoyed a helping of tea and buttered toast.

'So young Master Montacute turns out to be Catherwood's son!' said Crabb, when Ravenscroft had finished his narrative.

'Yes, and that probably explains the rivalry between the old banker and Catherwood – and would also go a long way to understanding the poor relationship between Rupert and his supposed father. Nathaniel must have known about his wife's association with Catherwood, but rather than divorce his wife and have to put up with all the ensuing scandal, he decided to do nothing and bring up the boy as his own,' explained Ravenscroft.

'That was why Catherwood remained here for all those years, instead of going back to Yorkshire,' suggested Crabb, taking another mouthful of toast.

'Exactly. At first there was the woman he loved, and when Enid died he no doubt felt that he had to remain in the town so that he could keep a watchful eye over his true son.'

'Do you think Rupert ever knew who his real father was?' asked Lucy, pouring out another cup of tea.

'I doubt it – and Catherwood could do nothing about the matter whilst his great rival still lived,' replied Ravenscroft.

'So that's why Catherwood turned up for the reading of the will, to see if Rupert had been provided for,' said Crabb.

'Only to learn that he had been left nothing.'

'Mean spirited of the old man,' said Lucy. 'Nathaniel could have left Rupert something. He was, after all, his wife's son.'

'Yes, but I suppose he could never forgive the wrong that his wife and her lover had committed against him all those years ago,' said Ravenscroft.

'Do you think Mr Catherwood was responsible for killing Nathaniel?' asked Lucy, passing over the toast rack to Crabb.

'We cannot discount that possibility. By poisoning his old enemy, he would not only have been gaining his revenge but would also be able to acknowledge Rupert as his own son.'

'But Catherwood was not there the night that Montacute was killed, and you said that Mrs Leewood saw no one enter or leave the room,' said Crabb.

'That would appear to be true, but Catherwood could still have attended the ball and gone unnoticed. He could have disguised himself either as one of the guests, or even as one of the lamplighters. There is also another door at the end of the ballroom which opens out on to the landing at the top of the back stairs. Catherwood could have slipped in that way, making sure that Mrs Leewood had not seen him, put poison in Montacute's glass and then slipped away when no one was looking,' said Ravenscroft, neatly folding his napkin and placing it upon the table.

'The same could be said of Rivers,' suggested Crabb.

'That is true. I still find it strange that the gamekeeper went out before midnight rather than remain in the kitchen with Mrs Chambers. I don't believe that he went out in the hope of catching poachers. Any other reasonable man would have been grateful for a warm hearth and a welcoming drink on such a cold night. I think we need to question him further.'

'You don't think, my dear, that the same person who killed the coachman also killed the banker?' asked Lucy.

'That was what I first thought. Two brothers killed within a few days of each other, one returning to the town of his birth carrying the important envelope, the second being the named recipient of the package. That would seem the obvious solution, but the more I thought about it, the more I became convinced that the two deaths were unrelated to one another.'

'Begging your pardon, sir, but you have not yet said what was in the envelope,' said Crabb, buttering another piece of toast.

'That, I'm afraid, I am not at liberty to disclose at present.'

'Oh, why not, sir?'

'The envelope contained a letter addressed to the senior partner of the bank. After examining the remaining contents of the envelope, Mr Montacute, Mr Midwinter and I swore an oath agreeing that we would never disclose the nature of its contents to anyone.'

'It's no good, Tom, you won't get him to tell you. I have tried myself to obtain the information from him and met with no success,' laughed Lucy.

'It is better that you do not know, my dear.'

'You believe Robertson's killer will make a second attempt to recover the envelope?' asked Crabb.

'Almost certainly. I have posted two of our men inside Midwinter's office. When he returns they will be more than ready for him, and as an additional precaution, the envelope no longer resides there – it's in the vaults of Cocks and Biddulph. If he should succeed in breaking into Mr Midwinter's safe then he will be disappointed. In the meantime we can continue with our investigations into the banker's murder, when you are ready, Tom.'

'There's something else, sir. You remember when that fellow attacked me, and I said I thought I had seen him somewhere before? Well, the more I thought about it, the more I became convinced that I had indeed seen him before.'

'Go on, Tom,' urged Ravenscroft.

'Well, he kind of reminded me of that fellow Cranston.'

'Cranston!'

'Yes, sir, we came across him last year in Worcester.'

'I do indeed remember him. He was a nasty individual on all counts. He said that he worked for the Worcester Porcelain Company as a salesman.'

'I can't be absolutely sure it was him. It was very dark, but the more I thought about it, the more likely it seemed that it was him.'

'What on earth was Cranston doing here in Ledbury? Why would he want to kill Robertson?'

'Well, sir, that is what I thought, so I decided that I would make some enquiries yesterday. I went into Worcester and visited the porcelain works. It seems Cranston disappeared one day last autumn without giving in his notice and they haven't seen him since.'

'This is interesting news, Tom. Well done! So it looks as though Cranston is Robertson's murderer.'

'As I said, sir, I can't be absolutely sure it was him.'

'If it was this Cranston, why would he have killed the coachman?' asked Lucy, looking into her husband's eyes.

'To acquire the packet. He no doubt thought that Robertson still had the package about his person. He could have been working for someone, I suppose. Perhaps the same people in London who were trying to recover the envelope from Robertson? Anyway, we shall learn the truth once we have the fellow behind bars. Are you ready, Tom?'

'Ready when you are, sir. Thank you for your hospitality, Mrs Ravenscroft,' said Crabb, quickly drinking down the remaining contents of his tea cup.

'You are more than welcome here at any time, Tom,' said Lucy, smiling up at the constable before turning towards her husband. 'Do you know what time you will return, Samuel?'

'I cannot tell, my dear, in what direction our investigations will take us,' said Ravenscroft, rising from the table. 'I will try and send you a message if I am not able to return before dark.'

Crabb and Ravenscroft left the cottage in Church Lane and made their way down the narrow way towards the marketplace.

'Where to first, sir?' asked Crabb.

'I feel we should return to The Gables. I think we will have words with Mr Rivers, and try and ascertain why he left the kitchen before midnight, and where he really went to.'

'He may not be forthcoming, sir. He seems quite a hard nut to crack—'

'Do you notice something, Crabb?' interrupted Ravenscroft, suddenly coming to a halt.

'Not that fellow watching us again?'

'No, quite the opposite. We have just walked down here into the marketplace, and it has been the first time in three days that I have felt sure that no one has been observing us.'

'Perhaps the fellow has decided to give up trying to steal the package, and has gone back to London?'

'Maybe – but let us hope not, or we may never have the opportunity of placing him behind bars!'

'Good morning to you, Father Bannerman.'

'Good morning to you, my son.'

'I trust you are enjoying your stay here with us in Ledbury, Father?' said the receptionist at the Feathers Hotel, looking up at the middle-aged clergyman dressed in black clerical attire of a well-worn nature.

'Yes, indeed, Ledbury is a very pleasant town. It has many interesting old buildings. I particularly found your church most appealing,' replied the priest in what the clerk discerned as an Irish accent.

'Have you visited any of the neighbouring towns, Father?'

'Yesterday I took the opportunity of visiting Malvern, and the day before I went to Hereford on the train. Fine places, both of them. The cathedral there is most awe inspiring.'

'May I be so bold, Father, as to enquire how much longer you intend staying with us here at the Feathers?'

'I think perhaps one more day will suffice,' replied the cleric, peering through the darkened lenses of his large spectacles. 'Yes, I have a little private business to attend to today, which I expect to bring to a satisfactory conclusion before the day is out. Much as I would like to remain here for a few more days, I fear that would not be possible. My flock will be wondering where I am if I stay away too long.'

'I quite understand, Father. Be careful how you go, sir. It's still rather slippery outside.'

'I will indeed. Thank you for your concern,' he replied, putting on his black gloves and pulling his large hat further down on to his forehead before walking out of the doors of the Feathers.

In the marketplace, he observed that the traders were already busy selling their wares, and as he walked across the road, he paused to look up at the unexpected bright winter sun and felt its warm glow against his face. Temporary blinded by the sun's rays, he stepped cautiously on to the pavement.

Suddenly he felt the force of another coming into contact with him, and was unable to stop himself falling towards the ground.

'I'm so sorry, Father. Here, let me help you up,' said the stranger, reaching out for his arm and steadying him back on to his feet.

'Thank you, my son. It was the sun. I should have looked where I was going – so foolish of me,' he said, brushing away a few wet flakes from his clothes.

'It is easily done, Father. The roads are still treacherous after the night frost. I trust you are not injured?'

'No, not at all. Thank you, my son. You are most kind,' said the priest, turning quickly away.

'Your hat, Father,' said the stranger's companion, bending down and retrieving the item from the pavement.

'Thank you again.'

'Good day to you, Father,' said the first speaker.

'Good day to you both, gentlemen.'

The priest watched as Ravenscroft and Crabb went on their way, then slowly made his way up Church Lane. As he passed by the front of the little cottage, he caught a fleeting glimpse of a young woman standing before a fire, and could not resist allowing himself a brief smile before continuing on his journey.

'Good morning to you, Mr Rivers.'

'Morning to you, Ravenscroft,' replied the gamekeeper, looking up briefly from the cleaning of his shotgun.

'I've come to thank you for your valuable assistance in the wood.'

'It was nothing. Least I could do.'

'Nevertheless, without your being able to guide us along the pathways, we would not have been able to have found either Leewood or Master Rupert. How is the young master this morning?' asked Ravenscroft.

'Doctor says he should make a full recovery, so Mrs Chambers tells me,' replied Rivers, continuing with his cleaning.

'I am pleased to hear that. It was fortunate that we found him when we did. I doubt whether he would have survived another night in those conditions.'

'You haven't come here today just to indulge in idle gossip?'

'You are very observant, Mr Rivers,' said Ravenscroft, smiling.

'You want to know where I was that night,' said the gamekeeper, laying down the gun on the table and coming straight to the point.

'You say you left Mrs Chambers in the kitchen at around a quarter to twelve?'

'That's what I said.'

'Why did you not stay in the warm to see in the New Year?'

'I've told you that already – I was out trying to catch poachers. We get a lot of that here. If you don't keep a tight grip on it, we would have them all coming up from the town and helping themselves,' replied Rivers, pushing past Ravenscroft as he replaced the shotgun in its case on the wall and took down another.

'Surely you could have waited until you had seen in the New Year?'

'And lost some of our best game in the process?'

'And did you manage to apprehend anyone?' asked Ravenscroft.

'Didn't need to. As soon as folks know you are on the lookout, they quickly move on elsewhere.'

'So you spoke to no one?' asked Crabb.

'That's what I said.'

'So we have no proof that you were in the grounds at the time Mr Montacute was being poisoned?'

'Just my word for it,' replied Rivers grudgingly.

'Perhaps that won't do?'

'Best I can manage.'

'There would have been ample time for you to slip down into the town after leaving the kitchen, enter the Feathers and slip poison into your employer's glass,' suggested Ravenscroft, becoming annoyed by the gamekeeper's lack of co-operation.

'Now what would I want to go and do that for?' said Rivers, looking up from his work and staring full into Ravenscroft's face.

'I don't know, Mr Rivers. Perhaps you could tell us the answer?'

'This is all stuff and nonsense, Ravenscroft. Mr Montacute has always been a good employer – one of the best – and I had no cause to wish him ill. If you think I killed the master, then you best set about proving it. There are others who had more cause to see him dead than me.'

'Who exactly?' asked Ravenscroft.

'Not my purpose to say,' replied the gamekeeper, turning away.

'Come now, Rivers, you are playing loose with us. First you cannot provide us with a satisfactory alibi for your movements at the time of Mr Montacute's death, then you say there are more deserving candidates, but won't say who they are. This won't do at all,' said Ravenscroft forcefully. 'Perhaps if you were to accompany us to the police station, your memory might be revived.'

'Onslow for a start,' snapped Rivers.

'Major Onslow? Why would Major Onslow want to see your master dead?'

'Arguing, they were.'

'Could you elaborate?' asked a frustrated Ravenscroft.

'On the afternoon before Mr Montacute's death, I was walking along the path outside the house and happened to look across towards the summer house. The major and the master were shouting at one another.'

'Did you hear what they were arguing about?'

'I didn't catch much of what they were saying, but I do recall the major say he was damned if he was going to let the master get away with it.'

'What were his exact words?' asked an interested Ravenscroft.

'"I'm damned if I'm going to let you get away with it. You've got away with it for far too long". That's what the major said and I remember he was shouting and raising his fist in the air.'

'And what did Mr Montacute say?'

'He said that the major was not to be so silly and that the matter would be soon resolved.'

'Did he say anything else?'

'No. They must have realized that I had just heard what they had been saying. The major muttered something under his breath and then strode away.'

'What did your master do then?' asked Crabb, looking up from his notebook where he had been recording the gamekeeper's remarks.

'Nothing. He just looked over in my direction and then walked away back across the garden and into the house, without saying a word.'

'Was that all that happened between the two men?' asked Ravenscroft.

'There was nothing else,' replied Rivers, resuming his work.

'Very well. We will leave you to your cleaning. If you think of anything else you think we should know, I would be obliged if you would tell us straightaway. It is a great pity you did not inform us about this disagreement between your master and the major some days ago. It may have been useful to us.'

'It slipped my mind. Been rather busy,' muttered the gamekeeper.

Ravenscroft and Crabb walked away from the outhouse at The Gables and began to retrace their steps back towards the town.

'Do you think he was telling us the truth, sir?' asked the constable.

'I don't honestly know, Crabb. Either our Mr Rivers did witness such an argument between the two men or he has a guilty conscience and was making up the story in order to deflect suspicion away from himself.'

'He certainly was not very forthcoming. Why did he wait so long before informing us about the disagreement?'

'It could be as he says. He just didn't think it was important enough until we started to put pressure on him.'

'Can't say I trust the fellow,' said Crabb.

'I think it is time we paid Major Onslow a visit, so we can discover whether Rivers was telling us the truth about the disagreement and find out what the argument was about. Do you happen to know where he resides?'

'I think he lives in a large rambling house about a mile or so out of the town, along the Ross road,' replied Crabb.

'Then we will need to secure some transport.'

'I'll have that large piece of fish, if you please,' said Lucy, addressing the tradesman in the marketplace. 'My husband is rather partial to it.'

'Good choice, madam. Freshly arrived in the town this morning, off the express train,' replied the man, wrapping the requested item in a sheet of paper. 'I trust Mr Ravenscroft is well?'

'He is indeed, I thank you, although rather busy at the moment.'

'That will be the Montacute case then?' said the fishmonger, smiling.

'Yes, I believe so.'

'Terrible business. Who would want to go and kill Mr Montacute like that? Man did nobody any harm.'

Lucy said nothing as she handed over a coin.

'Thank you, ma'am, I hope the inspector enjoys his fish.'

'I'm sure he will. Thank you,' said Lucy, placing the package in her wicker basket before moving away.

'Good morning. I could not help hearing the name Ravenscroft. Forgive me, my good lady, for my intrusion. You are, I assume, Mrs Ravenscroft?' asked a clerical gentleman dressed in black attire.

'Yes – and you are?' enquired Lucy cautiously.

'Father Bannerman at your service,' replied the priest, raising his large black hat and nodding in her direction. 'Are you in any way related by marriage to Inspector Ravenscroft, formerly of the Whitechapel Constabulary in London?'

'My husband did indeed work in Whitechapel for a number of

years before he came to reside in Ledbury,' replied Lucy, her curiosity aroused.

'I too resided in Whitechapel for a while, during which time I made the acquaintance of your husband upon several occasions. We would often meet in the evenings and enjoy a drink or two in one of the local taverns,' said the gentleman, smiling and peering through his darkened glasses in Lucy's direction.

'I will mention your name to my husband,' said Lucy, anxious to move on.

'I would be most obliged, my dear lady. Perhaps I might call upon you one evening, to renew my acquaintance with your husband?'

'You say, Father, that you and my husband were great friends?' asked Lucy, feeling uneasy in the stranger's presence.

'Acquaintances rather than friends, my dear Mrs Ravenscroft, but close acquaintances I would like to think.'

'I will certainly inform my husband of our meeting, Father.'

'Then that is all I can ask of you, my dear lady. I wish you good day, Mrs Ravenscroft,' said the priest, again raising his hat and giving a slight bow in Lucy's direction.

'Good day to you, Father,' said Lucy, moving away.

The priest walked over to the other side of the road, and leaned forward to pick up a small leatherbound book which lay on one of the market tables. As he turned over the pages with his black gloves, he peered over the top of the volume and observed the policeman's wife making her way back up Church Lane.

Ravenscroft and Crabb found themselves in a large courtyard situated at the rear of an untidy, rambling house, which had the name 'Bengal' in large letters at its front entrance.

'This must be where he keeps his horses,' said Ravenscroft, looking across towards a stable block before pulling down the long bell handle at the back door.

'Best keep a look out for the tigers,' joked Crabb as they waited.

Presently the door was opened by an Indian servant dressed in a turban and long flowing robe.

'Inspector Ravenscroft and Constable Crabb to see Major Onslow, if you please. I take it your master is at home?'

'Certainly, sir. If you would care to step inside,' replied the servant, giving a bow and sweeping his arm before his chest as an indication that the two policemen should enter the building. 'If you would care to wait here in the hall, gentlemen, I will see if the major is available to see you.' He bowed again before disappearing from view.

Ravenscroft looked up at the walls, which were adorned with animal trophies and faded photographs of groups of hunters and soldiers taken on what he supposed to be the Indian continent.

'Looks as though the major was rather fond of the shooting when he was in India,' said Crabb, shrugging his shoulders and looking up into the open mouth of a dead tiger.

'Ah, there you are, Ravenscroft! What can I do for yer?' said Onslow, suddenly flinging open one of the doors that led off the hall and striding forward to greet the detective. 'Can't give yer long, I'm afraid. Got to go hunting in a few minutes.'

'I would have thought the weather was rather too cold for that kind of activity?' suggested Ravenscroft, shaking the major's outstretched hand.

'Nonsense, man. Bit of cold weather keeps the foxes frisky! Makes the dogs all the more eager. Suppose yer best come in here, then.'

Crabb gave Ravenscroft a quick glance out of the corner of his eye, before the two men followed their host into a large room, the walls of which were hung with numerous hunting prints and animal heads, and the centre of which was dominated by a horsehair sofa and a large glass case containing a stuffed tiger.

'What do yer think of him then?' said Onslow proudly, patting the top of the case. 'A fine beast. Caught him in Bengal and had him stuffed and sent back here. Yer won't find another one like it in all the county.'

'Major Onslow, I'd like to ask you a few questions concerning the afternoon before Mr Montacute's death. I understand that you and Mr Montacute had a heated argument?' said Ravenscroft, ignoring both the animal and the major's boast.

'Yer don't beat about the bush, do you? Like that, I do. Always best to come straight to the point, I say. I've got no time for those folks who mince their words. Glass of whisky?'

'Not for me, thank you.'

'Think I'll have one. Need something warm inside me before

galloping over them fences,' replied Onslow, pouring himself a large drink from the decanter. 'You should join us for the hunt, Ravenscroft. Good for the constitution and all that.'

'What was the argument all about?' asked Ravenscroft, trying to return the conversation to his line of questioning.

'What argument? Don't remember any argument. New Year's Day, you say?'

'No, Major, on the afternoon before Mr Montacute's death. I have a witness who says he saw you and Mr Montacute in a heated exchange outside the summer house at The Gables.'

'Can't recall the occasion,' replied Onslow, sipping his whisky and rubbing his forehead.

'Constable, if you please,' said Ravenscroft, turning towards his associate. Crabb took out his notebook from the top pocket of his tunic and began to read from one of the pages. 'I saw Major Onslow raising his fist in the air and shouting, "I'm damned if I'll let you get away with it. You have got away with it for too long." To which Mr Montacute was heard to say, "Don't be so silly, the matter will soon be resolved."'

'Well, Major, do you now recall your conversation?' asked Ravenscroft.

'I remember that I did go to The Gables that afternoon to see Nathaniel, and that we did exchange a few words together outside the summer house, but it was not as you have just described.'

'Would you like to tell me about the nature of your conversation?'

'A few months before, Nathaniel had suggested that we should both invest in a small mining company in Southern Africa. He said the prospects were good and once the diamonds were located, shares in the company would soon double and we would get a good return on our investment.'

'May I ask how much you invested in this company?'

'The sum is none of your damned business, Ravenscroft. Suffice it to say that it was a sizeable investment.'

'And how is the company doing?' asked Ravenscroft.

'Not as well as we had hoped. Nathaniel said that it was early days, and if we held our nerve for a few more months we should both do well out of it. That was all our conversation was about.'

'You were seen raising your fist in a threatening manner.'

'Stuff and nonsense!' retorted Onslow, becoming red in the face.

'Do you deny shouting that Mr Montacute had "got away with it for too long"?'

'Never said anything of the kind.'

'That's not what our witness said.'

'Then yer witness is a damned liar! There was no shouting or anything of the kind,' grumbled Onslow, taking a large swig from his whisky glass.

'Why did this conversation take place outside in the garden, near the summer house? It was a very cold afternoon, if I recall. Surely it would have been more comfortable inside – or did you not want to be heard by the family and servants?'

'When I arrived at The Gables, I found Nathaniel was out walking in the grounds. That's why we had our conversation outside. Look here, Ravenscroft, this is all nonsense. Someone obviously saw us talking and has grossly exaggerated what they saw and heard. Nathaniel and I were on the best of terms. If you are implying that I wanted to see him dead, nothing could be further from the truth.'

'I have to say, I am not satisfied with your account, Major Onslow, and that we intend making investigations into the deceased's business affairs.'

'Do as yer wish, Ravenscroft – and be damned! If you can't believe the word of a gentleman against that of some snooper, then it's a great shame. This has taken up far too much of my time. If you'll excuse me – can't keep the hunt waiting.'

'Very well, Major. I will need to speak with you again later,' said Ravenscroft, beginning to take his leave.

'Ranjit, show these gentlemen out,' snapped Onslow, turning his back on the detectives whilst pouring himself another whisky from the decanter.

'Well, Tom, what do you make of our major?' asked Ravenscroft as he and Crabb made their way back towards the town.

'Plays his cards tight to his chest, I should say.'

'I'm inclined to agree with you. He certainly wanted to make light of his argument with Montacute. Either Rivers has deliberately made more of their encounter to draw attention away from himself – or the major and Montacute did really have a falling out. If Onslow felt that Montacute had given him bad financial advice then that might have resulted in him seeking his revenge. We need to dig further into the banker's affairs and see what we can discover about this mining company in Southern Africa.'

As Ravenscroft and Crabb arrived at The Gables, a light flurry of snow began to drift steadily downwards, giving a thin covering to the lawns and gardens of the big house. Ravenscroft rang the bell and, after explaining the reason for his visit, was shown into the study, where Maurice Montacute sat writing at his desk.

'Mr Ravenscroft, what brings you to The Gables?' asked Maurice, rising from his chair.

'Mr Montacute, I'll come straight to the point. Did your father ever mention anything about a mining company in Southern Africa? We believe he may have had shares in the enterprise,' said Ravenscroft.

'My father had many business interests in a number of concerns, but I'm afraid he said very little about his investments to me, unless of course the business enterprise involved the bank in any way.'

'Nevertheless, your father did make a number of such investments on his own account?'

'I would not have expected otherwise,' replied the banker.

'Where would your father have kept the papers relating to these business investments, Mr Montacute?'

'In the small safe in the corner, I believe.'

'May we examine the papers there?'

'That may not be possible. The only key belonged to my father.'

'And where would such a key be now, sir?'

'I have no idea. I think my father always kept it upon his person.'

'What happened to your father's personal effects after he died?' enquired Ravenscroft.

'I think one of the servants collected everything together and placed them in an envelope.'

'Where might we find such an envelope?' asked Ravenscroft.

'I don't know – although it could have been placed here inside the desk.'

'Would you oblige us, sir.'

Maurice Montacute opened the top drawer of the desk and searched amongst its contents. 'Ah, here we are, Inspector,' he said, placing a large envelope on top of the desk and running the blade of a paper knife along the flap before tipping out its contents before them. 'And this must be the key you are looking for, Inspector.'

The three men walked over to the safe. Maurice placed the key in the lock and opened the door. 'May I, sir?' asked Ravenscroft.

Maurice nodded as Ravenscroft reached into the safe and withdrew a number of documents. 'With your permission, sir, we will just go through these papers.'

The men returned to the desk, where Ravenscroft spent the next few moments examining the documents. 'Are you looking for anything in particular?' asked the banker.

'Ah, here we are – the Colesberg Mining Corporation. Let's see what it says. Yes, here we are. Two thousand shares purchased by Mr Nathaniel Montacute and Major John Onslow on 3 May 1888 giving them each a twenty-five per cent interest in the company.'

'So they were business partners,' said Crabb, peering over Ravenscroft's shoulder.

'My father had known Major Onslow for a number of years – they were good friends,' added Maurice.

'This makes interesting reading. Which ever of your father or Major Onslow dies first, then their shares in the company reverts back to the surviving member,' said Ravenscroft, looking up from the paper with a certain degree of satisfaction.

'So Major Onslow now inherits Mr Montacute's shares,' said Crabb.

'Thank you, Mr Montacute, you have been of great assistance to us. I suggest you place this document in your safe for the time being,' said Ravenscroft, returning the papers to Maurice.

'You are surely not suggesting that Major Onslow killed my father to inherit his shares in this dubious African mining company?' asked the banker, looking concerned.

'I cannot say that, sir, at this stage,' replied Ravenscroft, making his way over to the door.

'But the major?' began Maurice.

'I think it might be prudent, sir, if you were not to speak about this matter with anyone until we have carried out further investigations. I thank you once again, sir.'

A few minutes later the two detectives made their way back to the centre of the town.

'So Onslow stands to inherit Mr Montacute's shares in the mining company,' said Crabb. 'Good enough reason to kill the old man, I suppose.'

'Maybe, but that does not mean that he did. The shares in the company may be worthless. Perhaps that was what the argument was about? Onslow thought that Montacute had tricked him into paying a great deal of money for shares in a company that were not worth the paper they were written on, and had wanted to sell out his share, but the banker had urged him to hold his nerve. We know that Montacute had sought to ruin Catherwood all those years ago. Was he now doing the same thing again with Onslow?'

'We've only got Rivers' word that there was an argument. Onslow might have been telling us the truth all along when he said there was no argument between him and Mr Montacute, in which case it is Rivers who is lying,' suggested Crabb.

'Either way we need to find out more about Onslow's financial position. There is something else which strikes me as rather strange. Don't you find it rather odd that Maurice Montacute had not taken the trouble to open his father's safe since his demise?'

'But he said he didn't know where the key was.'

'But then he remembered that his father's possessions were in an envelope in his desk. Furthermore, he described the mining company as being "rather dubious" – how did he know that if he knew nothing about the company?'

'You don't think Maurice has anything to do with his own father's death?'

'I don't know, Crabb. Sometimes I feel as though we are going round in circles. Just as we unearth some fact which casts one of our gentlemen in a bad light, so we learn of more events which change the direction of our suspicions. However, I believe that our search for Montacute's murderer may soon be at an end. Let us call into the post office on our way back into the town. There may be something waiting for me there.'

Ravenscroft and Crabb made their way into the building. 'Good morning. I believe you may have some replies for me?' asked Ravenscroft, addressing the clerk.

'Ah yes, Inspector. This letter has just arrived from London in the morning post, and this telegram arrived not half an hour ago, sir.'

'Thank you.'

Ravenscroft opened the envelope and removed a sheet of paper from inside, which he studied for a few seconds before reading the contents of his telegram.

'Anything interesting, sir?' asked Crabb.

'Very,' replied Ravenscroft, placing the envelopes in his pocket. 'I think I may now have a very good idea who killed Nathaniel Montacute and why. The problem may be the proving of it, as no one saw the poison actually being placed in the glass. There may be only one course open to us, Crabb. We need to call together all those closely involved with the banker. I want you to send messages out to all our likely suspects as soon as possible, summoning them to a meeting in the ballroom of the Feathers at six o'clock tonight.'

'Who shall I inform, sir?' asked Crabb, taking out his pocket book.

'Maurice and Rupert Montacute, Mrs Montacute, Rivers and Mrs Chambers from The Gables, and in addition to them, Catherwood, Doctor Andrews, Midwinter and Major Onslow. Yes, that should be all,' replied Ravenscroft, deep in thought.

'Right, sir.'

'One of those nine people killed Nathaniel Montacute. Once we have them all together, we can begin to unravel this mystery. If we can apply pressure and extract a confession, we will have our killer behind bars before the day is out!'

# CHAPTER TWELVE

## LEDBURY, 9 JANUARY 1889. EVENING

He had kept watch on the small cottage up the narrow cobbleway of Church Lane for most of the afternoon, waiting for the darkness to descend so that he could begin the final act. When he had returned from London, a few days previously, he had been content to watch and follow the policeman, knowing that eventually he would lead him to the papers that his masters so desired. And so it had proved. Ravenscroft had eventually led him to the offices of the old solicitor and had even held the packet up to the window so that he had been able to confirm its place of safety. He should have realized then, of course, that a trap had been laid for his capture. Fortunately he had gone armed to the office, and in the ensuing struggle had wounded one of Ravenscroft's men – but he had failed to escape with the papers, and that failure had been a bitter pill to countenance. He was not used to others thwarting his well-thought-out plans, and for a while he had even contemplated abandoning his quest and of leaving the town immediately before his movements could be tracked, but his dislike of unfinished business and lack of success had only strengthened his resolve. He had kept his nerve, had assumed a new disguise and had continued to listen and learn, ever turning over the varied possibilities in his mind, as his loathing for the man who had attempted to entrap him had grown in intensity. Now, out of that bitterness and anger, there had grown the seeds of his deliverance. Ravenscroft himself would give him the envelope; would provide him with the final solution.

'Evening to you, Father,' said the old lamplighter, seeking to adjust the small flickering flame.

'Good evening to you, my son,' he replied, moving back into the shadows.

'Another cold evening, I'll be bound.'

'Yes indeed.'

It was time to move on, lest his loitering cause suspicion. He made his way slowly down the lane towards the marketplace, keeping his head low beneath his hat, replacing the glasses with their darkened lenses on the end of his nose so that his features would remain partially hidden. As he neared the small police station, he slipped again into the shadows, his black clothes being easily absorbed by the darkness of the night. He knew he would not have long to wait until Ravenscroft left the building and his work could begin. He pulled his scarf closer round his neck as the snow began to fall on to the pavement – and as he waited he remembered all the other nights when he had stood in the darkened alleyways of Whitechapel watching and listening before he had felt confident enough to encounter his victims. Now he had grown tired of the hours of cold and boredom, of damp and gloom, and had resolved that this would be his final mission. Tomorrow he would at last be free to leave the small drab town with its rundown buildings and creeping domesticity, and by the evening would return triumphant to the capital with the precious envelope and its contents. Then when he had received his payment from the grey faceless men who had become his temporary masters, he would leave for warmer lands – to Greece, Italy, even India or the Caribbean perhaps – where there would be light and warmth and where at last his restless soul might find the peace it had always desired.

The town clock struck the half hour between five and six as the door of the building opened. There was Ravenscroft and his assistant stepping out on to the pavement, talking with one another in quiet huddled tones, before striding off towards the marketplace and the Feathers. How he hated the man, with his dogged determination, boring temperament and cosy family. If only the silly man knew what was about to befall him, he would not have sounded so confident, so pleased with himself.

Now it was time to act!

He quickly retraced his steps up Church Lane and slipped unnoticed into the porchway of the ancient church. Within a few minutes he would be able to proceed with the next part of his plan. He opened the church door and entered the building. A quick gaze round the dimly lit building confirmed his expectations. At this time of night, the church was empty of people; the vicar would have departed for his home an hour before, and it was unlikely that any of the townspeople would have entered the cold, uninviting building to offer up their prayers.

He returned to the porch, leaving the door to the church partially opened behind him, and drew his cloak further round him as he felt the cold wind on the night air. The church clock struck the hour of six as he peered into the darkness, straining to hear the sound for which he had waited. Then suddenly he heard the noise of footsteps in the distance, and he knew then that the light from a dim lantern would shortly come into view. He stepped out of the porchway.

'Who's there?' called out the voice. 'Show yourself.'

'Thank goodness it's you, Constable,' he said, approaching the light.

'Who are you, sir?' called out the constable, lifting his lantern high so that its rays might fall on the intruder.

'My name is Father Bannerman. I am visiting the town for a few days.'

'Bit late to be out, Father.'

'I wanted to see the church before evening. I'm afraid I have something terrible to report, Constable.'

'Calm yourself, sir, and tell me what has disturbed you. The policeman drew nearer and saw that the stranger was in a distressed state.

'I don't quite know where to begin,' he began.

'Take your time, Father.'

'Well, a few minutes ago I came into the church and – such violation! The altar cross was lying on the floor, prayer books torn and scattered everywhere!'

'Did you see any signs of who might have caused this disturbance, Father?'

'I don't know. When I saw what had been done to God's house, I left as quickly as I could in order to fetch help, and that was when I saw your lantern. Thank goodness you have arrived.'

'I usually come past the church at this time of the evening on my patrol. I think we better go in and take a look.'

'That would be good. I would not like to enter the building alone.'

'I'll go first. You never know, whoever committed this crime might still be inside,' said the constable, pushing open the church door wider and entering the building.

'Step forward and show yourself! It's the law!' shouted the policeman, holding the lantern high so that its beams of light reflected back from the walls of the church.

'Perhaps the perpetrator of this crime left before I arrived?'

'You could be right, Father. Let's take a closer look.'

Quietly closing the church door behind him, he followed the policeman up the aisle, at the same time reaching into his pocket for the weapon that he knew was concealed there.

'I can't see any signs of a disturbance, Father. You say the altar had been violated?'

'Just a little further on, Constable.'

The two men inched forward along the aisle. Suddenly he lifted the cosh from out of his pocket, and raising it above his head brought it down quickly on the back of the other's neck. As the policeman let out a groan and began to fall towards the floor, he reached out, secured the lantern and placed it on one of the pews.

Monk allowed himself only a brief smile of satisfaction. So far, it had been so easy. The policeman had been simple prey, so gullible and trusting, but he knew now that he would have to work fast. There always remained the possibility that someone unexpected would enter the church at any moment. He bent down and pulled the unconscious man away from the centre of the church towards one darkened side of the building, where he knew they would be hidden from view. Then quickly turning over the body he removed his cape, tunic, boots and trousers, before discarding his own outer garments. Finally he hastily pulled on the policeman's clothes and boots. He had estimated that his victim would have nearly the same measurements as himself, but nevertheless he was relieved that the garments seemed to fit him so well. Dropping his darkened glasses to the floor, he ground the lens beneath his boots and then reached into the pocket of his former attire to retrieve the final part of his new disguise. After fixing the new moustache to his upper lip and combing his hair, he picked up the lantern and made his way out of the church.

Standing in the porch, he looked out across the churchyard, listening for any sounds that would indicate that his arrival there had been observed. After a few moments, he felt reassured enough to continue with the next part of his mission. Holding the lantern high, he made his way out of the churchyard and down the lane towards the cottage. He paused to look up at the flickering light in one of the bedrooms. How cosy and secure the interior of the building appeared – if only its occupants knew how their lives were about to be broken for ever! After allowing himself a brief smile of anticipation, he walked up the short path and knocked loudly on the wooden door.

'Yes, what can I do for you?' asked the maid, opening the door.

'Very important, miss, that I see Mrs Ravenscroft, without delay. It's very urgent.'

'Who is it, Sally?' called out a voice from the interior of the cottage.

'Mrs Ravenscroft, it's Constable Rogers,' he said, stepping quickly past the girl and into the hall. 'I am from the Malvern station. I'm sorry for the intrusion, ma'am.'

'How can I help you, Constable? I'm afraid my husband is not at home at present. I have not seen him since early this morning,' said Lucy, entering the hall.

'I'm afraid I have some rather bad news for you, ma'am.'

'Whatever is the matter?' asked Lucy anxiously.

'We have been out on the hills late this afternoon, arresting some villain by the name of Cranston. Dear me, I don't quite know how to tell you this, ma'am.'

'Please go on. Has something happened to my husband?'

'There was a struggle, Mrs Ravenscroft. Afraid your husband was shot through the chest.'

'Oh my God!' exclaimed Lucy.

'He's in a bad way, ma'am, I'm sorry to say. Doctor is with him now and says he can't be moved. Keeps crying out for you, he does, Mrs Ravenscroft.'

'I must go to him at once. Sally, you must stay here with Richard. Can you take me to him now?' said Lucy, tears forming in her eyes.

'Of course, ma'am. Constable Crabb says we should be quick. I'm sorry, Mrs Ravenscroft, to be the bearer of such bad news.'

The maid helped Lucy on with her coat.

'We can get a cab from down here,' he said as they set off at a brisk pace down the street, leaving the anxious maid looking after them on the doorstep.

'Is he greatly injured?' asked Lucy, distressed, as they arrived at the marketplace.

'I don't know, Mrs Ravenscroft. He seems to have lost a lot of blood, and keeps asking for you.'

'Oh no!'

Opening the door of a waiting cab, he gave instructions to the driver before helping Lucy into the waiting vehicle.

'Doctor is doing all he can for him,' he said, as they sat back in the cab.

'Pray God we are not too late!'

'Your husband is a strong man. I'm sure he will pull through, Mrs Ravenscroft.'

'Where are we going?'

'Out towards the British camp, Mrs Ravenscroft. The shooting took place inside a cottage near there.'

'How long before we get there?' asked Lucy, tears streaming down her face.

'Be about fifteen, twenty minutes, I'm afraid, ma'am. I came as quickly as I could.'

'Can't you instruct the driver to go any faster?'

The cab soon left the lights of Ledbury behind and began to climb steadily towards the upper reaches of the hills. Eventually the vehicle left the road and proceeded along a trackway, before eventually coming to a halt.

'Far as I can take you,' called out the cabman.

'We will have to complete the last part of the journey on foot, Mrs Ravenscroft,' he said, helping Lucy to alight and paying off the driver.

'Be quick!' she said, looking into his eyes.

'If you'll follow me, Mrs Ravenscroft, I'll go first and hold up the lantern. It's only another five minutes or so.'

'We must hurry!' she cried out in the dark.

He led the way along the path, which appeared to wind its way round the side of the hill before rising steadily upwards.

'Where?' shouted Lucy in desperation, looking all around her in the darkness. 'Where is this cottage that you speak of?'

'It's just over there, ma'am. You can see the light shining from one of the windows,' he said, pointing.

They ran towards the distant light, Lucy tripping over a branch in her haste.

'Let me help you up, ma'am.'

They raced forwards again, Lucy reaching the cottage first. She flung open the door and rushed into the room.

'Where? Where is my husband?' she cried out, looking frantically around the empty room. 'Tell me where my husband is!'

Monk slammed the door behind him and let out a loud laugh.

It had all been so easy – so very easy.

'Firstly may I thank you all for being here tonight,' said Ravenscroft, addressing the group of people who were seated round a large rectangular table situated in the centre of the ballroom at the Feathers hotel.

'Bit theatrical all this, Ravenscroft,' grumbled Onslow.

'The reason why I have bought you all here tonight will soon become apparent,' said Ravenscroft, continuing. 'By the end of the evening, I believe we will have arrived at the truth, and the poisoner of Nathaniel Montacute will be unmasked. However we first have to ask ourselves the question, why was Mr Montacute killed? In my experience people are usually murdered because of one of two reasons: money or revenge. If we look at the second area first – who hated Nathaniel Montacute enough to want to see him dead? Clearly you, Mr Catherwood, would fall into this category. Many years ago, shortly after your arrival in this town, you were persuaded by Mr Montacute to go into partnership with him in a number of financial enterprises, whilst at the same time forming a strong attachment to his second wife, Enid Montacute. Mr Rupert Montacute was the result of that liaison, and it soon became evident to me that once Nathaniel had discovered the truth about his supposed son he quickly set about gaining his revenge on you by ruining you as best he could. But instead of leaving the town you decided to remain, where you could continue your discreet association with Mrs Montacute whilst keeping a watchful eye on your true son. It must have been very frustrating for you, Mr

194

Catherwood, to see the woman and son you loved still living under the same roof as your enemy.'

'Who would have thought it,' uttered Mrs Chambers.

Catherwood said nothing but turned his head away as all the people around the table looked in his direction.

'You had good cause to see Mr Montacute dead. His death would allow you at long last to acknowledge your true son, whilst no doubt giving you a great deal of personal satisfaction.'

'You're forgetting one thing, Ravenscroft. I was nowhere near the Feathers that night,' said Catherwood indignantly. 'I was at home minding my own business.'

'So you say – and who are we to prove otherwise? So who else hated Nathaniel Montacute enough to want to see him dead? Certainly there was no love lost between Nathaniel and you, Rupert. Not only did he keep you short of money but he also appears to have actually disliked you.'

'Bravo, Inspector! Yes, I hated the old skinflint – and yes, I'm glad he's dead. He never did me any favours but I didn't kill the old miser. Though on reflection I wish I had!' said Rupert, throwing back his head and laughing.

'Be quiet, Rupert. You don't know what you are saying,' reprimanded Maurice.

'Then there was you, Major Onslow – supposed friend and business associate of Nathaniel Montacute. Did you hate him enough to want to see him dead?'

'Look here, Ravenscroft, this is all rather stupid. Montacute and I had been friends for years. I had no cause to see him dead,' protested Onslow, becoming increasingly red in the face.

'You and Mr Montacute were major shareholders in the Colesberg Mining Corporation. The shares must have cost you a great deal of money, Major Onslow. Perhaps you overextended yourself? Apparently the company is doing rather badly. Is that what the argument was about, on the afternoon preceding the murder? Had you discovered that Nathaniel Montacute had sold you shares in a worthless company? If so, that would have been a good enough reason for you to want kill the banker.'

'This is all stuff and nonsense! Nathaniel and I were on the best of terms. The mining company is currently looking for diamonds. When it finds them, I shall be rich. Best thing Nathaniel ever did for me. No, Ravenscroft, you've got hold of the wrong stick there!' laughed Onslow.

'But according to Mr Rivers here, you were having a rather unpleasant disagreement with Mr Montacute,' said Ravenscroft.

'Rivers don't know what he's on about!' protested Onslow.

'I knows what I saw and heard,' mumbled the gamekeeper.

'Mr Rivers, were you on good terms with your employer?' asked Ravenscroft.

'The best of terms. I have worked for the Montacutes as man and boy, as my father did before me.'

'Ah yes, so you keep telling us, but perhaps there had been some recent irregularities in your conduct?' suggested Ravenscroft.

'Irregularities? What irregularities? Don't know what you're talking about,' snapped Rivers, looking uncomfortable.

'Perhaps everything was not as well as it should have been on the estate – and your employer threatened to dismiss you after all these years?'

'Absolute nonsense, man. You're just making all this up. It has been obvious from the start that you have been trying to put the blame on me.'

'The other person who hated Montacute, of course, was Joshua Leewood, the escaped convict,' said Ravenscroft.

'Now yer talking!' exclaimed Onslow, banging his fist down on the table. 'Why the devil ain't he here tonight?'

'Leewood has been sent back to Hereford gaol, where he will continue to serve out the remainder of his sentence. He, more than anyone else, wanted Nathaniel Montacute dead. Sentenced for a crime he believed he had not committed, he protested his innocence only to be sentenced for a further term. He must have spent many a long hour in his prison cell plotting his revenge. Then one day he escapes and hides up in the hills in the old workmen's hut. At first it seemed to me that given his reduced circumstances, Leewood would have found it extremely difficult to have procured the poison, and for a while I even considered the possibility that his mother may have obtained it for him. After all, she has admitted that she was outside this room on the night in question.'

'Then why have you not arrested her?' asked Doctor Andrews.

'Because the more I considered that possibility, the more

unlikely it seemed to be.'

'Why ever not?' asked Maurice.

'The Leewoods are poor people, and revenge can be a costly business.'

'I'd still put my money on this Leewood character,' added Onslow.

'You mentioned a moment ago, Inspector, that money can be an important motive for the cause of crime,' said the solicitor, adjusting his spectacles.

'That is indeed so, Mr Midwinter. I next asked myself who stood to gain the most from Mr Montacute's death. Although both you, Major Onslow, and you, Mr Midwinter, had been left money in Nathaniel's last will, it did not seem to me that the amounts were enough to justify murder. The same applies to you, Mrs Chambers, and you, Mr Rivers, both left small legacies in gratitude for your long and loyal service. Neither Mr Catherwood nor you, Master Rupert, had been left anything in the will. Even you, Mr Maurice, had been left very little by your father, only his interest in the bank which was yours partially on your own account. No, the only person who stood to gain financially from Mr Montacute's death was you, Mrs Montacute.'

'Now see here, Ravenscroft, what are you implying?' asked Maurice indignantly.

'It's all right, Maurice, let the inspector continue,' said Edith, placing a hand on the banker's arm.

'Thank you. As I was saying, you, Mrs Montacute, stood the most to gain by your husband's death, but the more I considered that possibility the more it seemed implausible. You, after all, came from a rich landed family, the Henshaws of Cheshire, and had money left to you by your family in your own right. You had no need to kill you husband for financial gain.'

'I am very relieved to hear you say that, Inspector,' said Edith.

'Then I wondered whether Mr Montacute had made an earlier will, and if so, whether it differed in any way from the last will. After all, if there was someone who stood to benefit from the former will, he or she may have committed the crime under the impression that they still stood to benefit. You may recall, Mr Midwinter, that when I inquired into the nature of the earlier will, you replied that the terms were practically identical to the later version, except in one or two respects,' said Ravenscroft, turning towards the solicitor.

'That is indeed so.'

'Perhaps you would enlighten us, Mr Midwinter?'

'Yes, of course. The minor bequests to Major Onslow, Mr Rivers, Mrs Chambers, myself and to St Katherine's were identical in both versions of the will. In the earlier will Nathaniel had provided for his then wife, Mrs Enid Montacute, and in the last will he provides for you, Mrs Montacute. The other difference is the clause relating to you, Mr Maurice. In the earlier will you had been left The Gables and more of your father's property but in the last will these clauses are no longer there.'

'Thank you, Mr Midwinter. Can you think of any reason, Mr Montacute, as to why your father had changed his will, in respect of yourself?'

'I hope you are not suggesting, Ravenscroft, that I killed my father because I was under the misapprehension that I stood to benefit under the earlier will?' said Maurice, his face turning ashen in complexion.

'Perhaps you could answer that question for us, Mr Montacute?' asked Ravenscroft, facing the banker.

'When my father drew up his earlier will, some ten or twelve years ago, I had only just entered the bank. I was very much a junior, not even a partner then, and had a great deal to learn. I had very little money on my own account at that time. My father was merely safeguarding my interests. Since then I have become a full partner in the bank and over the years have benefited financially through a number of fortunate investments. When my father drew up his latest will, he knew that I was already well provided for, and quite naturally wanted to protect the welfare of his new wife. In fact, I remember my father discussing this with me when he drew up his last will, and I told him I had no objections,' replied the banker, recovering his composure.

'But of course, Mr Montacute, we only have your word that such a consultation ever took place at all,' said Ravenscroft.

'That is so, but you have my word as a gentleman of honour that this conversation did indeed take place,' said Maurice firmly.

'I want to turn to the night when Mr Montacute was poisoned, here in this very ballroom. Whoever killed Nathaniel Montacute knew the exact nature of what would take place at midnight; the lights would be extinguished, the room plunged into darkness, and the opportunity would arise to pour the poison into the glass before the lights were relit. Whoever killed the banker could have easily undertaken the crime at an earlier time and in another place and still gone undetected, but by committing the crime in a crowded ballroom the killer was deflecting suspicion away from him or herself by ensuring that there would be more suspects than ever. And so it proved. Many of you were present on the night in question, and in the ensuing darkness any one of you could have slipped the poison unnoticed into the glass. But then what if the murderer had only been in the room for a short while? It only took a few seconds for the poison to be placed in the glass, and by the time the lamps were relit the killer could easily have slipped away. Mrs Leewood stated, however, that she saw no one enter or leave the room either shortly before or after the poisoning – but then there was the other small door at the back of the room. Although it opens out on to the landing, where Mrs Leewood was situated, it is nevertheless far enough down the corridor for her not to have noticed anyone entering or leaving, particularly if she was being distracted by what was going on inside here in the room. The only people not here at the ball that night were Mr Catherwood, Mr Rivers and Mrs Chambers.'

'Lord above, he thinks I killed the master!' cried out Mrs Chambers.

'All this speculation is getting quite out of hand, Ravenscroft!' said Onslow, glaring at the policeman.

'Any one of you could have slipped into the room by the back stairway. Mrs Chambers, you still say that Mr Rivers left the kitchens at a quarter to twelve that evening?'

'Yes,' replied the cook.

'I was out catching poachers. I've told you that already,' said Rivers forcefully.

'Indeed you have – but again we have only your word for it. There would have been ample time for you to run down to the Feathers, poison your master and return to The Gables unnoticed in the darkness – after all, the lamplighters had put out all the lights in the town. What wonderful cover the darkness could have provided for our killer.'

'I've told you before to arrest me if you have any evidence. I've had enough of this nonsense,' said Rivers, angrily rising from the table and beginning to walk across to the door.

'Mr Rivers, I advise you to sit down. My constable has instructions to prevent anyone leaving this room,' said Ravenscroft firmly.

The gamekeeper stared wildly at Ravenscroft before resuming his seat.

'Thank you, Mr Rivers.'

'Look here, Ravenscroft, is this going to go on all night? Seems to me yer just going round and round in circles, man!' said Onslow irritably, shuffling around in his chair.

'I agree. I think it is time we all left. We don't appear to be getting anywhere with all this conjecture,' added Doctor Andrews.

'On the contrary, it is only by going over the evidence again that one can eventually arrive at the truth. Already I have established that one person in this room tonight has lied to us,' said Ravenscroft, pausing for the full effect of his words to register with the assembled group.

'Well, go on then. Get on with it, man!' snapped Onslow.

'When I first began my investigations, I was under the impression that I was dealing just with one murder – that of Mr Nathaniel Montacute – but then we found a second body in the woods – the coachman. For a while it seemed as though the two deaths were linked together, and even more so when I eventually discovered that the coachman was none other than Mr Montacute's long departed brother and that he had returned to the town of his birth with the intention of depositing a packet of great importance with you, Mr Midwinter. It clearly seemed that whoever killed the coachman, Robert Montacute, must have also killed his brother, Nathaniel – but that of course was nonsense. The killer of Robert would have no cause to kill Nathaniel, for at the time of the banker's death Robert Montacute's murderer would have been completely unaware of the relationship between the two men, let alone knowing where the packet was lodged. No, the murders of the two brothers, although close together in time, had no connection with one another.'

'It does not take a genius to work that one out,' said Catherwood.

'Indeed so, Mr Catherwood. So we are then left with two separate murders – or so it seemed – but the more I considered this case, the more I came to the conclusion that there were not just two murders to solve but three!'

'Three? I'm at a loss, Ravenscroft,' said Maurice, looking bewildered.

'Why, yes. There had always been three murders in this case. The first murder had been that of Enid Montacute!'

'But that is a ridiculous statement to make, Ravenscroft. Enid died of a fever,' interjected Catherwood.

'A fever, yes. That is what everyone said. Enid died quite suddenly as the result of a fever. I have forgotten how many times that remark has been said to me during the past few days, but I believe that Enid Montacute did not die of natural causes. She was in fact cruelly murdered!'

'Go on, Inspector,' said Catherwood, leaning forward.

'When Mrs Montacute fell ill, she was attended by you, Doctor Andrews, I believe?' said Ravenscroft, turning in the doctor's direction.

'That is correct. I was called to Mrs Montacute's bedside when she fell ill,' replied Andrews.

'So you said, Doctor. I recall that you also said there was little you could do for your patient.'

'That is indeed so. The fever was quite advanced when I was called into attendance. I was powerless to save her. She died two or three days later. There was nothing out of the ordinary regarding her death. The fever was quite prevalent in the town at that time. I don't know what you are implying, Ravenscroft.'

'Doctor Andrews, it might interest you to know that I have examined the burial registers for the time of Enid Montacute's death. There is no increase in burials at that time to suggest that there was an epidemic in the town.'

'I don't know how, and when, she contracted the condition. She was in the habit of attending the sick and the poor. It would have been quite easy for her to have become infected with cholera,' said Andrews, looking uneasily around the room.

'You wrote out the death certificate, I believe?'

'Of course. I was the attending physician at the time of her death.'

'Look here, Ravenscroft, you say Enid was murdered? What

evidence do you have?' asked Catherwood.

'I have no evidence at all—' began Ravenscroft.

'Well, there you are, then,' said Andrews, throwing up his hand and relaxing back into his chair.

'However, I believe Mrs Montacute was poisoned. I have today applied for an exhumation order for the recovery and examination of Mrs Montacute's body!'

'Good God, man! You can't do that. She's been dead for nearly three years!' exclaimed Maurice.

'Arsenic poison preserves the body, I believe,' announced Ravenscroft.

'This is terrible!' said Mrs Chambers, bursting into tears.

'There now, Mrs Chambers, don't you distress yourself,' said Rivers, placing a comforting arm round the cook's shoulders.

'Look, Ravenscroft, this is all quite ridiculous. Enid Montacute died of a fever. She was not poisoned. I should know, I was there at the time. I would have known if anyone had administered arsenic,' said Andrews forcefully.

'As you say, Doctor Andrews, you would have known,' said Ravenscroft, allowing himself a brief smile.

'If you are suggesting that I killed Mrs Montacute, then I'm afraid you have failed to take two things into account,' protested the doctor.

'And they are?'

'Firstly I did not choose to attend Mrs Montacute in her illness. It was the family who called upon me.'

'But you were the only doctor available in the town at that time, Mr Andrews. Your predecessor had died the year before. If Mrs Montacute was ill, it would have been quite natural for the family to have called you in,' said Ravenscroft.

'Secondly, what possible reason would I have had for wanting to kill Mrs Montacute?' replied Andrews, ignoring Ravenscroft's last remark.

Ravenscroft said nothing but walked away from the table, deep in thought.

'Precisely! I had no financial incentive in seeing Mrs Montacute dead. The whole idea that I somehow poisoned my patient is quite ridiculous,' said Andrews, shaking his head.

A long silence followed. Ravenscroft removed his spectacles and after polishing the lens, stared out of the window, knowing that the assembled group all believed that he had failed. Even Crabb looked down at the floor and shuffled his feet.

'Well, Ravenscroft, if that's all yer can come up, we might as well all go home,' said Major Onslow, standing up from the table.

'I must say I'm inclined to agree with you,' said Maurice, doing likewise and offering his arm to Edith.

'There is someone here tonight who has been lying to us,' said Ravenscroft, suddenly turning round and producing some papers from his inside pocket. 'If you would kindly all resume your seats, I will explain.'

Onslow looked across at Maurice as the two men sat down once again at the table.

'Thank you. I promise not to detain you for very much longer. After the death of Enid Montacute, Nathaniel Montacute travelled alone to Rome, where he met you, Mrs Montacute?'

'Yes, we were staying together in the same hotel in Rome,' replied Edith, giving a slight smile.

'After a few weeks you fell in love and married?'

'Yes, but you know all this, Inspector.'

'You returned to Ledbury shortly after your marriage, where you were quickly accepted by the family. After all, it was plain for everyone to see that you brought your husband a great deal of happiness, so much so that after a year of marriage you persuaded him to make a new will in your favour.'

'I did not persuade my husband, Inspector, to change his will. I had no knowledge whatsoever that he was even thinking of changing his will,' replied Edith.

'For that assertion, of course, we have only your word,' said Ravenscroft.

'See here, Ravenscroft, this is a gross slur on a lady,' said Maurice.

'Ah, Mr Montacute – always springing to the defence of your stepmother. A very protective and quite commendable attribute. Could it be that one day you would hope to eventually marry the lady?'

'I regard that remark as highly offensive, Ravenscroft,' replied the indignant banker. 'Someone has to look after my stepmother's interests.'

'Mrs Montacute, your former name was Henshaw. Edith Henshaw, I believe?'

'I have told you all this already, Inspector,' protested Edith.

'Yes, of course – the Henshaws of Nantwich, Cheshire. Your father and your mother have both passed away in recent years, leaving you a very rich woman, I believe?'

'That is indeed correct, Inspector.'

'If that had indeed been the case, why would your husband have felt the need to alter his will entirely in your favour?' asked Ravenscroft.

'I don't know, Inspector. You would have to ask him that question,' replied Edith calmly.

'And of course your husband is dead – so we cannot question him on that point. I have here in my hand the reply to a telegram I sent to the police in Nantwich. Do you know what it says, Mrs Montacute?' said Ravenscroft, opening the paper.

'I have no idea, Inspector,' replied Edith, blushing.

'I asked my colleagues in Nantwich to make enquiries regarding the Henshaw family. I do not think it would surprise you to learn that there are no landed gentry of that name in the town, or anywhere else in the county for that matter. There was however a Kitty Henshaw born in the town twenty-five years ago – and far from being an orphan, she still has a mother who is alive and well. The mother in fact keeps a small dressmaker's establishment in the town!'

'Good heavens!' exclaimed Onslow.

'You must be mistaken. You clearly have the wrong family, Inspector,' said Edith, looking anxiously round the table. 'I was formerly Miss Edith Henshaw, daughter of Mr Joseph Henshaw, Gentleman of Nantwich. Maurice, you believe me, don't you?'

'I don't know what to believe,' protested Maurice.

'Then let me enlighten you. Far from coming from a rich landed family in Cheshire, Miss Henshaw, your origins come from a far more humble source. There was no money and no property to inherit. Your father died twenty years ago, leaving your mother, a seamstress, to struggle to bring up her only daughter alone in this world. Then one day, you leave the town of your birth and travel to Rome where you meet an old man who has recently lost his wife and where you deliberately set about entrapping him until he is persuaded to marry you and bring you back to his home town of Ledbury.'

'It was not like that at all. Yes, my real name is Kitty Henshaw, but it is not a crime surely to come from a poor background and to want to rise in this world,' said Edith, looking desperately at Maurice.

'A noble sentiment. You are correct, it is not a crime to be ambitious, to better oneself in society. It is a crime, however, to commit murder,' said Ravenscroft firmly.

'I did not kill Nathaniel. I loved him!' exclaimed Edith, tears beginning to form in her eyes.

'I believe you deliberately poisoned your husband when the lights were extinguished. When I asked you if anyone else was standing next to you at the time, you mentioned Major Onslow's name, but when I questioned you, Major, you remembered standing in a different part of the room entirely. I think you deliberately implicated the major in order to draw attention away from yourself, Miss Henshaw.'

'Good Lord!' exclaimed Onslow.

'No! No, this is all so untrue!' exclaimed Edith.

'You still don't have any proof for all this?' interrupted Doctor Andrews.

'That is indeed true, Doctor. No one saw the poison being administered. It was, after all, quite dark,' said Ravenscroft, smiling.

'Then all this is pure guesswork,' said Catherwood.

'Not quite. I am arresting you, Kitty Henshaw, for the murder of Nathaniel Montacute. Crabb, put the cuffs on her,' said Ravenscroft, leaning across the table and staring hard at his quarry.

'No! I'm innocent, you must believe me!' pleaded Edith, looking anxiously at the others seated around the table.

'Crabb, do your duty!' instructed Ravenscroft, turning away.

'No! No! For God's sake, tell them, James, that it wasn't my idea!' screamed Edith, looking in Doctor Andrews' direction as Crabb stepped forward to place the handcuffs round her wrists.

'I don't know what the devil she's talking about,' protested the doctor, rising from his seat.

'James, for God's sake, will you tell them it was all your idea!' shouted Edith frantically as Crabb snapped on the cuffs.

'The woman is deranged!' laughed Andrews, moving away from the table.

'I don't think so. It is all over, Doctor. I have in my hand a copy of a marriage certificate dated 3 February 1885, for the union of a Doctor James Andrews and Kitty Henshaw, a marriage that took place in the town of Nantwich in Cheshire!' announced Ravenscroft, flinging the paper down on to the table.

'Damn you, Ravenscroft!' shouted Andrews. 'Damn you!'

'You see, ladies and gentlemen, it was all part of a very clever plan. Four years ago Doctor Andrews and Miss Henshaw were married. A year later you came alone to Ledbury, Doctor, to take up a new position – and where you quickly made yourself known to the Montacute family. When Enid Montacute fell ill with some minor complaint, you took the opportunity to poison the good lady, and when you recommended that the distraught widower embark on a tour of Italy, you made sure that your wife was there at the hotel waiting to entrap him.'

'My God, Ravenscroft!' exclaimed Onslow, as the cook burst into tears.

'Tell me one thing, Andrews – had you and your wife already formulated this plan before you came alone to Ledbury, or did the idea of murder occur to you once you were here?' asked Ravenscroft.

'For God's sake, tell him everything!' screamed Edith, trying to break free from Crabb's grasp.

'Shut your mouth, you stupid woman!' snapped Andrews.

'Doctor James Andrews, I am arresting you for the murder of Enid Montacute and for your implication in the murder of Nathaniel Montacute—' began Ravenscroft.

'You'll have to catch me first!' shouted the doctor as he rushed towards the door.

'Sergeant!' yelled Ravenscroft, as Andrews flung open the door to be confronted by two policemen barring his way. 'This is Sergeant Stephens and Constable Smith from Hereford Central Police Station. Gentlemen, if you would care to put the bracelets on him and escort both the doctor and Miss Henshaw to the station, Constable Crabb and myself will be with you shortly.'

Two hours later, Ravenscroft and Crabb stood outside the police station in Ledbury, watching a police wagon making its way out of the town.

'They should both be locked up safely in a cell in Hereford gaol before the night is out,' said Ravenscroft.

'Suppose they'll both hang?' suggested Crabb.

'Not until a jury has found them both guilty of their crimes.'

'No doubt about that, sir.'

'I would hope so. Andrews is still protesting his innocence, but with Kitty's full confession, a conviction would seem inevitable. Not even the esteemed Mr Sefton Rawlinson could achieve an acquittal in this case.'

'Who is Sefton Rawlinson?'

'Oh, just a slippery brief I have encountered on more than one occasion in London. But enough of all this, Tom. It has been a long day. Come home with me and partake of a nightcap before you make your way back to the Wells,' said Ravenscroft, letting out a deep sigh as the two men began to walk up Church Lane.

'Thank you, sir, I don't mind if I do. So Mrs Montacute wasn't legally married to Nathaniel at all?'

'That's right. Her real name was Kitty Andrews, although she was born Kitty Henshaw. As she was still married to Andrews at the time she married Nathaniel, then her second union is invalid. The more I think about it, the more I'm convinced that the couple must have formulated their plan before they arrived here in Ledbury, otherwise Kitty would have accompanied her husband when he took up his new position. He was clearly on the lookout for some rich widower who he could later introduce to Kitty. When he learned of the wealth of the Montacutes he decided to speed things up by poisoning Enid Montacute – and once Kitty had persuaded Nathaniel to alter his will in her favour, all they then had to do was wait for some public occasion, such as the Lamplighters' Ball, when they could poison Nathaniel without implicating themselves in any way. I have no doubt that once the police had failed to catch Nathaniel's murderer and things had settled down, Andrews and Kitty would have gone through some form of sham marriage in order for both of them to inherit the Montacute money and property.'

'It was a very clever plot, sir. It's Maurice I feel sorry for. He clearly had designs on the lady as well!' added Crabb.

'You noticed how he was always springing to her defence, Crabb? He was clearly infatuated with her.'

'It was a bit touch and go in there tonight, sir. At one stage I thought it was all over for us. How were you so sure that you would catch the two of them?'

'I wasn't. After all, no one had seen either Andrews or Kitty commit their crimes, but I knew that if I kept my nerve I could confront them with the telegram and the copy of the marriage certificate and then one of them would break down and confess, and furthermore implicate the other – and so it proved to be.'

'All we need to do now, sir, is to apprehend this Cranston fellow,' added Crabb.

'I must confess that in all the excitement I have forgotten that we still had to bring that villain to account, but that can wait until the morning. If he makes his move tonight, he will meet with two armed constables from Hereford who will be waiting for him in Midwinter's offices,' said Ravenscroft, opening his front door.

'My God, sir!' exclaimed Sally the maid, rushing to meet the two men. 'My God, sir, you're supposed to be dead!'

'Far from it, Sally, for as you can see I am alive and well!' replied Ravenscroft, laughing.

'But you're supposed to be shot through the heart and dying, out on the hills!' said the frustrated maid.

'Sally, what is all this about?' asked Ravenscroft, suddenly realizing that the servant was sincere in her misapprehension.

'Just after six o'clock tonight, sir, one of your men knocked on the door and said you had been seriously injured whilst undertaking an arrest on the hills.'

'What policeman? I sent no policeman here,' stated Ravenscroft anxiously. 'How was he dressed?'

'He wore a police tunic, and cape, just like they do, and said he had come over from the station at Malvern.'

'Good grief!' said Ravenscroft, suddenly realizing the seriousness of the situation and fearing the worst. 'Where is Mrs Ravenscroft? For God's sake, girl, where is Mrs Ravenscroft?' he shouted.

'She's gone with him, sir! He said you were dying out on the hills, and that you had asked for her – and so she went with him, sir,' replied the distraught maid.

'Oh my God, Crabb, do you see what this means? It's Cranston – and he has Lucy within his power!'

# CHAPTER THIRTEEN

## LEDBURY, 10 JANUARY 1889

Ravenscroft stood silently at the window of the cottage in Church Lane, waiting for the dawn to break so that he could begin the desperate search for his wife. Several hours previously he had learned how Cranston had first assumed the disguise of the Catholic priest, and then that of the constable, in order to lure Lucy away from the safety of their home. Then he and Crabb had quickly returned to the Feathers, in the futile hope that Cranston would have taken refuge there, only to learn from the receptionist that their guest had left the previous afternoon. Now Cranston had Lucy at his mercy, somewhere out on the hills, and Ravenscroft felt utterly powerless in his attempts to find her. Furthermore, he cursed himself for his own stupidity. Whilst he had been busily engaged in bringing Nathaniel Montacute's murderer to book, Cranston had seized the opportunity to lure Lucy away from the safety of their home on his false pretext. He ought to have seen that the man would have stooped to such an evil design in order to secure the envelope. He should have offered his wife his protection; should have realized that Cranston would have struck at the very heart of his own family. Through his own negligence and stupidity he had placed the life of the woman he loved above all other at the gravest risk.

'If it is any consolation, sir, I don't think the fellow would have killed Mrs Ravenscroft,' said Crabb from the armchair. 'Not while he still wants that envelope.'

'I pray you are right, Crabb. If he has harmed her in any way, I

210

swear I will kill him, Tom, and let hang the consequences. But where can he have taken her? Where do we start to look?'

'My guess is that he has left the town.'

'I think you are right there, Tom. We will have a word with the cab men, when it is light, and see if they know or saw anything yesterday evening. According to Sally, Cranston intended taking Lucy out somewhere on the hills. One of the men could have taken them out there. Now they could be anywhere! God, I have been so stupid, Tom! Why did I not see that Cranston would do something like this? I should have realized that he would not have made any further attempts on Midwinter's offices and that he would have resorted to more desperate measures.'

'You were not to know that, sir.'

'But I should have known, damn it!' said Ravenscroft, bringing his fist hard into the base of his other hand, anxiously pacing up and down the room. 'I should have known!'

'It will be daylight soon, sir. I'll have every available man out searching the hills until we find them,' said Crabb, trying to sound confident.

'It will be like looking for a needle in a haystack. No, Cranston has us just where he wants us. He knows we will be waiting here, and that we are powerless to act. If he wants that envelope and its contents, he will have to make his next move soon.'

'I'm sure you're right, sir.'

Suddenly there was a loud knocking on the front door of the cottage. Ravenscroft looked across at Crabb, before the two of them dashed quickly into the hall. A postboy was handing a letter to Sally the maid.

'Letter for Ravenscroft,' said the boy.

'Who gave you this letter to deliver?' asked Ravenscroft, anxiously taking the envelope from the maid.

'No one, sir. It was left at the office yesterday afternoon, with instructions that it was not to be delivered until early this morning.'

'Thank you,' replied Ravenscroft, giving the boy a silver coin before returning to the living-room.

'Could be from Cranston, sir?' suggested Crabb.

'I don't recognize the handwriting,' said Ravenscroft, examining the envelope. 'If it is from Cranston, then he must have written it and deposited it at the post office yesterday, before he abducted Lucy.' He tore open the envelope and read aloud its contents.

*Ravenscroft,*
*When you receive this letter you will know that I have your wife.*
*The pretty young thing is well looked after!*
*I can assure you that no harm will befall her, provided you do exactly as I instruct.*
*You know what I want – a fair exchange – your wife for the envelope!*
*You are to take a cab from Ledbury at ten this morning. When you arrive at the British camp, you are to pay off the cab man, and follow the path that leads round the side of the large hill until you arrive at the Giant's Cave. There inside you will find further instructions left within an old tin box. It is important that you bring the envelope with you, and that you come unarmed – and alone! I will be watching your every move, and if I find that you have sought to entrap me, then your wife will die!*
*Believe me, Ravenscroft, it will be an easy thing for me to kill your wife, should you attempt not to fulfil these conditions.*
*If you wish your wife returned to you, safe and well, you will do as I have instructed. There is no other way.*

'Well, at least he has not harmed your wife, sir,' said Crabb, trying to sound reassuring.

'You are forgetting one thing, Crabb. He wrote this letter before he seized Lucy. We only have his word that he has no intention of harming her,' said Ravenscroft, laying the letter down on the table.

'What will you do now, sir?'

'We know that Cranston has Lucy somewhere near the old cave on the hills. I can see no alternative but to comply with his instructions.'

'I'll have some men out on the hills. We will have him as soon as he shows himself.'

'No, Tom. From up there he will see our men for miles around. He will know that we are closing in on him and will carry out his threat to kill Lucy. I cannot take that risk.'

'Then at least let me come with you in the cab. I could follow you up the hill, keeping at a safe distance. I could make sure that he never saw me.'

'No, Tom. I know you mean well, but you must stay here. I have to go alone, as he says, otherwise he will kill Lucy.'

Crabb looked crestfallen and turned away.

'Dear Tom. We have been through a great deal together, and you know how I value your service – and your friendship – but now I must see out this business alone, for Lucy's sake. I cannot put her at risk. I hope you will accept that, Tom?'

The two men looked at one another.

'Very well, sir,' said Crabb.

'Good. Then this is what we must do. What hour does the bank open?'

'Just after nine, sir.'

'Then we will go to the bank, and persuade Maurice Montacute to let us have the coachman's envelope from his safe before I leave for the camp. There is nothing more we can do now before nine, so I will ask Sally to prepare some breakfast for us. Cheer up, Tom, once I have Lucy safe and sound, we will have all the time in the world to lay our hands on Cranston. He cannot escape us for ever.'

The town clock struck the hour of ten as Ravenscroft and Crabb stood by a cab in the marketplace in Ledbury.

'Well, Tom, I best be on my way. You know my instructions? Neither you nor anyone else is to follow me. A life will depend upon it,' said Ravenscroft firmly.

'Yes, sir, but I wish you would take this pistol with you, sir,' said Crabb, producing a weapon from the pocket of his tunic.

'No, Tom. If he sees that I have come armed, he will know that I have broken my word and will kill Lucy.'

'But how will you protect yourself, sir?'

'Once Lucy is safe, I'll think of some way in which I can move against him, although I must confess that at the moment I don't see how. I must trust that a suitable opportunity will present itself. Give me the packet, Tom.'

'It must be something mighty important in that envelope, sir, for him to go to all this trouble,' said Crabb, handing over the item to his superior.

'One day I'll tell you all about it. Be in good spirits, Tom. I'm sure both Lucy and myself will be back in time for lunch.'

'Yes, sir.'

'Then give me your hand, Tom – and wish me well.'

'I do indeed, sir, with all my heart.'

The two men shook hands vigorously.

Ravenscroft stepped into the cab, after first giving instructions to the driver that he was to be taken to the British camp.

Crabb watched as the vehicle turned the corner at the top of the High Street and disappeared from view. As he made his way back to the station, feelings of despair and loneliness suddenly swept over him, as he realized that circumstances had combined against him to prevent him from assisting and protecting his colleague and friend. If only Ravenscroft had allowed him to shadow his progress on the hills, he was sure he would have been able to tackle the villain Cranston, but he had been sworn to inactivity. All he could do now was wait and hope.

Ravenscroft let out a deep sigh as the cab began its slow journey towards the camp. Shortly he would be reunited with Lucy. He knew that Cranston would not release her until he had handed over the envelope, but once he knew that his wife was safe, he would think of some way in which he could retrieve the papers and somehow destroy the diary to prevent it falling into the wrong hands. Perhaps Crabb had been right after all, and he should have secreted the pistol somewhere upon his person, but the more he ran over that course of action in his mind the more he was convinced that he was doing the right thing. He knew that his adversary was a dangerous, evil man, who would not have the slightest hesitation in killing Lucy if he in any way thought that Ravenscroft had broken his promise.

As they journeyed ever steadily upwards, he looked across the fields of corn. The London train was billowing out smoke as it made its way along the track that ran from Malvern and Colwall towards Ledbury – and he reflected on how his life had changed in the past few months. A year ago his daily round had brought him into contact with people of all nationalities and all stations in life. Pickpockets, thieves, prostitutes and villains of every description had crossed his path over the years. Sometimes the noise, smells and violence of Whitechapel had almost overpowered him in their intensity. Now, looking back on that old life, he wondered what it had all been about, and what contribution he had actually made to making the area a better place in which to live – and it seemed that his busy existence then had little reason or meaning. But then all that had given way in recent months to the rural tranquillity of Ledbury, as he had been reunited with the only woman he had ever wanted in his life – and he had acquired a joy, contentment and purpose in life that he had never thought possible. Now, as the cab neared the end of its journey, he realized that this new life could shortly be taken away from him; that the happiness and love he had so tentatively secured could again slip away from his hands, leaving him bereft and alone once more.

The cab came to a sudden halt. Ravenscroft alighted and paid for his fare.

'Want me to wait, governor?' asked the cabman.

'I don't know how long I will be,' replied Ravenscroft, at a loss for words.

'Be over at the inn. Patch needs a rest, and I could do with a drink.'

'Then we may well see one another again,' said Ravenscroft.

He watched as the driver swung the cab across the road towards the inn that lay in the clearing between the hills, and then sought out the path that he knew would take him around the side of the Beacon Hill.

As the path took him upwards, he realized that in his haste and anxiety his breathing had become more laboured, and as his chest began to tighten he prayed that his old affliction would not now return to bring him down at this crucial hour. He paused for a moment by an old seat, to wipe away the sweat from his brow and to gaze upon the fields and hedgerows that stretched out across the wide landscape – and wondered whether his every move was being observed by Cranston from some higher vantage point.

Eventually his journey brought him on to the small plateau at the side of the hill, and quickly taking the path that ran along the ridge he eventually found himself standing outside the cave that he had visited on his previous visit to the hills. He had half expected to see Cranston emerging from the cave itself, but then remembered that the letter had instructed him to look for an old tin box within its interior.

He stepped into the cave and, adjusting his eyes to its darkness, he moved tentatively towards the back of the cavity until his boot suddenly came into contact with an old battered tin on the floor. He knelt down, picked up the container and removed the lid. Inside, he was relieved to discover a small piece of paper.

Retracing his steps into the daylight, he unfolded the sheet and read the words written there:

*So Ravenscroft, you have made the journey.*

*If others have followed you, or you have come armed, I will kill your wife! On that you can be assured.*

*Continue your way along the path, until you reach a place where five paths meet.*

*Take the first path on your left and follow it along until you reach the cottage.*

*Knock on the door twice and enter.*

*There you will find your wife.*

As he read the words, he realized that his hands were shaking and that his breathing was coming in short gasps. The fact that his beloved Lucy was but a short distance away from where he stood, and that his adversary was in all probability studying his every movement, made him all the more nervous and unsure. The knowledge that he was now facing the greatest challenge of his life had slowly sapped away his confidence and resolution but then as he refolded the paper and placed it within his coat pocket and walked purposely along the path, an inner strength began to build within him and slowly a new determination came to the fore.

Reaching the crossroads, he took the path on his left and after a few hundred yards saw the cottage coming into view. A thin trail of smoke was drifting upwards from its chimney. He paused for a moment to look all around him at the surrounding hills, to see whether Cranston was looking down upon him. Seeing no one, however, Ravenscroft concluded that his adversary was in all probability awaiting his arrival within the cottage itself, and he quickened his pace, anxious to see that no harm had befallen his wife.

Striding up to the door, he briefly looked around him before banging his fist on the woodwork. Receiving no reply, he gently to find the words as he attempted to brush the swirling mist from his eyes.

'Bravo! Fine words, my good fellow,' said Cranston, clapping his hands together. 'But may I remind you that you are in no position to make such empty threats. It is I, Ravenscroft, who now holds all the cards, who has the pistol at your wife's head.'

Ravenscroft could see the fear in Lucy's eyes as she groaned and attempted to free herself from the bound chair.

'Nevertheless, Cranston, I swear—' he began.

'Oh, be quiet!' snapped Cranston. 'I am tired of you, Ravenscroft; tired of all your attempted meddling in my affairs. For nearly two years our paths have crossed – in Worcester, Whitechapel and Dinard.'

'Dinard?'

'You remember the day you and your wife left the Hotel Gandolphi at the conclusion of your stay? A cab drew up at the front entrance, and an elderly bearded man alighted with his pretty young companion. I saw how you looked across at me, trying to remember where we had previously encountered one another – but as usual you were incapable of making the connection,' boasted Cranston.

Ravenscroft turned away, a sickening feeling of utter despair running through his body.

'You had previously sought to cross me in that dingy moth-eaten lodging house in Worcester, but that was not the first time we had met. Remember the darkened alleyway in Whitechapel? The young girl not yet cold, and how you looked up when you heard me move in the darkness. You could have apprehended me then, Ravenscroft, but you were too slow and stupid! If you had only succeeded in catching me then, you would have spared me from all the dark deeds that were to follow. You could have earned your place in history!' sneered Cranston.

Ravenscroft leaned his head back on the wall and let out a deep sigh of despair, as he saw and heard again the black cloak flowing along the darkened, crowded alleyways of Whitechapel.

'You always were a miserable failure, Ravenscroft. You have had so many opportunities and never realized how close you came,' said his adversary, continuing to mock him. 'And now the game is nearly over. The package! Give me the package.'

Ravenscroft reached into his coat pocket and pulled out the

envelope. Cranston rushed forward and snatched it from his grasp.

'Now let my wife go. I will remain here with you, but please let her go. She has done you no harm,' pleaded Ravenscroft.

'In good time,' replied Cranston, tearing open the envelope and tipping out the contents on to the floor. 'Ah, what have we here? A diary of some kind, written by some illustrious person, I have no doubt. My masters will pay well for this.'

'Now that you have the diary, let my wife go. Honour your side of the bargain,' pleaded Ravenscroft, speaking through the almost deafening pain in his head.

'Don't speak to me of honour, Ravenscroft. You silly, stupid man, did you really think I could afford to let you and your precious wife leave here alive?' replied Cranston in a voice full of anger. 'You know far too much. If I were to let you go now, I know that you would not rest until you had tracked me down. Do you really think I am that stupid?'

'My wife knows nothing. For God's sake, man, I implore you to let her go. You can do what you like with me. You must see that she is the innocent party in all this!' cried out Ravenscroft, attempting unsuccessfully to raise himself up from the floor.

'Innocence is an expendable commodity! No, Ravenscroft. I have decided that you both must die. My work is nearly completed. I cannot afford to leave any loose ends.'

'Please. I will do anything – but let my wife go free!' implored Ravenscroft, looking across at his wife with tears in his eyes, and realizing that there was nothing he could possibly do to save the woman he loved.

'I am so sorry, Ravenscroft. I know that you hate and despise me. You think I have no compassion, no feeling at all, but in that you are mistaken. I will shoot you first, Ravenscroft, so that you will be spared the sight of witnessing the slow death of your wife,' said Cranston, raising his pistol and pointing it in his direction.

'Let my wife—' began Ravenscroft.

'Prepare to die, Ravenscroft!' snapped Cranston, taking aim. 'How you have disappointed me. Your pleading is below contempt! I would have thought better of you, if you had been a worthier opponent!'

Ravenscroft allowed himself one final desperate look at Lucy before closing his eyes.

The shot rang out across the room.

Ravenscroft opened his eyes, and saw Cranston clutching his chest as he fell to the floor.

In the doorway, through the mist of his vision, he saw the distant outline of a figure holding a smoking pistol in his hand – and knew then that his life had been spared.

The figure said nothing as he walked over to Cranston and discharged another shot from a second pistol into the groaning body.

Ravenscroft wiped his hand across his eyes, struggling to see who his saviour was, but the figure seemed oblivious to their plight and bent down and retrieved the contents of the envelope from the floor.

'Help us, for God's sake!' cried out Ravenscroft.

The figure walked over to the fireplace. He removed the pages from the diary and threw them on to the blazing fire.

'Who are you?' asked Ravenscroft, unable to see the other's features.

The man remained silent as he stared into the flames. Only when the charred remains fell back on themselves did he walk over to Lucy and begin to untie the ropes and gag that bound her.

Lucy rushed forward, and knelt down at her injured husband's side.

'Samuel!' she cried, holding his head in her hands and kissing his lips. 'Oh, my dear Samuel!'

'Lucy! I thought I had lost you,' he replied.

'That blaggard won't trouble yer any more,' said the stranger, reaching out a helping hand towards Ravenscroft.

'Thank you. You saved our lives,' said the detective, struggling to his feet.

'Say nothing about it, old man. The scoundrel got all he deserved.'

Ravenscroft reached out and shook the hand of their saviour.

Major Onslow gave a brief smile in reply.

# EPILOGUE

## LEDBURY, 17 JANUARY 1889

The bright winter's sun of the late afternoon shone down on the churchyard as the group of mourners gathered round the Montacute family vault.

'It is rather sad to think that the coachman came back to his home town, only to be struck down in such a terrible way,' said Lucy, linking her husband's arm as they stood at the entrance, watching the events unfold.

'Well, at least he is reunited with his family. Killed within a few days of each other, by different hands, the two brothers will now lie side by side. Their differences had kept them apart for so many years, but now they will be reunited once more,' replied Ravenscroft.

'Good to see Catherwood here,' said Crabb.

'Yes, I have hopes that something good may come from all of this. Catherwood seems to have taken his natural son under his wing, so perhaps young Rupert may be guided in the right direction at last,' remarked Ravenscroft.

'To think that all three members of the family met their end in such a terrible fashion,' said Lucy, giving a shiver.

'You're cold, my dear, we should not stay long,' said a concerned Ravenscroft, laying his hand on his wife's arm.

'One thing that still puzzles me, sir—' began Crabb.

'Go on, Tom.'

'How was the major able to follow you on to the hills without being seen either by Cranston or yourself?'

221

'That I don't know, but don't forget that Onslow was used to stalking and hunting big game in India. He could have followed me up on to the hills, or he may have been there already. Either way, I'm certainly thankful that he turned up when he did. Another minute and it would have all been over. It was a damn close thing,' replied Ravenscroft.

'You never did tell me what was in that book that the major threw on the fire?' said Lucy.

'No, I believe I did not, but rest assured that one of these days I may be at liberty to tell you everything,' teased Ravenscroft.

'It's no good, Mrs Ravenscroft, he won't say,' said Crabb.

'Afternoon to you all,' said a familiar voice from behind them.

'Good afternoon to you, Mr Sanderson, sir' said Ravenscroft, turning round and recognizing the stonemason he had encountered in the churchyard a few days previously. 'It looks as though your services will be in demand once again.'

''Tis never a dull week in Ledbury. There's always someone who is on the way out. Who would have thought that another of them Montacutes would have turned up like that, after all them years.' The old lamplighter removed his cap and wiped his brow.

'Who indeed,' replied Ravenscroft.

'What I wants to know, sir, is what I'm supposed to put on that fellow's stone over there,' said Sanderson, pointing to the other side of the graveyard.

'I'm afraid I can't help you in that respect. We knew him as Cranston when he was in Worcester, but since then our enquiries have found that the real Cranston passed away in Stoke-on-Trent some four or five years ago. The Feathers said he gave the name of Father Bannerman when he was staying there. Then again, I believe that Major Onslow referred to him as Major Monk,' replied Ravenscroft.

'Well, sir, that's all rather confusing, like,' said the workman, scratching the top of his head. 'That's all very well. Am I to put Cranston, Monk or that Bannerman on his stone?'

'I'm sorry,' said Ravenscroft, giving a shrug of his shoulders as he looked across at Crabb for guidance.

'You're no help, then! You might as well put that fellow Jack the Ripper's name on it for all I cares! They never did catch him, did they?'

'No, they did not,' said Ravenscroft, smiling.

'Jack the Ripper, that would be something, sir – the murderer of Whitechapel buried in an unmarked grave here in Ledbury!' joked Crabb.

'You know, Crabb. You could just be—' began Ravenscroft.

'Oh, come on, you two, enough of this nonsense!' laughed Lucy, steering her husband away from the churchyard.

'Nonsense? You're probably right, my dear. You usually are.'

# POSTSCRIPT

Six months later an investigation concerning missing postal orders revealed that a number of post office boys had been supplementing their wages by working in a male brothel at 18 Cleveland Street in London. After the premises had been raided, a number of allegations were made against leading members of society. Lord Arthur Somerset, bachelor equerry to the Prince of Wales, discreetly retired to Dieppe. Strenuous and successful attempts were made to keep secret the name of one of the house's most illustrious clients – Prince Albert Victor.

Two years later, Albert Victor was made Duke of Clarence and Avondale. In December 1891 he became engaged to Princess Mary of Teck. He died a month later, reputedly of pneumonia resulting from influenza contracted in an epidemic. His younger brother, George, married Mary of Teck, and succeeded to the throne as George V in 1910. His granddaughter reigns as Elizabeth II.

Despite many theories advanced by learned scholars over the years, no one has satisfactorily been able to establish either the true identity – or the final resting place – of the man known as Jack the Ripper.

An unmarked grave is still to be found in Ledbury churchyard.